Meet the Marcelli family in a wonderful series that's warm, witty and stunningly sensual.

The Marcelli Bride ~ *The Sparkling One*

The Sassy One ~ *The Seductive One*

"Smart, sexy entertainment." —Christina Dodd

"The highs and lows of the Marcelli family saga have made this series extremely compelling and quite unforgettable."
—*Romantic Times*

"The characters will charm readers . . . the story is indeed seductive; once you pick it up, you won't want to put it down." —America Online

"A heartwarming story with some surprises along the way."
—Romance Reviews Today

More praise for the novels of this beloved *USA Today* bestselling author!

Married for One Month

"*Temptation Island* meets Oprah in [this] contemporary romp. . . . This sweet story will delight as it provides food for thought." —*Publishers Weekly*

Sweet Success

"[A] sweet tale from beginning to end. . . . A delightful read." —*Rendezvous*

***The Marcelli Princess* is also available as an eBook**

Also by Susan Mallery

The Marcelli Bride
The Sparkling One
The Seductive One
The Sassy One
Married for One Month
Sweet Success

SUSAN MALLERY

The MARCELLI PRINCESS

POCKET STAR BOOKS
New York London Toronto Sydney

An *Original* Publication of POCKET BOOKS

A Pocket Star Book published by
POCKET BOOKS, a division of Simon & Schuster, Inc.
1230 Avenue of the Americas, New York, NY 10020

ISBN-13: 978-0-7434-9958-3
ISBN-10: 0-7434-9958-1

This Pocket Star Books paperback edition March 2007

10 9 8 7 6 5 4 3 2 1

Cover illustration by Craig White

Manufactured in the United States of America

ACKNOWLEDGMENTS

This books exists because readers asked for Mia's story. They asked a lot and they were extremely vocal about it. So here it is. For each of you who wanted to know what happened to the wild girl who planned to take over the world.

And to my editor, Megan McKeever, who made it so much better.

The MARCELLI PRINCESS

1

Mia Marcelli was used to sleeping alone so it came as something of a shock to wake up with a strange man in her bed. She did what any other self-actualized, self-defense-trained woman would do—she screamed and jumped to her feet.

"Big mistake," she yelled as she backed toward the door. "You shouldn't have broken in here. I have access to weapons, and grandmothers who don't like this sort of thing. My brother's a former Navy SEAL."

The man sat up and smiled at her. "I see you still talk too much, Mia. When an unknown man appears in your bed, you should run."

He knew her name. That startled her nearly as much as the fact that he was giving her advice. It didn't seem like normal behavior for a guy intent on raping and pillaging. Assuming anyone really pillaged these days.

She paused by the door and pushed her bangs out of her face. There was something familiar about the man. The hair and eye color were all wrong, but the shape of his face reminded her of someone. And that mouth—she would remember it until she died.

"Diego?" she breathed, knowing this stranger *couldn't* be him. Diego was dead. She'd seen the bullets hit his body, had watched him fall to the ground. There'd been so much blood.

"Am I that different?" the man asked as he stood and smiled at her. "Has so much changed?"

It *was* him, she thought, too stunned to do much more than gasp. "H-how is this possible? Why aren't you dead? I saw you die. Dead people don't have conversations."

"It is a long story. Perhaps one I could tell you over breakfast."

That voice. She would know it anywhere. It had haunted her dreams for the past five years.

Dead people also don't eat. "Get back," she said, feeling both shocked and angry. When in doubt, get pissed off. It was a philosophy she'd learned worked for her. "I don't know what this game is, but I'm not playing it."

"Mia, it is I. You must recognize me."

"Must I?"

Right now she didn't have to do anything but keep from having a heart attack from the shock, and wish she kept a weapon in her room. Something big and scary.

The bedroom door flew open and her two grandmothers burst inside. Grandma Tessa had a fire poker in one hand, and Grammy M threatened Diego with a rolling pin.

"Call Joe," Tessa ordered Mia. "He'll take care of this scumbag."

Scumbag? Someone had been watching just a little too many police dramas.

"I'm not sure he's a scumbag," Mia said, still finding it difficult to believe her own eyes. "I might know this guy."

"You do know me," he said, his voice washing over her like a familiar and welcome memory. "Mia, it is I."

Diego? Was it possible? Conflicting emotions raced through her. She wanted to run into his arms and have him hold her forever. At the same time she wanted to grab the poker and beat him over the head with it.

"You're supposed to be dead," she said, still confused and angry, and maybe just a little scared. Because if this guy really *was* Diego, she was going to have a lot of explaining to do.

"So you keep saying," he told her, sounding more amused than anything else. "Would you be more happy if I were?"

"It would make more sense. I don't believe in ghosts . . . or vampires."

He actually smiled. "Good, because I am neither. Mia,"—he took a step toward her—"trust your eyes and your heart. I am the man you knew as Diego."

"We don't trust people who pretend to be someone else," Grandma Tessa said with surprising force despite her small stature and advanced years. "Who do you think you are now?"

"I know I am Rafael, Crown Prince of Calandria."

Mia rolled her eyes. Great—a crazy man in her bedroom, and she hadn't even had coffee yet. "Right, and I'm the Sleeping Beauty."

This had gone on long enough. Mia took the poker from her grandmother and held it out in front of her. "That's it. I don't know who you are or what you want, but you're in big trouble. Grammy M, call Joe." She shook the poker at the intruder. "As for you, big guy, you stay right there or I'll take you out. Don't think I can't. I've had professional training."

The man who looked amazingly like Diego had the balls to smile at her again. "I'm not going anywhere, Mia. I came to see you. I've waited five years to be with you again. I can certainly wait until you're willing to listen to reason."

Reason? "Not my strong suit. I'm more into react now, say 'Oops' later. If you're who you say you are, you should know that."

"I know many things, including the fact that you once wore a silver ring bought in a market. It was a foolish trinket, yet oddly valuable to us both."

Mia's gaze involuntarily darted to the bottom drawer of her dresser. She remembered the ring and the man who bought it for her.

He took a step closer. "I know other things," he said, his voice low and seductive. "I know how you like to be kissed and touched and where you like to—"

"Hey," she said loudly, doing her best to both shut him up and break the spell he attempted to weave. "Grandmothers present. Let's avoid too much information."

Slowly she lowered the poker and looked at him. He was the right height and physical type. His voice was the same, as was his arrogance. His smile made her thighs go up in flames, which hadn't happened even once in the past five years. She wanted to believe because once she'd loved him so much, she'd thought knowing he was dead was going to kill her, too.

But what about the other changes? The color of his eyes, the hair, the scar? Then she remembered her brief time in a world of deception and secrecy, where people could easily be made to look different. Contact lenses, a quick dye job, and little glue—voilá, a new man.

"I assume you have some ID on you," she said, trying to hold on to her anger, because it was safe. Only she was feeling more confused than anything else. Shouldn't she get coffee before an event like this? And maybe a cinnamon roll?

"Walk to the window," he said.

She raised the poker again and shook it at him. "You walk to the window."

He sighed. "I see you are still stubborn. Very well, Mia, we will walk together."

She eyed him warily as he moved to the window and pulled open the drapes. Keeping him at arm's-plus-poker length, she glanced down and saw a very shiny black car complete with what looked like flags flying from the front. Flags amazingly similar to the royal coat of arms of Calandria.

"So you have access to a limo, and an active imagination. That proves nothing." Actually, it kind of proved something, but she wasn't going to admit that.

He raised both hands. "As you wish. May I show you my passport?"

Her throat tightened and her mouth went dry. Man, she really wanted to brush her teeth and take a shower and get some coffee. Because after all those normal activities, none of this would be real anymore.

"Sure," she muttered. "Whatever."

But her heart began to beat faster. She didn't know if she accepted the premise that he was Diego, back from the dead, but she was halfway to being convinced. Which made no sense and gave her a stomachache.

If Diego wasn't dead, then where the hell had he been for the past five years and why hadn't he found her and told her the truth? She'd mourned him and ached for him, and what, he'd been off being some prince?

Because that's what scared her the most. That he really was Diego and Diego was in fact the prince of Calandria. The knowledge would rock her world and she didn't know how she was going to recover. Because having the child of a bad boy turned art thief was one thing, but having the child of an heir to a throne was quite another.

He pulled his passport out of his suit jacket and handed it to her. She glanced at the cover, then nodded at Grandma Tessa. "Let her read it."

Mia told herself she didn't want to look at it because she needed to keep her attention on Diego . . . or possibly Prince Rafael of Calandria. But in truth, she didn't want to see the words printed there.

Tessa opened the passport. Grammy M moved in close and stared over her shoulder.

"A very flattering picture," Grammy M said, smiling at him.

"Thank you."

He was all graciousness and confidence, and he didn't seem the least bit intimidated by the poker in Mia's hand, which made her want to bonk him with it.

Grandma Tessa stared at the print on the page, then looked at Mia. "It says he's the prince. Crown Prince Rafael of Calandria. *Prince* is even listed as his occupation."

Oh God. This couldn't be good.

"Of course it could be a fake," Tessa said cheerfully. "People do it all the time. A couple of hundred bucks and you have a new passport."

Definitely too much TV, Mia thought.

"A prince," Grammy M said, eyeing Rafael. "There'll be a castle, then, with the title?"

He nodded. "Of course. We're also very rich."

Grammy M beamed at Mia. "So, maybe you'll be inviting your friend the prince to breakfast?"

Mia wanted to scream. "He broke in to my *bedroom.* We don't know who he really is. The last time I saw him, he was dead, and you want to invite him to breakfast?"

Grammy M slipped her arm through Diego's . . . or Rafael's . . . and walked him to the door. "So, how will you be taking your coffee?"

Mia watched them go, then dropped the poker to the floor. "Somebody shoot me now. I know matchmaking is a time-honored Marcelli tradition, but could we please first find out the man in question isn't an ax murderer?"

Grandma Tessa handed her the passport. "You're the one who'd know that. Is he who he says he is?"

Mia stared at the picture. So much the same and yet so much different, she thought. Was it possible Diego hadn't died that night? That he was really the Crown Prince of Calandria?

"I don't know," she admitted. "I don't know anything."

Grandma Tessa moved to the door. "He was supposed to have been killed five years ago?"

Mia nodded.

"So he's Danny's father."

She nodded again.

"Then this is going to be interesting."

Twenty minutes later Mia walked into the kitchen. She'd showered and dressed in record time. She would have been down sooner, but she'd debated both putting on makeup and blow-drying her hair. On a normal summer morning she wouldn't have bothered with either, but this was hardly normal. Besides, if Rafael was really who he said he was, a little mascara and lip gloss were probably a good thing.

She found the man who claimed to be Diego sitting at the kitchen table, being force-fed coffee and toast. Judging from the yummy smell coming from both ovens, fresh scones and cinnamon rolls were already on the way.

"Morning," she said as she approached the table.

Rafael immediately stood and smiled. "Mia."

He sounded so pleased to see her, as if he'd been waiting for this moment forever. But he couldn't have been. They'd been apart for years, and he hadn't once gotten in touch with her. She had a feeling she was only a simple Google away from being found, so why hadn't he looked before? And why was he here now?

"Your prince is very charming," Grandma Tessa said as she held out a cup of coffee. "Too charming, if you ask me."

"No one did," Grammy M said tartly. "You're always looking for the bruise on the apple. Sometimes there isn't one."

Grandma Tessa sniffed. "How can you be as old as you are and still so foolish about the world?" She narrowed her gaze as she looked at Rafael. "Crown prince or not, what do we really know about him?"

At that moment, Rafael's lineage was the least of Mia's problems.

"This has been fun," she said, and grabbed Rafael's coffee cup along with one for herself. "Let's go for a walk."

"Stay close to the house," Grandma Tessa told her. "I've called Joe. He'll be keeping an eye on you."

"Joe?" Rafael asked as they left the kitchen and stepped into the sunny late June morning. There was still dew on the flowers, and the scent of grapes from the acres of vineyards filled the air.

"The ex-Navy SEAL brother I mentioned before."

"He lives nearby?"

She handed him his coffee and nodded toward a large house on a hill, less than a quarter mile away. "He lives there."

"A very close family," Rafael said.

"You have no idea." She clutched her coffee in both hands and turned to the man walking next to her. "Who are you and why are you here?"

"I told you. I am the man you knew as Diego."

"As simple as that?" She tried to laugh, but the effort fell flat. Her mind wouldn't accept what was happening. She didn't know what to think, what to feel. Her anger had faded, leaving behind confusion and a sense of loss. As if seeing Diego after so long made her miss him all over again. "Nothing makes sense. You're supposed to be dead."

"You have mentioned that before. Are you disappointed to find otherwise?"

"I haven't decided." A lie. There were a thousand emotions swirling through her right now, but disappointment wasn't one of them. "I saw you die."

"You saw me shot and fall to the ground. There is a difference."

Not to her. That night was forever etched in her brain. The roar of the helicopter, the way the wind whipped up by the blades slapped her. She'd been crying, screaming, afraid. And then the gunshots. Diego had staggered back before falling. The world had slowed to just that moment, as he hit the ground and the blood poured out of him.

She'd yelled for the pilot to take her back. She'd tried to jump out of the helicopter, but someone had held her in place. She'd strained and clawed but hadn't been able to break free. They'd flown over Calandria. She remembered staring down at the bright lights, blurry through her tears, knowing that the hole his death had left in her heart would never heal.

"Mia?" He touched her arm.

His voice jerked her back to the present. She pressed her hand on his shoulder and shoved him back. "Dammit, Diego, you lied about dying? You lied and let me suffer all this time and never once thought maybe you should drop me a note saying 'Hey, not as dead as you'd think'? I *mourned* you. I didn't think I was ever going to recover."

She wanted to hurt him the way she'd been hurt. She could handle anything but betrayal and being played for a fool. She wanted to demand to know why he hadn't come after her, but she couldn't seem to ask that. Maybe because his sudden return from the dead illustrated the possibility that he hadn't loved her as much as she'd loved him.

Or maybe he hadn't loved her at all.

"Was this just a game?" she demanded. "Let's jerk around the American girl. It will be so much fun."

"It wasn't like that," he said, staring into her eyes. "I swear. I wanted to tell you the truth. I left Calandria to find you. It took me some time to learn your real name and then to convince your government to give me any information about you."

Right. Because he wasn't the only one keeping secrets.

She hadn't been the ditzy American tourist she'd led him to believe when they'd met. She'd been a newly trained operative, working for the United States government on her first assignment. In the words of James Bond, she had been a spy.

Not a very good one, she could admit now. She'd botched the assignment from the beginning. Fortunately, the only items of value on the line had been Calandrian artifacts, not lives. Not until she'd thought she'd seen her lover die.

"Allow me to start at the beginning," he said, his voice low and slightly accented.

She was willing to admit she remembered that voice. If she closed her eyes and simply listened to the words, it would be easy to believe, to get lost in a confusing mist of past and present. She almost wanted to—because back then her choices had been the relatively simple right and wrong. Now everything was complicated.

"My cousin Diego never accepted the fact that due to an ancient rule and a quirk of birth order, he would not rule Calandria. As he grew older, he vowed his revenge, on whom I do not know. Perhaps on the country herself. No one could reason with him, not even me, but we were, until our early twenties, close."

"But if you're the heir"—a fact she wanted confirmed by a reliable outside source, because thinking about it was just too crazy—"wouldn't he have resented you the most?"

"In a way he did. Yet we were friends. No matter how I tried to make Diego feel welcome, to give him something to do in our government, he remained bitter. He turned his energy to researching our ancient past and discovered a treasure trove of antiquities just beyond the waves. That discovery itself could have made him a very famous and wealthy man, but for Diego, it wasn't enough. Instead of announcing his find, he kept the knowledge secret and sold the jewels and artifacts on the black market."

"I know that part," Mia said. "That's why I was sent there—to help uncover the ring of thieves." She'd been thrilled to get an undercover assignment so quickly after finishing her training. "But *you* were Diego."

"Not at first. After he was killed, the director of intelligence came to see me."

Tiny Calandria had a director of intelligence? The island was barely the size of Manhattan.

"He and his men had decided the best way to trap all the would-be thieves was for me to go in and pretend to be Diego. We told no one. Not even the Americans who were assisting us. As no one knew Diego had died in a car accident outside of Paris, it was easy for me to step into his place."

She walked to the wooden railing at the edge of the vegetable garden and rested her arms on top. Her head hurt from trying to get all this straight. "You were a plant?"

"Yes."

"Then you were never the bad guy."

"Not in the traditional sense."

Mia would deal with that later. When she was alone, she would pick apart his story, piece by piece, and try to get her mind around the fact that Diego hadn't been bad at all.

She looked at him, then wished she hadn't. Listening was safe, but seeing the differences in his appearance startled her. Not that he wasn't good-looking now, but everything was wrong.

"You set me up. You wanted me to see you die so I would report that little tidbit back to my government. You used me."

"I didn't want to, but there wasn't another way. Per the plan, the authorities arrived to arrest everyone. You escaped, Diego's people watched Diego die, and the heritage of my country was restored."

All very tidy, Mia thought, except for the fact that she'd been in love with Diego. She'd gone against all her training and her beliefs when she'd found herself falling for the man she thought was the enemy. Torn between what her head told her was right and what her heart begged her to claim, she'd barely been able to function.

Anger returned. She glared at him. "You must have been so delighted that I conveniently fell in with your plans. Imagine how difficult things would have been if I hadn't fallen for you."

"Mia, no. I never meant to hurt you or use you. I wanted to tell you the truth."

"I know, but you were just so busy. There wasn't any time." She took a step back. "I suppose the moment you were pushing me onto the helicopter wasn't convenient enough? Or what about afterward, when I was falling apart? I thought I loved you. I thought you were special, and you walked away and let me think you were dead for five years?"

"I wanted to come after you," he said. "I needed to tell you the truth. You must believe me."

"Not a chance. How hard would I have been to find?"

He set his coffee on the fence post. "Your government

was not exactly forthcoming. You were an operative and they insisted on protecting your identity. In desperation, I went through diplomatic channels. I used every power of my office to find you. At last I received word from a source I trusted that you had been killed only a few weeks after you had left Calandria."

"Bullshit."

He reached for her again, but this time she stayed back.

"I'm not lying," he said. "I was devastated. I could not imagine a world without your laughter." He shook his head, then looked away. "I know what I felt and I will not explain myself further."

If he'd tried to convince her, she wouldn't have believed him, but the arrogant tilt of his head, the lack of concern for her feelings, sort of made her wonder if he was telling the truth.

Rafael was right—the United States government didn't give out personal information on intelligence personnel to foreign governments. Even intelligence personnel who quit after their first job.

He stared at the vineyard. "If they hadn't told me you'd died, I never would have stopped looking. I believe that's why they made up the story. The source was someone I trusted. I had no reason to question the information."

"So you knew who I was," she said.

"I knew you were with the American intelligence community. I knew you were there to get information on the thefts. I knew we were both on the same side."

"Wish *I'd* had that information," she murmured. "So what happened next? You returned to your life?" She shook her head. "Are you really the crown prince?"

He smiled. "You have seen my identification. Speaking of which, I will need my passport returned to me."

"Sure thing." She glanced at the driveway and saw the front of the large, long limo with flags fluttering. "You'd better not be lying about that being your car. Even as we speak, my brother is running the plates."

"Then he will be able to confirm the truth of my statement." His smile deepened. "Would I really lie about being a prince? Something so easy to prove or disprove?"

He had a point. She sipped her coffee and wished she could take a couple of days to absorb all this.

"Why now?" she asked. "Why did you come back?"

"I found out you were still alive. I came right away, Mia. I came for you."

Not quite as good as Kyle Reese coming across time for Sarah Connor in the first *Terminator* movie, but when spoken in Rafael's soft accented voice, it was a close second.

"There was a picture in the newspaper," he said. "President Jensen's sixtieth birthday, I believe. You know the president of the United States?"

Mia knew exactly what picture he was talking about. It had been taken at a private party for the president. President Jensen had picked up Mia's son and tossed the boy in the air. The photo showed him as he caught the boy. They were both laughing, with Mia standing just behind them, clapping at their fun.

The picture had been on the front page of *USA Today*, with a line about the president enjoying a family outing on his birthday. Who knew the newspaper's distribution went all the way to Calandria?

"Yes, well, that just sort of happened. The president's daughter was threatened and she came here to hide out.

She and Joe fell in love. When they got married, we all became relatives."

She shook her head. If Rafael had seen that picture, he'd also seen Danny.

"What have you been doing?" he asked. "I know you left the agency. You would not have had your picture in the paper if you had not."

"What? Oh, right. No press photos of operatives. I quit as soon as I got back to the States. After you died, after I thought you died, I couldn't do it anymore. I came home and tried to make peace with everything."

"Did you?"

No. She'd fallen apart—a new experience for her. She'd grown up confident and ready to rule the world. But something had happened in the short weeks she'd spent pretending to be an American looking for adventure.

"I thought you were the bad guy," she told him, still furious that she'd been lied to. "I thought I was betraying my country by falling for you."

He stepped toward her. "Mia, do not distress yourself."

What was she supposed to do? Be happy? "If I can't believe who you were, how can I believe who you are?"

"Perhaps you don't have to. Perhaps we could start at the beginning. Meet now." He held out his right hand. "Good morning. I am Rafael, Crown Prince of Calandria. And you are?"

She sighed. "Sorry, no. That isn't going to work. We can't just start over. There's too much messy past between us. Too many years."

"So I should not have come? You are not happy to see me?"

"I'm . . ." Annoyed, confused, furious, shocked. "I'm not really a morning person."

"Of course. You want me to leave."

He turned, as if prepared to walk to his limo and disappear from her life. Only she wasn't ready for that. Not yet.

"Wait," she said. "I . . . What do I call you? Prince Rafael? Your highness?"

"Rafael is fine."

"All right. Rafael. This is happening so quickly. I don't know what to think or believe. I need a little time. We have to talk. I'm still not clear on why you're here."

"To see you."

Was that all? "If you saw the picture, then you saw Danny."

He frowned slightly. "The boy? The child of one of your sisters."

Mia clutched her coffee. It was true that the caption hadn't identified the child in the picture, or her for that matter.

She didn't know if Rafael was telling the truth. She'd long since learned to be wary of the men she brought into her life. They were usually snakes. Diego had been no exception, but was Rafael different?

Did it matter? Either way, she had to tell him. He deserved to know.

"Danny is my son," she said, doing her best to keep her voice even. "And yours."

Rafael timed his reaction carefully. To show too much shock would be to put Mia on her guard. To show not enough would mark him as an indifferent father.

"My son?" he asked as he took a step back. "What are you saying?"

"I was pregnant when I left Calandria. Only a week or so along. I didn't know, obviously. When I came home, I was pretty broken up about everything. Finding out I was pregnant saved me."

He saw the pain in her eyes as she spoke and knew he had no reason not to believe her. Besides, he and Mia hadn't been lovers for more than a couple of weeks before the sting had ended.

"I had no idea," he said, willing his expression toward disbelief. "You had a child? Your government kept that from me as well?"

"I'm not sure they knew," she told him. "I quit and came home. That was the end of my relationship with the agency. Unlike in the movies, they didn't spend a lot of time begging me to return to my old job."

"Someone should have told me," he growled, not having to fake the anger he felt. What Mia didn't know was that it was directed at himself. He'd been the one who hadn't bothered to follow up with her. To make sure there were no consequences of their time together. For the past four years his son, his *heir*, had existed and he hadn't known.

"I would have, except I thought you were dead," she said sharply, then sighed. "Sorry. I don't mean to be crabby. This is all so much. Too much. I don't know what Danny's going to think. All his life, I told him his father died before he was born." She looked at him. "You're not questioning your paternity. I'm not lying, but you'll probably want to check this all out. It would be a big deal for any guy, but I'm guessing an even bigger one for a prince."

She was telling the truth. Before sneaking into Mia's room, he'd visited the boy. The child had slept soundly and it had been easy to check the small of his back. There, just to the left of his spine, was the small star-shaped birthmark all the men in his family possessed. The child was his, but better to play along and pretend to not be sure.

"I have never doubted your integrity," he said. "But under the circumstances proof will be necessary. I'm sure we can arrange for a DNA test of some kind."

"Circumstances?" she repeated. "You mean the one where you're a prince and heir to a throne and I'm just some commoner from California?"

"I would not describe you thus," he said, moving close and taking her hand in his. Her skin was warm and he enjoyed the contact.

Five years ago he'd claimed Mia as his own because it had pleased him to do so. Now he would claim her for other reasons, but the task would still be most pleasant.

"Great," she murmured, then took a sip of her coffee as she carefully pulled free of his touch. "Let me recap. You might be Diego, and hey, an heir to the Calandria throne. You're also not dead. In the short time we were together five years ago, I managed to get pregnant, because that's just how my luck goes. Now you're back and we're parents together. Did I miss anything?"

He remembered the first time he'd met her. Even then he'd been unable to decide which he admired more—her spirit or her beauty. His dilemma had not changed.

"Those seem to be the salient points," he said.

"Great. I need more coffee."

She took a step and stumbled on the uneven ground. He reached for her, grabbing her arm and holding her upright. She reached for him with her free hand—to steady herself, he was sure—which left them standing very close.

He found himself staring into her brown eyes. He could feel the warmth and enticing curves of her body. Her mouth called to him. Whatever else might or might not have happened with Mia, he had always wanted her. Apparently time apart hadn't changed that fact. How convenient.

"Mia," he whispered.

"Don't even think about it," she told him, but she didn't move away.

"Why would I think when action is so much more pleasurable?" he asked as he lowered his mouth to hers.

Her breath caught. She stiffened but stayed in his arms.

Then a loud voice cut through the morning and broke the mood completely.

"Step away from my sister. Do it slowly and I probably won't shoot you in the back."

2

Rafael straightened but didn't move away. Mia took advantage of his momentary distraction and stepped back so she could look at Joe.

Sure enough, her former Navy SEAL brother held a mean-looking handgun inches from Rafael's back. While she appreciated Joe's concern about her safety and that he was willing to be all macho and protective, she wasn't sure shooting the father of her son was an especially good idea. Not yet, anyway. Although she kind of liked seeing Rafael at the business end of a gun.

"I don't think he's dangerous," she said, only to gasp in surprise as two large and burly men in dark suits rounded the side of the house. Each of them had an equally impressive-looking handgun. They shouted in Italian, then in French, for Joe to drop his weapon.

In a move too fast for her to see, Joe grabbed Rafael and held his gun to the base of his neck.

"Get behind me," Joe told her. "Who the hell are you?" he asked the other two. "What do you want?"

Okay, this was quickly getting out of hand. Mia looked

at Rafael. "Let me guess—the bodyguards?" Traveling with protection certainly helped his credibility on the whole "I'm a prince" thing.

"Yes. Umberto. Oliver. There is no need to attack anyone so early in the morning. This is only a misunderstanding." Rafael, apparently unconcerned about the gun pressing into his neck, smiled at Joe. "Is it not?"

He sounded calm, which Mia respected.

The bodyguards, however, were not moved. They kept their weapons trained on Joe.

Just then the back door to the kitchen opened. Grandma Tessa walked out and planted her hands on her hips. "If you boys are finished playing, breakfast is ready." Her eyes narrowed. "It's getting cold."

Mia glanced at the men and realized this could take a minute. Rather than deal with the diplomatic disarming, she stepped around Joe and hurried toward the house. Maybe running away wasn't her preferred method of dealing with problems, but Rafael wasn't a normal problem. Besides, she had to be somewhere.

"Mia?" Rafael called after her. "Perhaps you could ask your brother to release me."

"You used to be a dangerous outlaw," she told him as she passed Grandma Tessa on the stairs. "You figure it out."

Once she was inside, she made her way to the second story. She'd grown up here—lived her life surrounded by these walls. At sixteen she'd gone to college but had still considered the hacienda home. At twenty-three she'd returned pregnant, emotionally devastated. Her family had taken her in and made her feel welcome.

In time she would leave again and take her son with

her. They would start a new life, but they would both always remember their time here.

When she reached the bedroom on the end, right across from her own, she paused in front of the closed door and pressed her hand against the painted wood.

Everything was about to change. She didn't know where they would end up, but as of this minute, her world had been tilted on its axis. Until this morning she'd wondered if her son would be interested in inheriting Marcelli Wine and the acres of vineyards around the house. Now, apparently, he might be next in line to inherit a whole country.

She opened the door and stepped into the colorful, toy-filled bedroom and smiled as her son sat up.

"Good morning, sleepyhead. Did you sleep well?"

"Mommy!" Danny held out his arms.

When she plopped down on the mattress, he climbed into her lap and leaned his head against her chest. Automatically she picked up his treasured stuffed tiger and handed it to him. He held it close while she wrapped her arms around him and rocked him back and forth.

"We have a busy day," she said softly. "So many things to do. Grammy M and Grandma Tessa have finished your costume."

He looked up at her and grinned. "For my play?"

"Uh-huh. I think maybe later we should practice your lines again."

"I know 'em."

She smiled. He knew his three lines about as well as any other child in his preschool class. Which meant the play would consist of a lot of parental prompting and giggles from the kids.

Danny snuggled close. She breathed in the scent of him,

knowing she could find him in the dark by smell alone. He was her child and her world. From the moment she'd found out she was pregnant, she'd known it would always just be the two of them. Well, as much as it *could* be the two of them, given her extended and loving family and the fact that she lived in the same house as her parents and both grandmothers.

"I want chocolate cake," he said.

She laughed. "Hmm, yesterday it was peanut butter."

"Grammy M said a peanut butter cake would stick to the roof of my mouth. So chocolate."

His fourth birthday was still nearly a month away, but Danny took the cake decision very seriously. As this was the first year he'd actually had an opinion, Mia was more than willing to let him pick.

"Chocolate it is," she said as she kissed the top of his head then set him on the floor. "Okay, big guy. Let's get you dressed."

Danny rubbed his eyes, set down his tiger, and tugged at his PJ shirt. He got it over his head, where it got stuck. Mia pulled until he popped free and grinned at her.

She pulled open a drawer and called out colors. "Blue, green, red, or yellow?"

Danny closed his mouth and blew through pursed lips. "Yellow."

She removed a bright yellow T-shirt with trucks on the front, a pair of dark gray shorts, and cartoon character–covered underwear.

He stepped out of his bottoms and underwear, then reached for the clean pair of little boy briefs. Next were the shorts, which he could pull on himself. She helped him with the T-shirt.

The familiarity of the morning routine allowed her to

momentarily forget the sudden appearance of Danny's father, but she couldn't ignore Diego . . . Rafael . . . any longer.

She tossed the dirty clothes into the hamper and grabbed the hairbrush from the dresser. Danny stood patiently while she smoothed his dark hair. When she'd finished, she looked at the familiar little face and knew he was very much his father's son.

The shape of their eyes was the same and they had similar smiles. Not that there was any doubt. Mia hadn't been in a relationship in months when she met Rafael. She'd fallen hard, even though she'd known it was the wrong thing to do.

Rafael might insist on a DNA test, but she already knew the truth.

"What, Mommy?" Danny asked, his face scrunching up in a frown. "Are you sad?"

"Not sad. I have to tell you something."

"I've been good."

She smiled. "Yes, you have. You're usually very good and I think that's great." She took the boy's hands in her own. "Do you remember me telling you how your daddy died before you were born?"

Danny nodded solemnly. "You were very sad for a long, long time."

"I was. But what I didn't know was he was playing a game. Not with me, but with some other people. He only pretended to die, but I didn't know. I thought he was gone."

Danny stared at her and she could see he wasn't getting it. Who could blame him? He was three weeks shy of turning four. She was twenty-seven and she was having trouble taking it all in.

She started over. "I thought your daddy was dead, but he wasn't. He was fine. But some people wanted to protect me and they told him . . ."

She sighed. Okay, this was getting worse by the minute. How to explain that while she'd thought Rafael was dead and he wasn't, he'd thought the same about her and . . .

"Your daddy isn't dead. He's here. Downstairs. He didn't know about you until today and he's very excited to find out he has a little boy."

Danny's face lit up as he pulled his hands free and clapped them together. "I have a *daddy*?" he asked with a reverence usually reserved for ice cream and puppies.

"Yes, you do. Would you like to meet him?"

Her son nodded vigorously.

"You sure you want to go there?" Joe asked from the doorway to Danny's room. "What about the DNA test and checking this guy out?"

"Uncle Joe!" Danny flew toward his favorite male in the whole world.

Joe grabbed him and tossed him in the air. "Whoa there. You grew in the night. I can tell."

Danny shrieked with delight as his uncle caught him. "I got a daddy."

"So I heard."

Mia stood. "So the four of you worked out your personal issues?"

Joe shifted the boy so that Danny sat on his shoulders. "Grandma Tessa bullied them into putting theirs away first. Then I was willing to play nice."

"Always the protector."

"I try. Aren't you being a little premature on the d-a-d-d-y front? What do you know about this guy?"

Mia couldn't answer that. Diego had been a notorious outlaw. Apparently Rafael was a prince. "I know what happened and I know Danny is his son. I'm not going to keep them apart."

"I want to check out the guy," her brother told her.

"I encourage that. Check away." But prince or not, Diego/Rafael had fathered her child. Although as Rafael had pointed out, why lie about being a prince?

"What's he doing here?" Joe asked her. "Why now?"

"It was that picture with the president. *USA Today* picked it up and apparently flashed it around the world."

"Yeah, them," Joe muttered.

"At least the Grands will be excited if he turns out to be a prince," she told him. "First you marry the president's daughter then I . . ." She glanced at her son. "Then I meet someone famous."

"Meet, huh? That's one way to put it." Joe grabbed Danny's ankles. "Ready to go downstairs?" he asked.

"Go fast," Danny yelled. "As fastest as you can!"

Joe obliged by racing down the stairs. Mia followed, wondering how it was possible that her perfectly ordinary life had just taken a turn for the incredible.

Rafael did his best to hide his amusement. Oliver and Umberto were highly trained bodyguards who were used to controlling every situation. Now they were held at bay by a tiny woman with a rolling pin. It wasn't that the two men couldn't take Grandma Tessa, as Mia had called her, but that their own sense of family, not to mention his orders to stand down, put them in an uncomfortable situation.

"Tessa, please," the other grandmother—Grammy M—said with a sigh. "You'll be frightenin' our guests."

"They're not guests. They have guns." Tessa's eyes narrowed as if she wanted to whack them both on the back of the head to teach them a lesson. "There will be no guns in this house."

"Joe had a gun," Grammy M pointed out.

"He's family. That's different."

Rafael enjoyed the blend of Tessa's slight Italian accent and Grammy M's lilting Irish voice.

"They're here to protect me," he said, hoping to smooth over the situation.

"I can see why you'd want protection from two old women," Tessa chided.

Grammy M sighed. "You'll have to be forgivin' her, your highness. Tessa's not one to deal well with change."

"I suppose you expect us to feed them, too," Tessa grumbled as she put the rolling pin on the counter and ignored the other woman's comment. "You show up without warning, claiming to be . . ." She shook her head. "I, for one, don't believe a word of it."

He'd spent the past couple of days researching Mia's family. His time working with the Calandrian intelligence department had taught him to know his enemies better than he knew any of his friends. Not that Mia or her relatives were necessarily enemies. Perhaps wild cards would be a better description.

He'd studied the names and faces, along with facts provided by the director of intelligence. But seeing a two-dimensional picture was very different from meeting the person in question.

He liked that Tessa mistrusted him. Her wariness showed a sensibility that would do well for his son. While Grammy M's soft and accepting heart was slightly less useful when it came to ruling a country, it might serve Daniel well in romantic matters.

"How can I convince you of my true identity?" he asked. "You have already seen my passport. Unfortunately, princes are not issued identification cards at birth."

"Too bad," Tessa said with a sniff. "But not to worry. Darcy has put a call in to her father. We'll soon know everything about you."

He pretended a confusion he didn't feel. "Darcy?" he asked, knowing exactly who she and her father were.

"The daughter of the president of the United States," Tessa said sharply. "She's married to Joe. My very sensible grandson. Good thing he takes after me and not some flighty people I could name who are won over by a couple of flags on a long black car and a title that may or may not be real."

Rafael bowed his head slightly and tried not to smile. "I have nothing to hide," he said. At least nothing they would find out by calling the president.

Grammy M walked to the table and poured him more coffee. "Don't let her be botherin' you. She's always been a bit of a crab."

Tessa ignored them and retreated to the stove. Rafael decided to use the moment to cement Grammy M's support.

"When did you leave Ireland?" he asked.

Grammy M glanced at the two bodyguards standing by the back door, then took the seat across from his at the large table.

"When I was a girl. I married young and my husband, God rest his soul, moved us here."

"A change from the beauty of those green hills," he said.

"'Tis true, but this is home now. It has been for a long time. My family is here. My husband died here, as did

Gabriel, a man I knew. He passed on a couple of years ago. Now Tessa and I are two old women waiting till the end of our days."

"Speak for yourself," Tessa snapped. "I'm waiting on Joe to throw that man out. All your smooth talking isn't going to convince me of anything."

Rafael knew he would have to charm Tessa into neutrality, if nothing else, but before he could start, Mia walked into the kitchen.

He stood and smiled at her. She acknowledged him with a nod of her head but nothing else. Instantly, both grandmothers were at her side, offering tangible support.

Five years ago Mia had come to his country to help rout out the thieves who were stealing Calandria's history. Her assignment had been to pose as a foolish but rich American tourist looking for adventure while collecting information on those who plotted against his country.

She'd been smart, irreverent, and determined. She'd also been a beauty, with streaked hair and big brown eyes. While the hair color was now darker, the eyes were the same. She hadn't lost her curves, but the air of joyous exuberance seemed to be missing.

"You'll want to meet Danny," she said.

He nodded, then felt an unexpected quickening of his heart. His son. His heir. Blood from dozens of kings and princes pumped in the boy's veins. Daniel . . . Rafael sighed—the boy's name would have to be changed to something more royal. Daniel was the hope of his country's future.

Mia retreated into the hallway, then returned leading a small boy by the hand. Although Rafael had seen him sleeping only an hour or two before, he hadn't taken the time to study the child's features.

Even without the telltale birthmark, the truth was there in the features, the shape of the body. Danny reminded him of Diego and Quentin when they had been young.

Still holding the boy's hand, Mia crouched next to the child and smiled. "Danny, do you want to say hello?"

Danny stuck his forefinger in his mouth and regarded Rafael thoughtfully. "Are you really my daddy?" he asked softly.

"Yes, I am. I am Crown Prince Rafael of Calandria and you are my heir."

Danny frowned. "I'm not air. I'm a little boy."

Mia smiled. "He means you're going to be like him when you grow up."

Danny turned and buried his face in her shoulder. Mia wrapped her arms around him. "Sorry," she told Rafael over the boy's head. "He's not usually shy, but this is a big deal."

"Of course. Anyone would be confused by the situation."

"You'd think a boy would know his own father," Tessa said, glaring at him.

"Rafael *is* his father," Mia said. "I don't have any doubts."

"We should have breakfast," Grammy M said. "Come on, Danny. I've made hot chocolate."

The boy let go of his mother and went with Grammy M to the table. He glanced at Rafael several times, as if trying to figure out what having a father meant.

Mia stood. "It's going to take time for all of us to adjust," she said.

He was close enough to inhale the scent of her skin. Something floral with the hint of a woman's heat. Instantly he could remember what it had been like to be with her. They'd come together in a fiery passion that had defied logic and some of the laws of physics.

Did that fire still exist between them? He would not mind if it did. Seducing Mia would not only be pleasurable, it would aid his plan.

"I do not mean to rush anyone," he said. "We will—what is the phrase?—make it up as we go along."

She smiled. "I'd like that."

"Good."

She had known him as Diego as well as anyone, he thought. But she didn't know him as Rafael. If she did, she would realize that he never allowed himself to simply go along with circumstances. He always had a goal and he always achieved it.

Danny's eyes were wide, but he didn't squirm.

Mia crouched in front of her son and took both his hands in hers. "Remember when you had to get a shot and I told you it would hurt?" she asked.

Danny nodded.

"And when we went to the dentist for a cleaning and I said it wouldn't hurt and it didn't?"

He nodded again.

"This won't hurt at all. Okay?"

He looked from her to Umberto, then opened his mouth and closed his eyes. The tall, burly bodyguard stuck the swab into the boy's mouth and rubbed it against his cheek.

"I am finished," he said in thickly accented English.

Danny blinked. "That's it?"

Mia grinned. "Uh-huh. Did I say it wouldn't hurt? Did you believe me?"

As she spoke, she tickled Danny's sides. He laughed and pretended to push her away, while cuddling closer.

"It was okay," he said between bursts of laughter.

Umberto nodded and left with the swab. Joe stepped out of the corner.

"They'll rush it through," he told her. "It should only be a few days."

Mia pulled Danny onto her lap and glanced at her brother. "Still having doubts?"

"More like false hopes," he admitted. "I don't like this."

"I don't know how I feel," she admitted. Too much had happened too quickly. Four hours ago she'd been asleep in her own bed and now a man she thought dead and buried had strolled back into her life. And not just any man.

"Is he really a prince?" she asked.

"Pretty much."

Impossible, she thought. "I've never been very good at reverence."

"You'd better learn to curtsy."

She couldn't imagine *that* ever happening. "It's a new century. Royalty isn't like it was before."

Joe smiled. "They've let go of their love of a good beheading." His smile faded. "I don't know what to hope for," he admitted. "Danny needs a father, but this guy?"

"I do have interesting taste in men," she said, still unable to get her mind around all that had happened.

Grammy M walked into the dining room. "He's leaving," she announced. "Just like that. Prince Rafael is leaving."

"Going back to Calandria?" Mia asked, wanting him gone and not gone in equal measure.

"Worse. A hotel. Tessa says he's not staying here, which is just ridiculous. I've never seen her like this before.

She was always difficult and stubborn, but not like this. Imagine takin' an instant dislike to little Danny's father."

Danny looked up at Mia. "Daddy stays here."

She wasn't sure if it was a question or a request. She turned to Joe. "What does your military training say?"

"We can keep an eye on him in either place."

There weren't that many hotels around the hacienda. Santa Barbara was the closest town, and as it was summer, the main tourist season was in full swing. Would he even be able to find a room nearby? Did she care?

"He could stay in the house," Grammy M said eagerly, "and those other two can use the guest cottage. That will get them out of the house. We shouldn't have guns in the house. Not with little fingers about."

Or even the whole boy, Mia thought. Technically there was room. Her parents were gone for a few months and the hacienda was big. "All right. Sure. Invite Rafael to stay." Assuming royalty was willing to bunk with the common man.

Grammy M held out her hand to Danny. "Come on, then. Let's go see if we can be convincin' your father to grace us with his presence."

Mia let the older woman lead Danny away.

"I'm not excited about the 'gracing us with his presence' attitude," she admitted when she and Joe were alone. "The situation is already difficult enough."

Joe moved close and put his arm around her. "We'll be fine."

"You sure about that?"

"Almost."

"Great. What can we do to move you to be completely sure? Because I'd like that better."

"You scared?"

Scared? Sure. And nauseous and apprehensive and a whole lot of other things.

"I saw him die, Joe. I've spent the past five years feeling guilty about the fact that he saved my life only to lose his own. Now he shows up and tells me he's not who I thought, he's not dead, and hey, 'I rushed to your side as soon as I found out you were still alive yourself.' There should be a limit on surprises in a twenty-four-hour period."

"Agreed. I'm going to call in a few favors and get extra security around the house."

Mia didn't like the sound of that. "Is there a problem?" Her body tightened with sudden cold. "Do you think once the DNA test is back he'll try to kidnap Danny?"

"Don't go there. We don't know enough, Mia. I want to be cautious."

"Cautious is good. Be the king of caution. You're good at that. In the meantime, I'll try to muddle through. This is all good, right? Like you said, Danny needs a father and who better than his biological one."

"You don't sound convinced."

"I'm not. I should be, but I'm not. I feel like I'm over-reacting by expecting the worst. I don't know. It's all crazy."

He pulled her close and kissed the top of her head. "Don't worry. I'll keep you safe."

"Promise?"

"You bet. Nobody screws with my family."

3

"You don't like him," Mia said.

Grandma Tessa slammed the side of her knife against several cloves of garlic. "Liking or not liking isn't an issue. If he's Danny's father, then he's part of the family."

"There's no 'if,'" she told her grandmother. "The DNA test will prove that."

Mia half expected the older woman to reach for her rosary. It usually took a lot less than this to get her to take a trip around the beads. But her small hands continued to chop the garlic.

"I know you're disappointed," Mia said, feeling young and awkward. "That we . . . That I . . . About Danny." Which was a polite way of saying she was sure her grandmother was disappointed that Mia had not only had sex with a man she wasn't married to, but that she'd gotten pregnant.

Tessa glanced at her. "Why are you saying that now? You never cared what I thought when you brought your boyfriends around before."

Mia winced. "Things are different," she admitted. "I'm not that wild child anymore. I'm Danny's mother." She no longer brought home boyfriends to share her room. Shocking her family had ceased to be entertaining, even if she couldn't seem to stop doing it.

Her grandmother smiled. "You're a good girl, Mia. You're smart and independent and sometimes you act before you think. At least you used to. Since you had Danny, you've settled down."

"Become boring," she muttered. Her life was her son, her family, and law school. Or it had been. "Of course now I know a prince. That's going to change things."

Tessa's smile faded. "I don't like him."

"Really? I hadn't noticed."

Her grandmother narrowed her gaze. "You're not to be taking that tone with me, young lady."

Mia leaned down and kissed her cheek. "You don't scare me."

A floorboard creaked overhead. Mia glanced up. "I guess Rafael is settling in."

"I'm not sure his highness will like living in a real home with regular people. This isn't a palace, and if he thinks he's going to have us at his beck and call, he can think again."

Mia found herself torn between defending Rafael, who, technically, had not been unreasonable, and siding with Grandma Tessa.

"The bodyguards are in the guest house," she said. "That's something."

Tessa scooped the garlic into the heated pan and stirred the garlic and olive oil mixture. Mia had no idea what she was making. Practically every Italian dish began with garlic and olive oil.

"That was Joe," Tessa said curtly. "He's looking out for his family. Imagine those gorillas wanting to stay in this house with a little boy around. What if one of us got up in the night? They'd think we were after their precious prince and shoot us all in our sleep."

Mia thought about pointing out that anyone walking around was unlikely to be sleeping, but she liked that Grandma Tessa was on her side.

"Why don't you like him?" Mia asked.

Her grandmother went to work on a bowl of tomatoes, chopping them quickly and efficiently. "I don't know the man. It's for the Lord to judge him. That's not to say I'm willing to ignore my good sense just because he has a title, like some people I could name."

Mia knew the dig was aimed at Grammy M, who seemed happy to accept Rafael at face value.

Tessa nodded at the refrigerator. "There's corn in there. It won't be shucking itself."

Mia collected the bag and went to work. "I don't know what to think about all this," she admitted. "I know who he was, but I don't know who he is." She brushed corn silk into the trash can, then put the clean ear on the counter.

"Have you called Marco and Colleen?"

"No. I will. I want to tell them; it's just they've been looking forward to this trip for years and it took so long to arrange." Her parents, in charge of the overseas sales of Marcelli Wines, had just left for China three days ago. They were supposed to be gone two months. "I'm going to wait until they're in Beijing, then phone them at the hotel. I don't want them to come home early just for me. It's not as if Rafael is going anywhere."

Nor did she know if she wanted him to. While it would make her life easier, what about Danny? She wanted him to know his father.

"What about the girls?" Tessa asked, referring to Mia's sisters.

"I left a message for each of them already." There would be plenty of shrieking when they found out. "Brenna's out of town until tomorrow night, so Francesca and Katie will come over with her."

"They'll want to be with you," Tessa said. "They'll understand."

"I know." Sometimes her family made her crazy, but in situations like this, she appreciated the support. She wouldn't want to be going through this on her own.

Not that she even knew what "this" was.

The back door opened and Danny raced inside. Grammy M followed a bit more slowly.

"We picked berries," Danny said proudly as he showed off his red and purple fingers. "For dessert. Grammy M said I could help make it."

"I thought a berry shortcake would be nice for tonight," Grammy M said as she carried a basket to the sink. "I'm sure Rafael will appreciate some fine home cooking."

Tessa snorted. "I'm sure he's been longing for a little homemade dessert to chase away the flavor of all those five-star meals he's been forced to eat."

The two old women glared at each other. Mia took Danny by the hand. "Let's get you washed up," she said, more than willing to let them fight it out themselves.

"Is that man really my daddy?" Danny asked as they climbed the stairs.

"Yes, he is."

Her son looked at her, his eyes large and filled with questions. "Does he like me?"

Mia stopped and dropped to her knees. She took Danny's hands in hers and smiled. "Of course he does. You're a wonderful boy. Smart and funny and kind. You always help the Grands in the kitchen and you know your letters."

"I can write my name," he reminded her.

"Yes, you can. But even if you couldn't do all those things your daddy would like you because of who you are inside. Because you're his son."

At least she hoped that was the case. Honestly, how much did she really know about Rafael? Diego's background had been carefully spelled out during her briefings, but the crown prince had only been mentioned in passing. Who was the man inside?

After washing Danny's hands in the hall bathroom, Mia debated whether to return to the relative safety of the kitchen or to face Rafael. While the former had more appeal, the latter somehow felt right, so she smiled at her son and asked, "Want to go see your daddy?"

Danny nodded eagerly, but as they left the bathroom, he clutched her hand tightly.

They walked the few steps to the main guest room, the one with its own bathroom. The door stood open. She reached up to knock anyway when she saw Rafael placing what looked like socks in a dresser drawer.

He might be a prince now, but when she first knew him he was a big, bad thief with a reputation for killing the competition. She couldn't imagine either man putting away his own socks.

"I guess this is really different from living in a palace," she said.

He smiled. "In some ways, but if you are curious, I assure you I will survive without my butler."

"Good to know." The man had a butler? Sure. It probably came with the prince thing. Someone had to be responsible for his formal wear.

"I'm sure you have dry cleaning nearby," he said.

"Yes. I can show you. Or will the bodyguards take care of that?"

"They will. And my laundry."

"How nice. Proficiency with handguns and knowledge of the delicate cycle. They truly are the contemporary version of the Renaissance man."

Rafael raised his right eyebrow in a gesture that was so familiar, her breath caught. In that moment she was transported back to her days with Diego after they had become lovers. She remembered sitting through a long planning meeting, barely able to stay awake because they'd been up all night making love. He'd caught her yawning and had raised his right eyebrow. The gesture, so unlikely in a dark and dangerous man, had caused her to giggle. Then he had smiled. The meeting had ended suddenly and he had ushered her back to his room.

She shook off the memory and her body's visceral reaction to it. Ignoring Rafael, she glanced at Danny.

"What do you think?" she asked.

The boy didn't speak.

His father crouched down in front of him. "This is a very unusual situation. It isn't every day that a man finds out that he's a father. We're going to have to take some time and get to know each other."

Danny's eyes widened slightly, but again he didn't speak.

"I am very fortunate," Rafael continued. "Some fathers never find their children. I'm glad that didn't happen to us."

"Do I look like you?" Danny asked.

Mia wanted to answer but sensed this was a moment when it was better to keep quiet.

Rafael looked Danny over, then smiled. "I think you do."

"Charlie looks like his daddy. So does Brandon. Billy looks like his mom." He glanced at Mia, as if wondering if she understood why that was a bad thing.

She smiled. "You have the same eyes and smile. The hair color could have come from either of us."

"You are my son," Rafael told the boy. "You are a prince and one day you will rule Calandria."

Mia didn't want to think of things in those terms. Right now she would be thrilled to get Danny to eat more vegetables.

"A prince?" Danny laughed.

"It's true," his father told him.

From the moment Mia had found out she was pregnant, she'd thought of her child as a Marcelli. But he wasn't anymore.

Danny lunged at his father, arms open, body quivering. Rafael pulled him close and they hugged.

She stood a little distance away, watching the moment, equally happy and sad. Of course she wanted her son to have a father, but at the same time, she realized that nothing would ever be the same again. It was no longer just the two of them against the world. They were no longer a pair—in a matter of seconds, they had become a family.

"It is very beautiful here," Rafael said later that afternoon as he and Mia walked through the vineyards by the house.

"Things are about to get crazy," Mia told him. "The grapes are ripening and soon Brenna will begin compulsively checking to see which are ready to harvest. From that moment on, it's a rush to get everything picked and pressed and put into barrels."

She forced herself to stop talking. It was one thing to

be nervous around Rafael, it was another to let him know. But jeez, Rafael here? Nothing felt real.

"We don't make wine in Calandria. There is not enough land. That which is used for agriculture is used to grow our olives."

"Ah, yes. The famous Calandrian olives. Worth their weight in gold."

He smiled at her. "Almost. If the price of gold is down that week." He stopped and looked at her. "How are you—what is the phrase?—holding up?"

"I'm good. A little shell-shocked but recovering." Give her six or eight weeks and she'd be an old pro at dealing with him.

"Me too," he admitted with a shrug. "A short time ago, I was a carefree bachelor."

"You're still that."

"Not so much. I have a family."

Exactly how she'd thought of them earlier. Why did it make her uncomfortable coming from him? "We have Danny in common," she told him. "But nothing else."

His mouth curved into a smile. "Once you would not have said that."

"It's been a long time. We're different people now. You more than me."

"Because I am not the dark and dangerous Diego?"

"That's part of it."

He reached for her hand. "Perhaps we should get to know each other again. We have a child together, Mia. That is a bond that will never be broken."

She was as mesmerized by his low, seductive voice as by the gentle pressure of his hand holding hers. He laced their fingers together.

There *was* Danny to think about, she reminded herself. Parents who got along were better than parents who didn't. Did she want that? To get to know him? Did she have a choice? She was drawn to Rafael but couldn't figure out how much of it was him as he was today and how much was the past.

"I agree that becoming friends is a good idea," she said carefully.

"Excellent. Then let us begin. Tell me about your family."

"Did you find out about them before you came here?"

"I have some basic information, but I want to hear about them from you. One can read a guidebook about a city, but until one has talked to a native, one cannot understand the flavor."

Interesting point. "Okay. This land has belonged to the Marcellis for nearly ninety years. Not impressive by European standards, but it's a big deal for us. My father is the third generation, and Danny the fifth. Obviously we're Marcelli Wines. Our neighbors are Wild Sea. That's the Giovanni family. Brenna, one of my sisters, married Nic Giovanni. The businesses are kept separate, but Brenna's the wine queen and pretty bossy, so things are changing at Wild Sea."

Rafael kept hold of her hand and began walking again. "Wild Sea is a much bigger company."

"They're huge. Brenna complains Nic is more into volume than quality, while he complains she's morally opposed to making a profit. Neither is totally true. But it's their passion and they argue all the time. They have five-year-old twins, Amy and Parker. Brenna's a twin herself. The other half of that is Francesca, who's married to Sam."

She paused to draw in a breath. "You really want to know all this?"

"Absolutely. Brenna and Francesca are twins. Go on."

"Okay. Francesca's a psychologist. Sam's a security expert. He has a daughter from a previous marriage—Kelly. She's a dancer and I adore her. They also have twins. Eric and Haley are seven. Then there's Katie, who's my oldest sister. She's a party planner in Los Angeles and is married to Zach. He has a son from a previous marriage, David, and they have two kids of their own. Valerie's six and Liana is three."

Rafael laughed. "Four girls. Your brother Joe was either very much in charge or tormented."

Mia wrinkled her nose. "You'd think, but Joe didn't grow up with us. It's complicated, but my mom got pregnant while still in high school and she gave up the baby. Then she and my dad got married and had us and finally realized they had to find their son. But he's a Marcelli now. He works in the winery. Darcy, his wife, is the president's daughter, which is how I was in that picture and you saw me."

"What if I hadn't?" he asked, sounding as if the thought distressed him. "I could have missed finding you."

There was an intensity that both drew her in and made her uncomfortable. In truth, she liked being with Rafael more than she should. But Grandma Tessa was right—what did she really know about the man? Still, there was enough of Diego in him to weaken her defenses. She couldn't be with him and not remember how much she had once loved him. Or at least the man he had pretended to be. Strong, intelligent, difficult.

"Where are your parents?" he asked. "Still alive?"

"Very much so. They've just left for China. It's a special trip for them and I hate to call them back. I'm sure you'll meet them, though."

"I want to." He looked around the vineyard. "I like this place. It is quiet and peaceful."

"Not much nightlife, though."

"Do you like that sort of thing?"

"Sometimes. The past few years, I haven't had the time or the energy. Even with all the help I have, Danny keeps me busy. And I've been going to law school. I have one year left."

"A lawyer. I wouldn't have guessed that."

"The spy business turned out not to be for me."

He squeezed her hand. "Mia . . ."

"I don't want to talk about what happened, Rafael. Not yet."

"As you wish. Then we will change the subject. What would you like to know about me?"

She had a thousand questions, but at that moment, she could only think of one. "Are you married?"

He stopped and faced her. "Mia, you do not have to ask me that. I would not have joined you in your bed if I had been."

"Oh. Right. That would have been tacky, huh?"

He smiled and touched her face. "You are different, and yet so much the same. I remember the first time I saw you in the plaza. You wore a very short dress and you were laughing. That is what I remember most, the sound of your laughter."

She felt herself getting lost in his eyes. Blue, she thought hazily. How could they be blue? She remembered how dark they had been. Contacts, of course. She'd never guessed.

He moved closer. She had a fleeting thought that he was going to kiss her, which immediately inspired panic.

Getting along with Diego in bed had never been a problem. She doubted she would have a difficult transition with Rafael. But she wasn't the same impulsive young woman she'd been back then. Now she had responsibilities.

"Tell me about your family," she said as she took a step back. Her body trembled slightly as heat filled her. Why was doing the right thing always such a bitch?

"I am an only child. My mother died when I was three and my father never remarried."

"How horrible."

He shrugged. "It is the world I know. I was raised with my two cousins. Diego and Quentin."

Like Chanel and Versace, Quentin didn't need a second name. "We all love his clothes," she admitted. "I can't afford them, but I love them."

"I will be sure to let him know."

"Absolutely. And if he ever has any couture overstocks, he should feel free to send them my way."

Rafael laughed. "As you wish."

They turned back toward the house.

"You have made a good life for Danny here," he said.

"I can't take all the credit. My family has been great. My mom and the Grands helped with everything from midnight feedings to babysitting. Now he's in preschool, which he loves. In fact, he insisted I sign him up for the summer program so he wouldn't miss anything. Not that he lacked for company before. With so many cousins around his age, he's had plenty of kids to play with."

"Do you enjoy law school?"

"It's interesting. I'm looking at international corporate law. My ability with languages could really be a plus."

"That's right. You are the language expert. How many do you speak now?"

"I'm fluent in about eight and I can get by in another five or six. I don't have the time to study new languages the way I used to."

"When we met you were studying Russian. I was most impressed."

"The language was nothing. It was that damn alphabet that really did me in."

As they approached the house, Mia saw a red BMW 3 series pull up. Instantly Umberto and Oliver appeared, guns drawn and shouting at the driver to show his hands.

Mia rolled her eyes. "Those guys desperately need a hobby," she said as she hurried forward.

"Relax, guys," she yelled. "He's family."

A rush of longing filled her. Another familiar face. Why did she suddenly feel the need to surround herself with people she could trust?

Rafael instructed the men to step back. They moved away from the car but kept their guns in plain sight. The driver's door opened and David Stryker stepped out.

"It's never boring here," he said, glancing from the guns to Mia. "I'm sure there's a perfectly logical explanation."

"There is," she said as she flew into his arms and clung to him.

"Hey, you're happy to see me." He hugged her back, then stared into her face. "Everything okay?"

"Fine."

He looked from her to the bodyguards, then at Rafael. "Why don't I believe that?"

"Not a clue." Mia bent down and waved at the slender blonde sitting in the passenger seat. "Hi, Amber."

David's fiancée gave a halfhearted wave back.

"It's the guns," David murmured in Mia's ear.

"Sure. They'd put anyone off." She turned to Rafael. "Want to call off the goon squad?"

Rafael winced. "They do not like to be called that," he said in English, followed by instructions in Italian. Umberto and Oliver reluctantly complied.

Rafael waited while Mia helped the blond woman from the car, then nodded politely as they were introduced. There was something about the younger man . . . a familiarity he had with Mia that Rafael did not like.

"Complications," Mia said brightly.

"You said they were family." His gaze narrowed. "Family by blood?"

"Not exactly. David is my sister Katie's stepson. In fact, David and I are responsible for bringing Zach and Katie together."

Rafael had a feeling that David sensed his mild annoyance. The other man slipped an arm around Mia and grinned.

"We were engaged. My dad thought we were too young and vowed to break us up. Katie took the other side of the argument. It was love at first sight for the two of them."

Mia shook her head. "If love means a lot of arguing. Although the sex was hot. At least that's what she implied."

David took a big step back. "No details, Mia. We have a deal. Parental unit sex is an unacceptable topic for discussion."

"Sorry. I keep forgetting. Katie's just a sister, so I don't have the same ick factor." Mia smiled at Amber. "Are we scaring you again?"

The pretty blonde smiled. "Of course not. I love all of David's family."

Rafael would not have been willing to bet on that fact.

Mia turned to him. "Rafael, this is Amber. She and David are going to be married in a couple of months. The Grands are going crazy, wanting to plan everything. Actually, they get along great with Amber's mom, which helps a lot."

"The wedding is to be held here?" he asked.

"David thought it would be beautiful and, of course, I agree," Amber said.

Rafael wondered if her concerns ended with Mia or did Amber dislike all the Marcellis?

"The Grands made two different kinds of cake for you to sample," Mia said. "I hope you're hungry."

Before Amber could protest, Mia led her inside. David chose not to follow. Rafael turned to the younger man and held out his hand.

"I'm Crown Prince Rafael of Calandria."

David raised his eyebrows. "That's a mouthful. It also explains the guys with guns. Interesting. You know Mia?"

"I am Daniel's father."

"Since when?"

"Since the night he was conceived."

David didn't look surprised or intimidated, which annoyed Rafael.

"You've been away a long time," David said.

"I was not aware that Mia or the child lived."

"Interesting story. I'll get the details later." David's gaze was steady. "You and Mia getting back together?"

"That is the plan."

"Does she know?"

Rafael resented the implication that Mia was not delighted to be once again in his presence.

"Is it your concern?" Rafael asked.

"Only as a brother. Mia and I are still close."

"A fact that must delight your fiancée."

David stiffened. "Met Joe yet? He's a pretty tough guy." He glanced at Umberto and Oliver. "If it came down to a fight, I'd bet on Joe."

With that, David turned and walked into the house. Rafael stared after him, then reached in his pocket for his cell phone. He dialed a number by heart, then walked away from the house as the call was answered.

"My father, please."

Seconds later, the king came on the line. "Do you have the boy?"

"Not yet," he said. "The situation is more complicated than we had realized."

"But you are there."

"Yes. I've seen the child. He is mine."

"An heir. You must bring him home at once."

"I will, Father. However, buying off the family is out of the question. They are wealthy in their own right, and they are not the kind to let the boy go easily."

"That is unacceptable. The heir to Calandria must be raised here. He must understand his duties."

Rafael knew all about those duties. He'd been raised with them as ever-present ghosts.

"They are a powerful family with close ties to the president. But do not concern yourself. I have a plan."

"Which is?"

"I will marry Mia."

4

Brenna Marcelli Giovanni checked the coffee table. "Cookies, chocolate, wine, glasses. I think that's everything."

Mia had been patient while her sisters met Rafael. Then the four of them drove over to Brenna's house for an afternoon of girl talk and wine.

"Well?" she demanded. "What do you think?"

"We need more wine," Brenna said. "Definitely another bottle."

Mia threw herself on the sofa and covered her face with a pillow. "Somebody kill me now."

"Don't say that," Katie told her as she settled next to her and put an arm around her. "Why would you want to be dead just when things are getting interesting?"

"She has a point," Francesca said. "Besides, death really isn't your style. Maybe you should start streaking your hair again. That would be a statement."

"A tacky one," Brenna said, returning with another bottle of Four Sisters pinot noir. "Everyone have what they need?"

There were murmurs of assent. Brenna sank into a club chair and motioned for Francesca to open the first bottle.

Francesca did the honors, poured them each a glass and passed them around. When everyone had appreciated the aroma, the color, and the subtle blend to Brenna's satisfaction, Francesca took her seat, then turned to Mia.

"So, you slept with a prince. That's new."

Mia threw the pillow at her. "Not helpful. Aren't you the one with the degree in psychology? Shouldn't you be making the situation better?"

"That seems like a natural assumption, but in this case, not so much."

Brenna and her twin grinned at each other. Katie tugged on Mia's hair. "Don't let them get to you. They're just having a little fun. You have to admit, this isn't normal, even for you. You haven't been on a date since you found out you were pregnant with Danny. You'd told us his father had died. Suddenly he's back and he's a prince. I think a little humor is in order."

"I know, it's just that I don't know what I'm thinking or supposed to think. Or feel, or any of that. He was dead. I saw him die. Only none of it was real and now he's here and I don't know what I'm supposed to do." Mia looked at Katie. "What did you think of him?"

"He was pleasant. Not pretentious."

"Good-looking," Brenna added, "which is always a plus. I mean if you have to look at them every day, why not get one who's pretty?"

"That is shallow, even for you," Francesca told her. "He said all the right things, Mia. What we have to figure out is if he means them."

Katie looked at Mia. "How are you handling this, aside from the death wish?"

"I don't know. It's been two days and I'm in confusion mode. The whole situation doesn't seem possible, but he's here and it's happening. He's Danny's father. Whatever else happens, I have to deal with that."

"Yes, there is the whole 'sperm meets egg' that changes things forever," Brenna said. "Why don't you start at the beginning and tell us how you met him. You were pretty vague when you got back from that assignment."

Mia knew her sister was being kind. She hadn't been vague, she'd been completely devastated. Because she'd been in the field as a covert operative—a reality she still had trouble grasping—she hadn't been able to tell her family anything. In theory, that truth hadn't changed. Except according to Rafael, nothing had been as it seemed.

"My first assignment was in Calandria," Mia said, figuring that was as good a place as any to start.

"Was it a dark and stormy night?" Brenna asked.

Mia grinned. "It was raining."

"You should always pay attention to atmosphere," her sister told her.

"I will now," Mia said, then wondered what it meant that it had been sunny the morning Rafael had shown up. Of course this was California. Where she lived, sunny was the norm.

"My job was to infiltrate a group of thieves who were taking newly discovered artifacts out of the country. I was supposed to play a bored, rich, ditzy American looking for trouble."

"Were you scared?" Katie asked.

"I don't think I knew enough to be scared," she admitted. "I thought it was a pretty easy assignment. I wasn't supposed to stop anyone, just get on the inside and then report back with what I knew. I flew into Calandria with the name of a contact. He was going to introduce me to a few key people in Diego's ring and then I was to take it from there."

"Diego's the bad guy, right?" Francesca asked. "Or the bad guy in disguise?"

"Right. The real Diego had been working this job for almost a year. He's the one who found the treasures and then got the divers to start bringing them to the surface. He had a reputation for being ruthless and dangerous."

"Your kind of guy?" Katie asked gently.

"I figured I was done with bad boys," Mia told her honestly. "After the disaster with Ian, I'd pretty much sworn off relationships period."

No one said anything, which Mia appreciated. She'd had six years to deal with the guilt of inadvertently bringing a domestic terrorist in close contact with the daughter of the president of the United States. She'd told herself there was no way she could guess that boring Ian, who had gone to grad school with her at Georgetown, was also secretly working to overthrow the government. Even the Secret Service had vetted him and come up with nothing. But she kept thinking she should have known her summer boyfriend was not a nice man.

"I spent a couple of days learning my way around town and sort of checking out Diego's people. He was too well known to come into town, so I didn't meet him at first. I did make contact with a couple of the women. As planned, a local policeman recognized one of them and began to arrest her. I started a fire in a trash can, which distracted him, and ran off with the women."

Brenna's eyes widened. "You were really a spy."

"Not a very good one. I lasted all of one assignment and fell in love with the bad guy. No one offered me a promotion."

"Don't be so hard on yourself," Katie said. "You weren't ready for what they asked you to do."

Mia agreed with that assessment. She should have been given a desk job for a while or at least a few low-level courier assignments. Instead, she'd been thrown into the middle of a gang of thieves, and their leader had mesmerized her from the start.

"They took me back to their hideout," Mia said. "Apparently that was considered a bad idea, because there was a lot of screaming. They discussed killing me as a way to keep me silent, which terrified me."

Her sisters stared at her. "They almost killed you? You never said anything."

"I wasn't supposed to. I probably shouldn't be telling you this now. But before anyone could shoot me or stab me, Diego came in and told them to let me go."

She still remembered everything about that moment. They'd been speaking in Italian, assuming she wouldn't understand them. Of course she had. Italian, Spanish, French. To her they were practically the same language.

Diego had asked how Mia had met the others, and when he heard about the fire, he crossed to her.

"Why did you help them?" he asked.

His voice had given her goose bumps. Her fear had faded in the heat generated by his nearness. To this day she couldn't say why she'd fallen for him in that second, but she had. She was sure there was some chemical explanation involving pheromones and the position of the moon or something, but it had happened. Hard, hot need had swept through her until all she could think about was giving herself to him. She would have been anything to him—lover, slave, sycophant. Anything, as long as he let her exist within the sphere of his world.

"They were nice to me," she'd said instead, proud that she'd been able to form words at all. "I'm loyal to my friends."

"What do you want with us?" he'd asked.

"Nothing. I don't even know who you are."

She'd lied, of course. She knew all about him from her briefing reports. Even more important, in that moment, staring into his dark eyes and willing him to take her right there, she understood the man.

He was darkness and she should be afraid of him, but she couldn't ignore the power of her need. If necessary, she would be in the darkness with him.

"I am Diego," he said, then watched sharply as if waiting for a reaction.

"Mia," she said with a shrug. "I'd offer to shake hands, but I'm kind of tied up."

He glanced at the handcuffs and smiled. "Do you travel alone?"

"I'm pretty independent. But don't get too comfy with the idea. If I don't check in with my dad every couple of days, he goes completely insane. We're talking about notifying four-star generals. Did I mention my father went to West Point?"

Diego had smiled then. "Release her," he told the others, speaking Italian. "She amuses me. She may stay. But make sure she doesn't go out by herself. And monitor her phone calls."

"I understood him, of course," Mia said to her sisters. "I thought he was the bad guy. I thought he was the one I was supposed to watch."

"Isn't the fact that he wasn't a good thing?" Katie asked. "Doesn't that make you feel better?"

"It should," Mia admitted. "It's just . . ." She drew in a breath. "I agonized over what was happening. I knew I was falling for him and that it would affect my judgment. I got in touch with my contact and begged him to get me out of there. I said I was at risk of compromising the assignment. But they left me in play. Every day he was there and every day I tried to resist. One day I couldn't."

"Okay, that's the part I want to hear about," Brenna said with a sigh. "In detail. Speak slowly."

Mia grinned. "It was another dark and stormy night. I remember sitting outside on a porch. Nearly everyone had gone into town. It was late and there were so many shadows. Suddenly, he was there."

He hadn't said anything—he hadn't had to. They'd looked at each other and then they were kissing and touching. He'd taken her without saying a word.

"The next morning I wondered if I'd dreamed the whole thing, but when I went to breakfast, he had me sit next to him. We were together from then on."

There were so many memories. So many times when she'd tried to walk away.

"I didn't want to do the wrong thing," she admitted. "If you knew how I tried to stay strong, to remember why I was there. I knew I was breaking every rule, I knew I was going to get fired. I told myself it wasn't so bad because no one's life was on the line. But I was wrong."

Two weeks after she and Diego became lovers, a rival gang attacked.

"I knew about it in advance from my handler. I was supposed to use the confusion to bring Diego in. If he resisted, I was supposed to shoot him. I wanted to warn him. For two days I nearly told him the truth." She laughed harshly. "For all I know, he arranged the whole damn thing."

"You think it was part of the plan to get him out of there?" Francesca asked.

"Maybe. I'm not sure. I do know that when the moment came, when I tried to take him with me, he wouldn't go. When I pulled a gun on him, he told me I wouldn't be able to shoot him. He was right."

"Did you try?" Katie asked.

"I knew it was the right thing to do, but I couldn't pull the trigger."

Mia had agonized over that. During her debriefing, she'd been grilled again and again about why she hadn't shot him when she'd had the chance. Now, knowing who he really was, she wondered if he'd replaced her bullets with blanks. It sure wouldn't surprise her.

"The fighting got closer," she continued, remembering the noise of that night. The sharp sound of gunfire, the cries of those who had been injured, then the roar of her helicopter.

"I didn't want to leave him, but I had to get out. I knew that. I begged him to come with me."

He'd smiled at her then, had kissed her hard and told

her to remember him. Because he'd known she was about to "see" him die?

"He literally tossed me onto the helicopter," she said. "I don't think I would have gone otherwise. As we lifted up, two men rushed him. I screamed, but it was too late. They fired and he fell and there was so much blood."

She would remember that for the rest of her life. The sound of the helicopter, her own screams, and the bright light that showed the rapidly widening pool of blood as Diego died.

Except he hadn't died. It had all been an elaborately staged event. Like a Broadway show.

Mia shook away the past and glanced at her sisters. "I thought he was gone. I went through my debriefing, then I quit and came here."

"And someone in the government told him *you* were dead?" Katie asked.

"That's what he said. I know they're not likely to give out information on operatives, even lousy ones."

"Mia, you were put in an impossible situation," Francesca told her. "Give yourself a break."

"I understand that in my head," Mia admitted. "But in my heart, I think about everything I did wrong. That's what's so hard for me. That I fell for the wrong guy again. You'd think Ian would have cured me of that."

"*Is* he the wrong guy?" Katie asked. "He's not the enemy anymore. He's a nice guy."

Brenna raised her eyebrows. "Nice? I don't think he's normal enough to be nice. He's royal, Katie. Does the man even know how to put toothpaste on his toothbrush?"

"He's doing it now," Mia said. "Unless Grammy M is sneaking into his bathroom every night to take care of that. When he was Diego, he had to act like everyone else. I know he's a prince and all, but he knows how to exist in the real world. At least he did."

"So *now* what?" Francesca asked.

"That would be my question," Mia said. "I'm trying to reconcile who he is with who he was and figure out where Danny fits in all this."

Brenna raised her glass. "I'll give you this—none of the Marcelli women are boring."

"Something we can cling to," Katie said. "I'm not sure that helps Mia, though."

Mia drank more wine. "I might be beyond help. Right now I'm dealing with crazy situations. Rafael is Danny's father. I can't change that, even if I wanted to, and I'm not sure I do. He's interested in his son, which is a plus, but what do I know about him?"

"You were once in love with him," Katie said. "Does that count for anything?"

Mia tried to laugh, but instead made a sound suspiciously close to a sob. "Not when you consider that the man I fell in love with was supposedly a notorious thief with a reputation for killing the competition."

"Maybe you sensed his goodness," Francesca said.

"I'm not that intuitive," Mia muttered.

"Are you attracted to him now?" Katie asked.

Brenna rolled her eyes. "Well, duh. Of course she is. Did you see the man? Did you think about him being naked?"

"Of course not! I'm a happily married woman." Katie sipped her wine. "I would never do that."

Mia looked at her, as did Brenna and Francesca. Katie sighed.

"Okay. Maybe. For a second. Yes, he's pretty amazing in the studly department, but that's no excuse to give in a second time."

"Ah, isn't knowing how good the sex was and could be again going to work against her?" Brenna asked.

Katie looked at Mia, who sighed. "It doesn't help," she admitted.

"Trouble," Francesca said. "All this is trouble. But you'll get through it."

"I don't see a way not to. I'm just glad Joe is around."

"Did you call Mom and Dad?" Katie asked.

"Yesterday. They're understandably shocked, but happy. I begged them to stay in China. Rafael will still be around when they get back."

"He's staying that long?" Brenna asked.

"I don't have exact dates, but I got the impression he would be parked here for a while. Even if he heads back to Calandria, there are going to be visits back and forth."

"So you have time," Katie said. "You can consider your options. Think with both your head and your heart."

"Don't make the same mistake twice," Mia said, and meant it.

"I have something for you, Danny," Rafael said as he entered the family room.

Mia sat on the floor with the boy on her lap. They both looked at him and smiled, Danny with more excitement than his mother.

"What is it?" Danny asked as he eyed the long, cloth-wrapped package. "A truck?"

"Better than a truck. I had it sent over from the palace." Rafael knelt on the floor and peeled back the quilted fabric. When he'd exposed the gold-and-jewel-covered scepter, he paused expectantly.

Danny stared at the scepter. "What's that?"

"The royal scepter of Calandria."

Danny looked at his mother. "What's that?"

Mia cleared her throat. "Well, it's a very important and beautiful part of your heritage. It symbolizes who you are."

"I'm Danny."

"Okay, yes, but you're also your father's son. Which makes you his heir."

"I'm the Crown Prince of Calandria," Rafael said, determined to be patient with the child. It was not his fault he didn't already know this. "I will rule as king and you will rule after me."

Danny considered that, then asked, "Where's Calandria?"

Rafael had come prepared. He pulled a European map out of his pocket and spread it on the floor. "Here is Italy and France. This is Spain. This is the Mediterranean and here is Calandria."

Danny stared at the island and wrinkled his nose. "It's small. Can I be the heir to a bigger place? What about Australia? Mommy and me read all about it in a book. There are kangaroos and crocodiles. I want to heir Australia."

As he spoke he reached for the scepter and slammed it against the floor. Rafael winced.

"Okay then," Mia said, grabbing it from him. "Maybe we should put this on a shelf until you're a little older. Why don't you go see Grammy M in the kitchen? I know she's making cookies. Maybe she'll let you help."

"Okay."

Danny scrambled to his feet and ran off to the kitchen. Mia turned to Rafael. "Sorry about that. He's still pretty young. I don't think he's grasping the whole 'heir' thing, which isn't a huge surprise as the rest of us are having trouble with it as well."

"He will have to learn," he told her, remembering how many responsibilities he had had when he had been little older than Danny was now. He needed to get the boy back to Calandria, where his real education would begin.

But that journey was a few weeks away. He had best remember not to rush his plan.

"You have done well with him," he told Mia. "A woman alone with a child, especially a boy."

"Hardly alone. Once I knew I was pregnant, I moved back here. It worked out well. I had help and I'm close to the campus for my studies."

"What happens when you graduate from law school?"

"I'll get a job and move to Los Angeles. By then Danny will be in kindergarten." She paused. "Well, that *was* the plan. I guess now I'll be discussing things like that with you."

"There is plenty of time for that," he said. In truth she would most likely still get a job in Los Angeles. The only difference was that her son would be in Calandria.

But that conversation was for much later. First he had to convince Mia to trust him . . . and seduce her into wanting him again.

He looked forward to both activities, especially the latter. He still found her most appealing, although he'd never been able to say exactly why. She was attractive, but great beauties populated his world. She was more intelligent than most women of his acquaintance, not that he set a great store by a woman's mind.

No, it was something else. He remembered the feel of her skin and how that had aroused him. Her scent, even when she was fresh from the shower, had lingered in his mind long after she had disappeared from his life. He had been with a great many women and most of those encounters blurred. Oddly, he remembered nearly everything about making love with Mia, and that remembering made him want to be with her again.

If she were someone else, someone with even minor titled connections or the daughter of a great leader, he would consider making their marriage a permanent connection. But she wasn't, and when it came to whom he would have more children with, he had to consider his obligation to the throne. Still, they were together for now and he planned to enjoy every minute of it.

He reached for her hand and rubbed his thumb against her knuckles. "You have been most patient and understanding."

She smiled. "Not much choice there. You're Danny's father. The prince thing is a bit of a shock, although it doesn't come close to the one about you not being dead."

He shifted closer and let his gaze drop to her mouth. "Are you glad I'm not dead?"

"Of course."

"I can say the same about you. I was most distressed when they told me you were gone. And later, when I thought you'd been killed . . ." He hesitated just enough to give the words a sincere ring. "Mia . . . I had just found you."

"*Found* is strong," she murmured. "I was sort of thrust upon you by the agency. I was there to do a job."

"As was I. Instead we found each other."

He spoke easily, mostly because it was all true. He had been delighted to find her. He'd known about the American operative and knew the wisdom of beginning an affair with her as a means to ending his time as Diego. He would have seduced her regardless, but with Mia what could have been effort had turned into true pleasure. For both of them.

He had even missed her when he'd returned to his life at the palace. Perhaps not as much as he indicated, but more than he usually did. Under other circumstances, he would tell her that and know she would be grateful.

"Let us not be parted again," he whispered.

Her eyes widened. "Rafael, I—"

He touched her mouth with his finger. "Shh. I think we are done talking." Then he lowered his head so that he could kiss her.

A heartbeat before he finally claimed her with his mouth, he heard footsteps in the hallway and a familiar and irritating voice saying, "I sure have a habit of showing up at the wrong time, don't I?"

"Do I need to lecture you?" Joe asked when Rafael had excused himself and Mia had scrambled onto the sofa.

She leaned back against the cushions and sighed. "Maybe. I know it's crazy to get involved with him and I can't tell you how grateful I am that you appeared when you did."

"But?" he prodded.

"But knowing I shouldn't get lost in the past and *not* getting lost in the past are two very different things. He knows how to push all my buttons."

"Don't take it personally. He's a professional playboy

by career and temperament, Mia. He's had plenty of practice."

Not exactly what she wanted to hear. Still, the information needed to sink into her brain. "Keep telling me he's the enemy," she said. "Apparently I need help not making a fool out of myself."

There was something about Rafael. His physical appearance might be different enough to make her nervous, but the chemical attraction between them didn't seem to care about things like scars and a change in eye color.

Joe slapped down a folder on the coffee table. "The preliminary report on Rafael."

She eyed the pages inside. "And?"

"He's who he said. Heir to the Calandrian throne. Not married. Not even a fiancée waiting in the wings. There have been rumors of various arranged marriages, but nothing seems to happen with them."

"Good to know." What with the almost kissing.

"He was educated in Europe. Graduated from Oxford. No career, of course, if you don't count the whole soon-to-be king gig. He partied hard when he was in his early twenties—nothing too kinky. He's a thrill seeker, but that's calmed down, too. No dead bodies, no bastard children."

Mia shook her head. "Oh, there's at least one we know of."

"Okay, but aside from Danny, he's clean. Which means Danny's the real heir."

"What if he marries and has legitimate children?" She shook her head. "I can't believe I'm actually discussing this. Legitimate children. Like we're in Elizabethan times."

"There's nothing like dealing with a royal family to bring up the past," Joe told her. "Per Calandria law, it's the acknowledged firstborn son of the crown prince/king. Whoever he is at the time. So if Rafael doesn't marry you or he doesn't officially acknowledge Danny, then there will be no Marcelli rule of Calandria."

"Gee, and we were all so anxious to expand our winery business. What's involved in officially acknowledging?"

"Paperwork mostly, and a presentation to the parliament. He's taken the DNA test, Mia. My guess is he's going to acknowledge Danny as his heir."

"Swell."

"Look on the bright side. If Danny's a prince, you have to be something too, right?"

"Screwed. I believe I'm mostly screwed."

"It's not as bad as that."

She leaned forward. "In all likelihood my son is going to one day rule Calandria. How long do you think he's going to be allowed to have a normal life?"

"Whatever happens, you're his mom. You'll be there to protect him."

"I know, but king. Jeez. I better get going on teaching him to tie his shoes."

5

"What kind of a surprise?" Danny asked. "A big surprise? Is it a puppy? I'd like a puppy, Mommy. I'm big enough now."

Maybe he was, but she wasn't, Mia thought wryly, knowing that dealing with a puppy was exactly enough to push her over the edge.

"We talked about a puppy," she reminded him. "It will come under consideration when you're eight."

Danny sighed. "I know. But that's so far."

Twice his life. He was already growing so fast. He would be eight before she knew it.

"What surprise?" he asked again.

"I don't know," she told him. Rafael hadn't been clear. He'd only asked them to meet him at three-thirty and said there would be a surprise.

She knew he'd gone out. The huge limo was gone, as were the ever-present Oliver and Umberto. What a life—trailing after a crown prince, watching him have all the fun. Or did royal bodyguards have groupies who made things more interesting?

Just then the limo turned the corner. Danny squealed

and pointed. "I can see the flags, Mommy. Can we have flags on our car?"

She had a feeling that diplomatic flags were hard to come by but might be worth the effort, especially during tourist season in Santa Barbara when parking was impossible to find. No doubt with diplomatic immunity came freedom from parking tickets.

The vehicle pulled to a stop. Umberto climbed out of the front passenger seat and walked to the rear door. When he opened it, Rafael stepped out.

"How nice to see my family waiting," he said with a smile. "My very handsome son and his beautiful mother."

Mia reminded herself that it was his job to be smooth on command, but still, she liked the compliment and the way his gaze lingered on her.

"What did you bring me?" Danny demanded.

Mia winced. "How about some manners? You could say hello first."

"Hello. What did you bring me?"

Rafael walked to the trunk of the limo and opened it. Inside was a fully assembled three-wheeled bike with a horn and flags that matched those on the limo.

"Maybe they aren't so hard to get," Mia murmured, wondering if she could borrow them for her car when she went into town.

"Cool!" Danny cried as he raced to the bike. "Can I try it now?"

Mia cleared her throat. "Hmm, what do we say when someone gives us a gift?"

Danny wrenched his gaze from the bike and looked at his father. "Thank you very much." He turned back to his mother. "Now?"

She nodded.

Danny sat down and immediately started pedaling. The wide tires gave him plenty of traction on the driveway.

Rafael moved next to her. "I considered a real bike, but I knew he would have to learn to ride it. I wanted this to be fun for him."

"Making up for the scepter?"

He smiled. "You were right. He was a little young to grasp the significance."

"I'm not sure it's an age thing. *I'm* not clear on the significance. What does it do?"

"It is a symbol of the throne."

"You'd probably do better with an action figure."

"For Danny or for you?"

"Danny. I've outgrown action figures."

"And moved up to the real thing? Or do you prefer more adult toys?"

Tempting, she thought. Very tempting. But an intelligent woman wouldn't be sucked into the vortex of charm that was Rafael.

"Any other surprises for him in that trunk?" she asked.

His gaze sharpened, as if he acknowledged her attempt to change the subject and decided to let her. "No. I assume anything else will seem tame by comparison."

"He'll enjoy spending time with you. He's very excited to finally have a father."

"I am excited to know he is my son."

"You don't know that for sure. The DNA tests aren't in."

He stared into her eyes. "*You* are sure, Mia, and that is enough for me."

"Yes, well, I wasn't exactly sleeping around when me met. Or after. But you'll have proof soon enough."

He shrugged as if to say it didn't matter. "I wish I'd known sooner. I wish I could have been here with you."

"That would have been nice," she admitted. "I love Danny with all my heart, but I'm not all that maternal. Developing those instincts was difficult for me. If not for my family around me, I don't think I would have made it."

"Of course you would have. You are steel." He lightly stroked her cheek. "And silk. So many contradictions. I always liked that about you. How tough you were and yet so feminine. An ideal woman."

She took a step back. "Ideal is so not me. I'm totally filled with flaws. Flaw girl, that's me."

He chuckled. "I do not think so."

"Then you'd be wrong. And speaking of dinner, you do remember there's a whole big family thing tomorrow night. You've met my sisters. Now it's time to meet the husbands and kids. Brenna might even bring her dog, Max. You need to brace yourself."

"I have survived formal state dinners. I'm sure I'll survive your family."

"Ha. Formal state dinners have nothing on the Marcellis. You're gonna be scared. Trust me."

The next evening Rafael followed the sound of conversation from the stairs into the large formal living room in the Marcelli home. As Mia had promised, most of the family had assembled to meet him.

Although he'd dressed in a suit, he wasn't worried about making a good impression. He was, after all, Crown Prince Rafael of Calandria. How could they not approve of him?

He stood in the doorway, as yet unnoticed. He recognized Mia's three sisters and assumed the men standing near them were their husbands. Several young children ran around, including Danny. Rafael frowned. The boy should not be allowed to be so boisterous at events like these. He had to learn to understand protocol and respect ceremony.

The Grands were by the plates of appetizers, making sure all was well with the food. Grammy M saw him and waved. Grandma Tessa saw him and quickly turned her back. He still had not charmed the matriarch of the Marcelli clan, but he would. He had yet to meet a woman he could not win.

"Rafael," Mia said as she hurried toward him. "Are you braced?"

"More than that. I'm delighted to finally be meeting the rest of your family."

"Not the rest, actually. My parents are still in China, which you knew. Also Kelly isn't here. She lives in San Francisco. I left her a message, but I haven't heard back."

He didn't pay attention to her words; instead he concentrated on the woman speaking them. As always, Mia was pure energy. Life radiated from her eyes, her smile, the movement of her body. She was small, barely five three, and he was a man used to dating models. She had curves to their lean lines. Her face was pretty, and he often chose women for their classical beauty. Yet there was something about her, something that drew him. In a room full of strangers, she was the only person who mattered.

"You look especially lovely tonight," he murmured. "That color suits you."

She stopped in midsentence to brush the front of her green sleeveless dress. "Oh. Thanks. It's, um, not new or anything." She cleared her throat. "Okay, back to the family. Let's get you introduced." She took his hand and faced her family. "Hey, everyone. This is Rafael."

The room quieted and he found himself the center of attention. Danny raced toward him.

"He's my daddy and I'm the heir." Danny turned to one of his cousins. "That means I'm going to be a prince and you have to do what I say."

"Do not!" the older girl said as she stomped her foot. "Mo-om, I do not have to do what Danny says, do I?"

"No, Haley, you don't," Mia told her niece. "Danny, you're not in charge, okay?"

Rafael started to correct her. Daniel was in fact in charge. At least of the other children. The sooner he learned his importance, the better. But perhaps this wasn't the time.

"Everybody, pair up," Mia said. "Grab your kids and we'll go down the line. I think that will be easier."

"We should have name tags," Grammy M said. "Would you like that, Rafael?"

"I don't believe it's necessary, but it's very thoughtful of you to suggest it," he told the older woman.

Grandma Tessa shook her head. "I'm sure his shoes need polishing, Mary. Or you might want to ask how he's fixed for socks."

Grammy M ignored her. "Go ahead, Mia. Introduce the family to Rafael."

Mia worked her way through the names. Rafael had already met Mia's sisters. Now he had the chance to meet their husbands and children. Joe's wife, Darcy, greeted him enthusiastically.

"I'm so happy to have someone around more famous than me," she said with a laugh. "Now the press can follow you and make snide comments about *your* clothing choices."

"Does that happen often?" he asked politely.

"Joe keeps them off the property, but sometimes they tail me in town." She sighed. "I can't wait for my father's second term to be over. Once he's no longer president, no one will be interested in me."

"I'll still be interested," Joe told her.

Darcy smiled at him. Rafael watched the exchange and was surprised to realize the former SEAL was completely in love with his wife. He wouldn't have thought such a dark man would allow himself softer emotions.

"You've met Amber and David," Mia said, guiding him to the next group of people. "Amber and David are engaged. David is Zach's son and Zach is married to Katie, my oldest sister."

Katie winced. "I'm over thirty. You've got to stop introducing me as the oldest."

"How about the sexiest?" Zach asked. "Would that work?"

"Absolutely." Katie put her hands on the shoulders of two children. "These are my twins. Eric and Haley. They're seven."

Rafael nodded at the children and noted that Haley had been the one to protest Daniel's authority over her. He had a feeling she would grow up to be a most stubborn woman.

"That's everyone here," Mia said. "Are we ready to go in to eat?"

Grandma Tessa led the way. The large table in the

dining room had been set for the adults, while a smaller table by the window was for the children.

"There are so many kids now, we don't all fit," Mia told him. "It actually works out. We hire a sitter to keep the kids occupied. This way everyone has a good time. Of course on holidays, everyone manages to fit around the main table and it's complete chaos. But in a good way."

She handled herself effortlessly, with a natural grace he appreciated. He knew from past experience she could think on her feet. Once again he had the thought that under other circumstances, she would make a good match for him. At least their son would have had the opportunity to inherit her intelligence and style.

"You're over here, Rafael," Grammy M said. "Mia, you're next to him. Amber and David, right here."

Rafael glanced up and saw David's fiancée watching Mia. Amber noticed his observation and quickly looked away.

A few minutes later, everyone had been seated. Open bottles of Marcelli wine were passed around, and when the glasses were full, Joe stood.

"Before we begin our dinner, I would like to propose a toast to those who are no longer with us. To my grandfather, who is still missed every day."

"Grandpa Lorenzo died about five years ago," Mia whispered. "He was such a great man. Difficult and gruff, yet so loving. I wish Danny could have known him."

Before Rafael could say anything, Joe continued. "And to Gabriel Reese. You were a blessing to this family."

Mia raised her glass as she whispered, "That's Sam's grandfather. He and Grammy M fell in love. He died a couple of years ago. It's been hard on the Grands, but at least they have each other to grow old with. Like I'll have my sisters."

"Your sisters are married."

Mia shrugged. "Marcelli women live a really, really long time. We've already talked about it. When the men are dead, we're getting a house together by the vineyard. It will be great."

"I'm sure their husbands are delighted to know how you anticipate their demise."

She grinned. "They're used to it."

The toasts concluded with everyone drinking. Then the plates of food arrived, and Rafael was overwhelmed by delicious choices.

Katie leaned across the table and smiled at him. "This must all seem very different to you."

"I'm enjoying my time here. I am beginning to see where Mia inherited her charm."

Katie looked at her sister. "She wasn't always charming."

"That's true," Brenna added. "She was kinda bratty."

Mia hung her head. "Please, no. I beg you. Not the stories about what I was like when I was young."

"I would like to hear those stories," he told Katie.

"I'll just bet," Mia muttered. "I was very intelligent and precocious. I knew five different languages by the time I was eighteen."

"She was a good girl," Grandma Tessa said. "Very bright. She got all A's."

Rafael caught Amber rolling her eyes.

"But her fashion sense," Francesca said with a grin. "The constant streaking in her hair."

"It wasn't subtle," Brenna told him. "We're talking big chunks of bright blond. And the eye shadow. Katie was forever after her to blend, blend."

"I was finding myself," Mia said primly.

"I don't think so," Joe added. "You knew exactly what you were doing. Making trouble."

"Engaged at eighteen," Grammy M said. "That was exciting."

"Maybe we could avoid that story." David shrugged. "I don't do so well in that one."

"I'd like to hear all about that," Amber said. "David's never told me what really happened."

There was a moment of uncomfortable silence, followed by all the Marcelli sisters speaking at once. Rafael glanced from Mia to David and wondered what had caused the young couple to break their engagement. Even as he reminded himself that Mia's past had no value, save that with him, he was still curious.

Just then the dining room door opened and a tall, slender woman staggered inside.

"Am I late?" she asked as she leaned heavily against the door frame.

She was casually dressed, with long, curly red hair and pale skin that only emphasized the shadows under her eyes.

Francesca stood. "Kelly? What's wrong?"

"Wrong? Nothing. I'm here. Hooray." She took a step and almost lost her balance. An even taller, thinner man appeared behind her. He grabbed her around the waist and kept her on her feet.

"Hello," the man said, his voice faintly accented.

French, Rafael thought. Working class.

Francesca's husband stood. "Kelly, what the hell is going on?"

"I'm here for the party." Kelly looked at Rafael. "So you're the new guy. Cool. Mia, he's really, really cute. Is he rich, because rich is always such a plus."

"You're drunk," Francesca said, sounding stunned. "Kelly, tell me you're not drunk."

"I'm not drunk." Kelly took a step and found herself contained by the man's arm. "Oh, yeah. This is Etienne. We're lovers. But he's not rich. He's just a dancer, like me."

She turned in a slow, graceful move, then sank to the floor and passed out.

The dinner broke up early. Mia got Danny down for the night and then went looking for Rafael. She found him outside, leaning against the fence by the vegetable garden. Umberto and Oliver weren't around, but she saw lights in the guest house and figured they'd settled in for the night.

She paused at the bottom of the steps and stared at the large silhouette of the man who had once been her lover. She couldn't see his face, only the rough outline of his body, but it was enough to help her remember what she had felt when they had been together.

Between mourning his death, finding out she was pregnant, then dealing with a baby and law school, she hadn't been in a relationship since she'd been with him. For the past couple of years she'd wondered if that part of her was dead. But now, in the darkness, her body stirred back to life. Wanting filled her and she ached to feel his touch on her skin.

But it was more than that. She wanted to talk as well as

touch. They had different worldviews and had frequently argued. He'd never been intimidated by her intelligence.

He turned and saw her. "Mia."

There was pleasure in his voice, as if she were the one person he'd been waiting for.

"Daniel is asleep?" he asked.

"In theory. I read him two stories and then turned out the lights. After all the excitement at dinner, it may take him a while to zonk out."

"Ah, yes. The unexpected arrival. Very dramatic."

She moved toward him and stopped next to the fence. "I don't understand what's happening with Kelly. She's always been so together and mature. I'm not horrified that she drinks—she's on her own and most of her friends in the ballet company are a few years older—but that she would show up here drunk. She had to know everyone would be here."

"Perhaps she wasn't prepared to face the entire family. Responsibility can be daunting."

Mia rested her forearms on the fence railing. "Kelly's been a part of the family since she was a kid. No one scares her. She loves being here. She would come and spend long weekends here several times a year. I've never seen her like that. I wonder if it's the guy."

"Etienne?"

"Yeah. He's new."

"Would you like me to have Umberto, how do you say, check him out?"

She smiled. "That's really nice, but Joe's already on it. No one messes with his family." She thought about Kelly's boyfriend and shuddered. "He's too old, too dirty, too yuck. What does she see in him?"

"Few can see into the secrets of a woman's heart," he told her.

Kelly a woman? Was it possible? Mia still remembered her as the mouthy twelve-year-old who had been determined not to let everyone know how much she was hurting inside. Still, she was twenty and making her own way in the world.

"Sometimes I forget how complicated our family is," she said. "It's not usually this crazy."

"I suspect it is; however, that is part of the charm."

She laughed. "We're many things, but I'm not sure *charming* describes us."

"You are wrong. I am enchanted by the Grands, as you call them."

"Even Grandma Tessa?"

"Especially her." He smiled. "I like that she wants me to earn her respect. I prefer my women difficult. There is much love and concern, each of you for the other."

"That's true. We're excellent at meddling. I guess it's not like that in royal circles."

"No. My parents had an arranged marriage. My mother died when I was young and I do not remember much about her."

"Rafael." She touched his arm. "I know that was hard. I feel bad that I don't know that much about your life."

"You are not one to read gossip magazines, where my entire life has been detailed. I grew up prepared to one day rule Calandria. There are many responsibilities both then and now."

"Even when you were three?"

"Of course. I had to learn about my country's history,

the people. I had nannies and tutors. When I was eight, I was sent to England to begin my education."

Just like that. Sent away from all that was familiar. "Sounds barbaric."

He shrugged. "It was necessary."

"Because you can't get an education at home?"

"Because that is how things are done." He touched her chin, raising her head so that she looked at him. "You are too softhearted."

"Gee, no one's ever accused me of that before."

In the night, his eyes were dark, as she remembered them. Here in the shadows, the blurring of Diego into Rafael was more pronounced. The past seemed closer somehow.

"So now you're duty guy?" she asked, her voice low. "All for the crown and the people?"

"Something like that."

"Any arranged marriages in your future?"

"No."

"But you will be marrying a princess or duchess or some other kind of 'ess' woman."

"It is expected."

She really had to go check out those gossip magazines and learn a little bit more about Rafael, she thought, as he seemed to move closer.

"Since when do you do what is expected?" she asked.

"On occasion it has occurred."

"But an arranged marriage. What if you don't like her?"

"Then I will say no."

"You can do that?"

"Arranged is different from forced. I accept suggestions but the final choice is mine."

"And hers."

"Yes. Hers as well." He sighed. "Did you always talk this much? I remember more silence."

"Then you remember wrong. I've always—"

He cut her off with a kiss.

The moment his lips brushed hers, she felt her entire body begin to melt. He had been the last man to kiss her, to touch her, to make love with her. She had mourned him, knowing she would never want to give her heart again. Not when having it broken had nearly destroyed her.

Yet here he was, so familiar. In the darkness she could pretend he was Diego once again.

As he pulled her close, she went willingly, finding comfort and need in the familiar strength of his body. His scent aroused her nearly as much as the pressure of his mouth claiming hers.

He still kissed with a combination of imperiousness and passion that left her breathless. The light touch of his tongue on her lower lip had her parting instantly. Wanting had her clinging to him, desperate for more.

He plunged inside her mouth and claimed her. Waves of passion nearly brought her to her knees as she felt the familiar desire and tasted the man she remembered.

His hands were everywhere—down her back, on her arms, at her waist. She couldn't get close enough. She wanted to crawl inside of him and let the old emotional wounds of missing him finally heal.

"Mia," he breathed as he kissed her cheeks, her jaw, her neck. "How I have missed you."

It was too much. The need combined with that voice. The voice that had haunted her dreams for nearly five years.

Diego, she thought. Only not Diego. Rafael.

He raised his head. "So the fire still lives between us," he murmured. "Tell me you can feel it."

She drew in a slow breath. "You know I can."

He dropped his hand to the small of her back and drew her against him. Her belly brushed against his erection.

"This is what you do to me, what you have always done." He cupped her face and stared into her eyes. "My father has been parading all sorts of appropriate young women in front of me for years. Marry this one or the next one, he tells me. But I refuse. I know my duty to my people and yet I can't deny the hunger of my heart. I need more than an arranged marriage. From that comes only children. My father says to take a mistress along with my wife. But that is not for me."

He smiled. "Have you missed me?" he asked quietly.

"Every now and then."

"You tease me."

"A little. I was devastated when I thought you were dead. I didn't think I'd make it. Finding out I was pregnant saved me."

"I only had the memories of our love," he told her. "You did love me, didn't you? You said you did."

"More than I should have."

He kissed her. "So much lost. So much time wasted."

She felt as if she'd had too much wine, except she'd only had the one glass at dinner. Still, her head was spinning and she couldn't seem to think straight.

"What are you saying?" she asked.

"That we have been given a second chance, Mia. I have found you again. We have a son. Daniel will one day be king of Calandria. But to see him grow up as I did—

it cannot be. You would change that. You are strong enough to stand against tradition."

She took a step back. "Danny's not going to grow up like you."

"I know. You will not let him. We will not let him."

Sure, he was Danny's father, but Mia had trouble thinking of Rafael and her as a "we."

"It is you. It has always been you," he told her. He kissed her again, then took her hands in his. "Marry me, Mia. Marry me and be my princess."

An earthquake would have made sense. Hey, this was California and the earth moved all the time. Locusts might have even been okay because they were in the Bible and she had seen one once in a museum. But a proposal of marriage from Prince Rafael of Calandria? Not in this reality.

"You're crazy," she said as she jerked her hands free of his. "Marry you? I don't know you and you sure as hell don't know me. Rafael, it's been three days."

He laughed. "I know how many hours and minutes. Would you like to hear? I thought you were lost to me and now you are found. I cannot let you go."

He captured her hands again and kissed her knuckles. It was a pretty smooth move, but then he'd had prince lessons. What other guy stood a chance?

"Don't say no. Give me time to prove myself. We have another chance, Mia. How many people can say that? I don't want to lose you again."

She didn't know what to say. Marriage? Sure, he was the father of her child, but she'd been thinking along the lines of Danny's spending a couple of weeks each summer in Calandria.

"I have a life," she said. "School. Family."

Instead of responding, he stared into her eyes. She felt his presence as tangibly as if he'd thrown a blanket across her shoulders. There was warmth and protection. And the ever-present need.

She *had* loved him once, she reminded herself. Or at least the man he'd pretended to be. How much had been about playing Diego and how much had been real?

"Don't say no," he murmured. "Give us time. Is that too much to ask?"

It was crazy. Foolish. Impetuous.

It was irresistible.

"I won't say no, at least not right now," she told him. "But I don't want you to mention this to anyone."

"Of course not." He pulled her close and kissed the top of her head. "I will win you back, Mia. You will see. I will be all you have ever desired."

With anyone else, she would have had her doubts. But Rafael was a different kind of man. In this case, she wasn't sure she would be willing to bet against him.

6

Mia was up early the next morning. The Grands hadn't even stirred, which meant it was her job to get the coffee going. After pouring in grounds and water, she flipped the switch, then checked out the plastic-covered cookie sheets sitting in the refrigerator.

"Cinnamon rolls," she moaned as she hurried to the oven and dialed in the correct temperature. Caffeine and sugar. Was there any better antidote for a sleepless night?

She hovered by the coffeemaker until the hot liquid began to pour into the carafe. When there was enough to fill her mug, she pulled it out and claimed it for herself.

The first sip tasted heavenly. As the warmth slid down her throat and settled in her belly, she felt the first stirring of consciousness. Unfortunately with that came too-clear memories of the previous evening.

Had Rafael really proposed? She told herself he couldn't have, then took another drink of coffee and realized he had.

Marriage? She wasn't sure she wanted to get married. Besides, they barely knew each other, and while she had many really fabulous qualities, she doubted she would make much of a princess. She could barely find Calandria on a map.

Marriage? No way. She and Rafael were intelligent adults. They could find a way to share their son without resorting to what would only turn out to be a disaster.

"Good morning."

She looked up and saw the man in question standing in the doorway. His hair was damp from his shower, his body casually clad in jeans and a long-sleeved shirt, and his mouth . . .

Suddenly she couldn't stop looking at his mouth. Because whatever was the same or different about him, his mouth and his voice were exactly as she remembered.

Then, without meaning to, she suddenly recalled another kind of kiss from him. An intimate one that had her screaming out her release as he licked and—

"Morning," she managed through suddenly dry lips. She took a gulp of coffee and motioned to the nearly full carafe. "Help yourself."

"Thank you."

He poured himself a mug and took a drink. "Did you sleep well?"

"Not really."

"Anything in particular keeping you up?"

"An unnatural concern about interest rates and the latest drought in Africa."

"Really? I had no idea you were so concerned about current events."

"Sarcasm, Rafael. That was sarcasm."

He smiled slightly. "Yes, I know." He took another drink. "I did not mean to distress you with my proposal."

"*Distress* really doesn't cover it. I was confused—a pretty continuous state of affairs since you showed up in my bed." She frowned. "You could have just knocked on the front door."

"Perhaps, but far less interesting an entrance. Besides, I have not missed being at your front door."

Good one, she thought. The implication being he missed her bed. Or, one dared to assume, her in his bed.

"I, too, did not sleep well. You kept me up, Mia. I could not stop thinking about you."

"Yes, well, how interesting." She moved to the far side of the kitchen just as the oven beeped. Damn. Now he stood between her and cinnamon rolls.

He glanced at the appliance. "Are you baking?"

"Grammy M made cinnamon rolls last night. They need to go in the oven. They're in there."

She jerked her head toward the refrigerator. He crossed the room and removed them, then slid them into the oven.

"Better?" he asked.

"I will be in about twenty minutes." She glanced from him to the oven. "You know your way around the kitchen."

He grinned. "Yes, even I, Prince Rafael of Calandria, can find an oven in a kitchen. If you promise to show the proper amount of awe, I'll cut up some fruit later."

"You're making fun of me."

"I tease a little. I might live in a palace, but I do know how to exist in the real world."

"Unlikely."

"Why do you doubt me? I was on my own all through university. When I pretended to be Diego, I took care of myself."

"Barely. You had an entire harem of women. I distinctly remember being stunned by the number of otherwise intelligent women so eager to do the smallest thing for you."

He moved closer. "You are correct, but the leader of the pack always has his choice of the females. Diego was no exception. But you were not so willing to be my slave. You insisted I serve you."

"I have a very high IQ," she said primly. Mostly she'd refused to trail around after him in an effort to stand out. It had worked, although not in the way she'd imagined.

"One of them noticed I had my eye on you," he said. "She came after you."

"With a knife." Mia still remembered her fear and outrage when a tall blonde from northern Italy had called her some very disgusting names and ordered her to leave. Mia hadn't noticed the knife until she'd already told off the other woman.

"Do you still have a scar?" he asked as he placed his hand on her side.

The warmth of his fingers made it difficult to think, but she managed to nod. "It's pretty faint but still there."

"The cut was not deep, but there was much blood. You were very brave."

She'd been stunned by the swift attack. Rafael—a.k.a. Diego—had reacted with fury. The other woman had been sent away and told she would be killed if she returned. He had then taken Mia to his private rooms and had carefully stitched the cut. That night, he'd claimed her as his own. She still remembered how gentle he'd been, how careful so that she wouldn't feel any pain from her wound.

She'd already been half in love with him. His tenderness had pushed her over the edge. Afterward she'd been unable to sleep as she'd wrestled with the moral dilemma of her situation. She'd fallen in love with the enemy—a classic, almost clichéd, mistake.

As soon as she'd been able to get away, she'd contacted the agent in charge and explained that she was afraid of compromising the mission. She'd asked to be removed. Instead her boss had told her to suck it up and stay in play.

"There were no other women after you, Mia. Do you remember?"

His words made her more uncomfortable than the memories of her horror at being torn between her mission and the man she loved.

"I remember," she said softly, not wanting to let him get to her. Not again. Not until she was sure. Which might be never.

But he was telling the truth. From the second the two of them had become lovers, he hadn't looked at another woman. How long had it taken him to get over her?

He moved to the table and took a seat across from her. "My guilty secret," he said with a shrug. "I made you promise not to tell."

"I never knew why it was such a big deal. So you don't cheat. Most women consider that a good thing."

"My father has kept mistresses all his life. Usually two or three at a time. They know about each other and on the surface all is well. I was never comfortable with that. I could see the pain in their eyes."

He looked away, as if embarrassed by the turn in the conversation. That surprised her, and in a good way. She liked knowing that the imperious crown prince had a weakness or two. Twenty would be better but she would take what she could get.

"Tell me about life in the palace," she said, taking pity on him and changing the subject.

"It is not so different from your world," he said.

She laughed. "Oh, please. Royalty. It has to be different. Do you have your own wing or county or something?"

"I live elsewhere, in a private house on the edge of the sea. I am close enough to be reached quickly if there is an emergency, but I do not still live at home."

"I wouldn't have thought living in the palace would count as living at home."

"I learned very quickly that it was difficult to take girls to my room when we had to tiptoe past my father's quarters. At twenty, such things mattered to me."

"They would matter at any age. Okay, so you get up and one of your several harem women prepares you for your shower."

"I am sorry to disappoint you, but I do not have harem women."

"Not a good crop this year?"

"I get myself ready in the morning."

"What? No servants?"

"A handful. They prepare my breakfast and take care of my clothes."

"Nice work if you can get it. Then what?"

"Then I drive to the palace for my morning meetings with my father and officials from our government."

"Do Umberto and Oliver tag along?"

"I have bodyguards in a car following me."

This was one of the strangest conversations Mia could remember having. To her, none of what Rafael talked about was real, yet every bit of it was his life.

"So what happens after a hard morning of governing the little people?"

"You mock me."

"It's something I'm really good at. The reverence thing has always been a problem. Fortunately I don't run into many people deserving of that kind of attitude."

He sighed. "You are going to be difficult, but I expected as much."

"Really?" The thought pleased her.

"Of course. You forget, I know you. You are too smart for your own good and intimidated by no one. A dangerous combination."

"Ooh, let me guess. For a woman."

"For anyone. And to answer your question, which you have probably already forgotten, I lunch with different heads of state or visiting dignitaries. Sometimes I meet with officials in parliament. I spend my afternoons with charity work—I deal with three international organizations—or events in the city. Once a week or so there is an official dinner or fund-raiser of some kind."

"Sounds boring," she said. "What do you do for fun?"

"Polo, sailing, skiing, mountain climbing. I keep busy."

Her idea of excitement was a twilight stroll around the vineyards, followed by an extra glass of wine with dinner. They were practically twins separated at birth.

"I am in the unique position of training for a job that I may not have for years," he said. "I do not wish my father to die, yet this is the expected way of succession."

"Would he abdicate?"

"We have talked about it. He does not want me to wait indefinitely."

"So you would be king sooner rather than later?"

He nodded.

She didn't like the sound of that. Not with a proposal still hanging between them. Bad enough to be a lousy princess, but it was so much worse to be a horrible queen.

"You would do well," he said, reading her mind.

"I have many, many doubts. I could put them into categories and have them spiral bound for you, if you'd like."

"Calandria is a small country. Your duties—"

She cut him off with a strangled cough. "See, that's the thing. Any sentence that begins with the words *your duties* isn't for me. I'm not the duty type."

"There would be compensations."

She wasn't sure if he was going to talk about the wealth and relative power or the thrill of being married to him. Right now she didn't want to think about either.

"What about Danny?" she asked. "What would his life be like?"

"He would have tutors."

"Now?"

"Of course. There's much he has to learn."

That didn't sound good. She remembered what Rafael had told her about his years growing up.

"Just so we're clear," she said flatly, "he's not being sent away to some European boarding school. He can go to a regular school with other Calandrian children."

Rafael stiffened as if she'd slapped him. "My son is the heir to the Calandrian throne."

"Funny, because my son is just a little boy. Are you saying Calandrian schools are substandard?"

"Of course not. They are the best in Europe."

"Then think of the money we'll save. Besides, if Danny is going to grow up to rule the people, doesn't it make sense that he get to know them from an early age?"

She could feel Rafael winding himself up for some kind of princely tirade, so she quickly asked, "Did you like being sent away when you were all of seven? Didn't you miss your friends and your family? Do you really want that for Danny?"

"There are traditions," he began.

"There's also reality. It's a new century, Rafael. How about pushing the monarchy into it? I'm not sending Danny away to school."

She also was fairly sure she wasn't going to be marrying Rafael anytime soon, although the idea was fun to think about.

"You are right," he said, stunning her into silence. "I did not enjoy being sent away. I was angry and resentful. I vowed it would be different for my son."

"You might want to remember that," she said, trying not to melt at the thought of a scared and lonely seven-year-old Rafael.

"Was it too horrible?" she asked.

"I survived. I had my uncle Vidal, who visited me frequently. My father's brother," he added. "We were close. Much closer than I ever was with my father."

She imagined it would be tough to get close to the king. "It's too bad your father didn't remarry. Having a woman around would have helped."

"Perhaps, but my father had done his duty and saw no reason to do it again."

Marriage as duty—an interesting concept. "What about marrying for love?" she asked.

Rafael took her hand and lightly kissed the tips of her fingers. "Such a thing would not occur to him."

"What are *your* thoughts on the concept?"

His blue eyes darkened with emotion. "I have turned down three acceptable arranged marriages and I have been unable to tell my father why. Each of the women was exactly what I said I wanted, and yet when the time came, I was not willing to marry for duty."

"What did you say you wanted?" she asked.

He smiled. "You know that is not important."

"I want to know how close a match I would be."

"You are Mia," he told her. "That is enough."

Great response, she thought. He was good at saying exactly the right thing. She really was going to have to go online and become more familiar with his past. Was he serious about the three potential princesses?

"You worry for nothing," he said as he stood and came around to her side of the table. He pulled her to her feet. "Remember what it was like between us. Think of how it could be again."

Dangerous territory. She knew she could easily get lost in the past, and that wasn't a smart place to hang out. She had a pretty big present to worry about, including an almost four-year-old son who would—amazingly enough—one day rule Calandria.

"Rafael, I've been thinking, and it's the reason I'm up so early this morning. What you proposed . . ." Bad choice of words. "Your suggestion is really flattering, but I can't see how we could ever make it work."

"I will show you." He moved in close and wrapped his arms around her.

She already had a good idea of where this was going.

Not her favorite thing before she finished her first cup of coffee, but based on how great his kiss had been last night, she just might make an exception.

But before his mouth could claim hers, she heard footsteps in the hallway.

"Okay, that would be a chaperone on demand," she murmured as she stepped back and did her best not to look flustered.

David walked into the kitchen, took one look at them, and started back out. "Sorry," he muttered. "Just came down for coffee. Didn't mean to interrupt."

"You didn't. Really." Mia lunged toward him and grabbed his arm. "Rafael and I were finished."

Rafael smiled. "I would not say 'finished,' but we can certainly pick this up again later. Go ahead, David. Have your coffee. I will go and wake my son."

"Danny will like that," Mia said, more grateful for the interruption than she could say. Things were messed up enough without her getting lost in a sensual fog with Rafael. Sexual chemistry had never been their issue.

David crossed to the coffeepot and poured himself a mug. When Rafael had left, he looked at Mia.

"You always did do things in a big way."

She sighed. "This time, I didn't mean to. It was just one of those things."

He grinned. "Having a baby with the crown prince of a European nation doesn't just happen."

"It did to me. A week ago my life was perfectly normal. I had my plan. Finish law school, get a good job, get Danny into a nice private school in L.A., buy a condo. Suddenly I'm worried about co-parenting with a future monarch. It's unnerving."

"If anyone can handle it, you're the one."

She didn't feel like the one. She felt inadequate to the task and uneasy about Rafael. He was too charming, too everything. How was she supposed to resist him?

"It's good to see you," she said.

"I always like coming up here. The fact that we're planning a wedding here only gives me more excuses."

She wrinkled her nose. "Dinner turned into a disaster."

"What's up with Kelly? She was wasted."

"I don't know. I thought Francesca was going to pop a blood vessel. And Etienne. Yuck. Why is it some men think avoiding regular hygiene makes them sexy?"

The timer on the oven dinged. She grabbed a hot pad and pulled out the cinnamon rolls.

"You were always a frequent bather," she said. "I appreciated that. I just want you to know."

"Not a very high standard."

"I have others."

David was good-looking, in an easy all-American kind of way. While he and Mia were exactly the same age, their lives were so different. He'd graduated from college, gotten a great job at an investment firm, and had the perfect life. He was engaged to someone Mia liked a lot, owned his own home, and knew exactly where he wanted to be in twenty years.

She was a single mother, still living at home, with another year left in law school. Okay, yes, she had a master's and had been a spy, but she still felt as if she were waiting for her grown-up life to start.

David leaned against the counter. "I need your help."

She perked up. "Is this a shopping thing, because I am in the mood to spend some serious cash and it's always better if it isn't mine."

"It's not a shopping thing."

Damn. David had taken her with him to pick out Amber's engagement ring. They'd found the perfect set, with a 1.6 carat cushion-cut center stone. Mia considered it one of her crowning achievements in spending other people's money.

"It's Amber."

"What about Amber? She's fabulous." Mia grabbed the ingredients for frosting and set them on the counter. "Don't you dare tell me you're having second thoughts."

"I'm not," he said quickly. "How could I? Amber is incredible. Pretty and gentle and kind, and she thinks I'm funny."

"It's a miracle," Mia told him.

"Gee, thanks. She adores me, and I can't imagine ever loving anyone as much as I love her. I want to have kids with her. I want to grow old with her. I want to buy an RV with her."

"RV buying means it *is* serious." She measured out powdered sugar and butter. "So what's the problem?"

"You."

Mia paused in the act of pouring milk. "Excuse me?"

"She doesn't understand how I could have been in love with you once and not still be in love with you."

"Oh, please. You had me and realized you didn't want me."

He winced.

"I don't mean that in a bad way," she added quickly. "We were young and thought we were in love. We weren't. End of story."

"She doesn't see it that way. Every time we come here, she can't stop talking about you." He held up his free hand. "Before you say anything, I already thought about staying away, but we're supposed to get married here. It was Amber's idea. There are family holidays and gatherings. There's no way to avoid you."

"Kind of like flu season germs."

"You know what I mean."

"I do and I feel bad. Have you told her there's nothing between us? That we're like brother and sister—not that we were when we were having sex, because ick."

He grinned. "I've mentioned the brother/sister thing. And that you weren't very good in bed."

She glared at him. "Ha!"

"Mia, seriously. I need help."

"I'm not an expert," she told him. "Look, be honest with her. Tell her you don't want to lose her. Tell her no one else has ever mattered as much. That you'd be lost without her."

Sort of all the things she'd felt when she'd flown away in that helicopter after thinking she'd just watched Diego die. It had been the worst moment of her life.

"Tell her she's your world."

"You think?" he asked.

"I know. It'll work. Trust me."

"Thanks." He put down his coffee and held out his arms.

Mia abandoned her frosting and stepped into his embrace.

David felt good—solid and familiar. Like family.

"I mean this in a very nonromantic way," she said. "But I never stopped loving you."

"I know exactly how you feel."

Life being what it was, the short, friendly, comforting silence didn't last long. Mia distinctly heard a gasp. She turned just as David swore, and wasn't the least bit surprised to see a wide-eyed Amber quickly backing out of the kitchen.

David pushed Mia away with a speed that was almost comical. Mia watched him hurry after the woman of his dreams.

She finished with the frosting. Then, despite her earlier hunger for cinnamon rolls, she left them on the counter and climbed the stairs to her room. Once inside, she crossed to the dresser and pulled out the bottom drawer.

There were all kinds of mementos inside. Yearbooks, pictures from school, postcards from everywhere she'd traveled.

She wondered if she should help David explain, then shook her head. Nothing she could say would make a difference. The situation wasn't actually about her—it was Amber's inability to trust her fiancé and his feelings for her.

Funny how easy it was to see what was wrong with everyone else while she still wrestled with her own demons. Speaking of which . . .

She pulled out a small jewelry box from a corner of the drawer. Inside was a simple silver ring. Nothing fancy, no stones or engraving. But Diego had bought it for her one afternoon. He'd slipped it on her left ring finger and had kissed her.

"Now you are always mine," he told her. "For as long as the ring survives, so does our love."

She'd worn it nearly a year after she'd come back home. Then, after Danny had been born, she'd removed it and stored it away. The love that had been so precious to her was not destined to last.

Or was it? Diego was back, in a different form. The same man, a different person.

Could she trust him? Did he mean what he'd said? Did he want to marry her?

And if so, what did *she* want? Hadn't she just spent five years wishing for the impossible—the return of her one true love? Was she going to let him get away just because he happened to be the heir to a throne?

7

"That poor girl," Grandma Tessa said as she expertly stitched a bead into place on the piece of white satin she held in her hands.

Grammy M rolled her eyes. "She should be more trustin' of the man she's marryin', or she shouldn't be marryin' him a-tall."

"Trust is a tricky thing," Mia said, hoping to avoid an argument between her grandmothers. There was already enough tension between them about Rafael. "I see her point. I mean, hey, it's me."

Grammy M smiled. "You are a special one, Mia, but you're not all that."

Mia laughed. "Not all that? Where did you learn that expression."

"HBO," Tessa said with a grin. "We watch it all the time."

"Okay. Now I'm scared."

"Don't be," Tessa told her. "Amber is a sensible girl and she loves David. That's plain to see. But she's cautious."

"Why?" Grammy M asked. "David is a good man. She's lucky to be gettin' him."

"Sometimes a little caution is a good thing. A smart woman isn't taken in by a pretty face, fancy words, and an accent," said Tessa.

Grammy M put down her piece of white satin. "I suppose you'll be meanin' me when you make that remark. As if I could be taken in."

"You have been. What do we know about Rafael, eh? What he tells us. Charming manners are nice at dinner, but they don't say anything about his character. Mia is smart to hold back."

"Okay, I don't want to get in the middle of this," Mia said quickly. "Really. Let's change the subject. How about those grapes? Are they growing or what?"

"I don't think Mia should go running off with Rafael just because he smiles at her," Grammy M said, her voice clipped. "I'm saying she should give the man a chance to prove himself before she accepts his proposal."

There was a moment of perfect silence. Mia paused in the act of reaching for another bead. While her grandmothers sewed on the front of David's wedding vest, she'd been trusted with two tabs in the back.

She replayed that last sentence, lingering on the final word. How on earth did her grandmothers know about Rafael's proposal?

There was only one possible explanation. Damn the man. She'd *asked* him not to say anything. She hadn't wanted the pressure. She didn't know what she was going to do herself and she wasn't looking for advice.

"He told you?" She tossed the tabs onto the table and glared at them both. "He *told* you?"

"He might have mentioned it in passing," Grammy M said as she continued to calmly sew.

Mia couldn't believe it. "How, exactly, does that happen? You're discussing the weather and you ask if he's proposed recently, then he chuckles and says as a matter of fact he has?"

Her voice rose with each word until it ended on a shriek.

"Who else knows?" she demanded.

"No one," Grammy M said soothingly. "It was just the three of us in the kitchen. We were talking about you and how smart you are. Rafael seemed to like that. He mentioned you would be a beautiful and compassionate queen." She sighed. "Imagine. Our little girl a queen."

Right then Mia wanted to throw something, which didn't feel very royal to her. She turned to Grandma Tessa.

"What did *you* say? Do you think it's a good idea?"

"I think you should get to know the man before making any decisions that take you so far away."

"Okay, maybe. But doesn't it bother you that he told you?"

"Not as much as you *not* telling us," Tessa said.

Mia sank back into her chair. "I needed to think about it. No, I needed to find out a way to tell him no."

Grammy M dropped her needle. "No? But he's the father of your child, Mia. Danny'll be needin' a father as he grows up."

"He has Joe."

"An uncle isn't a father."

Mia looked at Grandma Tessa. "You can't want me to marry him."

"I want you to be happy. And sensible."

"He shouldn't have told you," Mia insisted. "It's not right."

"We're your family," Grammy M said, as if that explained everything.

But it didn't. Rafael went behind her back. What was up with that? Did he want to pressure her into saying yes?

Even as the thought occurred, she dismissed it. Hello, they were talking about royalty. Princes didn't need to push women into their lives. Women went willingly.

"I have to go talk to him," she muttered.

"He's outside playing with Danny," Grammy M offered.

Mia waved her thanks and stomped through the kitchen toward the back door. Something about this just didn't feel right. The word *manipulation* kept popping into her mind, which seemed both harsh and unfair.

She stepped out into the warm afternoon and immediately heard the sound of childish laughter.

"You're dead," Danny said gleefully as he poked at an action figure in Rafael's hand. "Dead, dead, dead."

They sat on a blanket in the shade. Around them were the remnants of what had obviously been a hard-fought war. Plastic soldiers lay discarded in heaps. Mia would bet that nearly every military toy had been hauled out for today's game.

"I die, I die," Rafael said in a high-pitched voice. "You shot me and I die."

Both he and his plastic soldier fell to the blanket. Danny doubled over with laughter, and Mia found herself smiling.

Interesting that the imperial prince had allowed himself to be defeated. So maybe Rafael was good with his son. That had to count for something, didn't it?

He looked up and saw her. "You are in time to attend my funeral. I am killed."

Danny grinned. "He's not a very good soldier."

Rafael pressed a hand to his chest. "How you wound me with your words. I am an excellent soldier. Perhaps you are simply better."

"I am!" Danny crowed. "I'm the best. I'm the heir."

Mia narrowed her gaze. "You are, huh? Maybe in Calandria but not here. Here you're just Danny Marcelli. Okay, kid. Why don't you head inside and ask the Grands to fix you a snack."

"Okay."

He scrambled to his feet and raced to her. She dropped to her knees for his kiss and hug, then stood as he ran into the house.

"He is the heir," Rafael told her from his place on the blanket. "Do not discourage him from knowing his own importance. He will one day be king."

"Not something I can readily imagine. Besides, he already has a very strong sense of self. Trust me, you don't want to make him feel any more important than he already does."

Rafael patted the blanket. "Join me," he said quietly. "It is very nice out here."

She glanced around. "Where are the boys with the guns?"

"Oliver and Umberto have taken a tour of the winery with Brenna."

"I'm surprised they were willing to let you out of their sight."

"I insisted. I wanted the time alone with my son. It is not good to always have bodyguards lurking."

"I agree." She sank onto the blanket.

He reached for her hand, but she slid away from him.

"Mia, what is wrong?"

"My grandmothers just informed me that you told them about asking me to marry you. That's not my definition of playing fair. I asked you not to say anything."

He nodded. "You are right. I should not have mentioned it. Believe me, I did not tell them in an effort to trap you or make you feel obligated. I don't want you to marry me because you think you have to."

He gave her a half smile that she found boyish and appealing, but she was careful not to respond in any way.

"Don't worry about forcing me into marriage. It won't happen."

"Good. As for what I said, the words slipped out. I was thinking about us being together and . . ." He shrugged. "I apologize."

Really? Rafael was many things, but he was not the type who apologized.

"I mean that," he said quietly. "I was wrong."

The W word. So rarely uttered by a male. The combination of his sincerity and his accent was difficult to resist.

"Okay," she muttered, not sure how to accept his apology without encouraging him. "I, ah, don't want you mentioning the proposal to anyone else."

"Agreed." He moved closer. "May I discuss it with you?"

"I'm not sure that's a good idea."

"But if I do not, how can I convince you that you belong with me in Calandria? I know you are not the type to be enticed by talk of jewels or riches, so instead I thought I would talk about my house at the edge of the island. Of the sound of the surf on the rocks and how beautiful your skin will be in the moonlight as we make love. I thought I would admit that I still dream about what it was like to be with you, of the feel of your body under mine and the way you clung so fiercely to me. As if you would never let go."

She remembered, too. The need to hold on to him had always overwhelmed her whenever they were intimate. Even now, after all this time, she recalled the weight of him as he plunged into her, taking her to the edge of the world and then jumping with her.

"I remember the passion in your eyes," he murmured as he moved closer still. "How sensually you touched me. Your fingers, your mouth."

He rubbed his thumb against her bottom lip. She couldn't help grabbing his wrist and holding him still while she gently bit down on his skin.

His breath caught as their eyes locked. Need filled her. Five years of missing this man exploded inside of her. Her breasts tightened, her thighs squeezed, and she reached for him just as he grabbed for her.

They fell onto the blanket, him on top, their legs tangled. He was heavy and strong and hard, so very hard as his erection rubbed against her belly. She slid her fingers through his hair and guided his mouth to hers.

She opened instantly, needing deep, dark, passionate kisses that would touch her soul. He read her mind, or perhaps he needed the same, because he thrust into her mouth and claimed her.

Her tongue circled his; then she closed her lips around him and sucked. He groaned, then shifted so his arousal pressed between her legs.

Her thighs fell open as she welcomed him home; then

she wrapped her legs around his hips and urged him to rub harder and faster.

"More," she gasped as she dropped her hands to his butt and squeezed the tight flesh.

He grabbed her, then shifted so that she was on top, her center resting on his erection. They were both panting, needy, and she couldn't seem to stop looking into his eyes.

Blue instead of brown, but she had grown used to that difference. The missing scars no longer mattered. On the surface, Rafael might look different from Diego, but her body recognized its most significant lover.

"Kiss me," he demanded even as he reached for her breasts.

She braced herself on the blanket and lowered her head. At the same time he cupped her curves and began to tease her tight nipples.

The combination of sensations—his tongue in her mouth, his hands on her breasts, her swollen wet center rubbing against his cock—was too much. Despite the fact that they were outside and fully dressed, she shuddered into orgasm.

The release stunned her, but she couldn't stop moving against him, couldn't stop kissing him, and would have killed him if he'd stopped touching her nipples.

But he didn't. As wave after wave of pleasure claimed her, he stroked her and kissed her and urged her on.

Somewhere in the house, a door slammed. Mia came back to reality with a thud. She wasn't a wild teenager anymore and she had a child to think about. Did she really want Danny running outside and seeing his mother acting like this?

Reluctantly, she straightened.

The reality of what had just happened slammed into her. How had a petting session gotten out of hand so quickly? And was she so damn needy that she was only seconds away from an orgasm, regardless of the circumstances or the fact that they hadn't even gotten naked?

"Second thoughts are not allowed," Rafael told her in a low voice, thick with passion. "I forbid them."

"You're not the boss of me."

"Very mature." He smiled. "Are you angry?"

She shook her head. "Just . . . embarrassed."

"No. Not that. Never that. You are so responsive. Each man likes to believe he is a master in the bedroom. I more so than most."

"All that practice," she said wryly.

"Perhaps. But with you, I know it to be true. However I touch you, you are pleasured."

As if to demonstrate, he slid his fingers between her legs and rubbed. He immediately found her swollen center and circled it. Another climax claimed her.

She sucked in a breath, then pushed his hand away. "Stop that," she said as she stood. "You've made your point."

He rose and grabbed her wrist. "I think not. You are fire, Mia, and there is no greater gift to a man than to burn for him." He brought her palm to his mouth and kissed it. "I have missed your flames. No one else burns as you do."

She still felt funny about what had happened. No one enjoyed being a living example of a life of celibacy. She doubted Rafael had done without for more than fifteen seconds.

"Whatever," she said as she walked away.

He grabbed her again. "Mia. Do not dismiss what we have together. It is magnificent."

She wanted to believe him. She very nearly did. For her part, he had been amazing. Not just because he knew how to arouse her and make her whimper, but because the chemistry between them was so powerful. That couldn't have gone away, she told herself. He had to have felt it, too.

So if he had then, did he now?

She stared into his eyes and willed herself to see the truth. There was need and desire and nothing else. No hint of secrets, no holding back. It was as if she could see down into his soul.

"All right," she said. "I won't do the regret dance, but we're not doing this again. It's a very powerful form of persuasion and I'm not interested in being coerced."

He smiled his agreement, then took her hand in his. "I will concede to your wishes on the condition you show me the regret dance. Do you perform it naked?"

She sighed. "It's a figure of speech."

"No. It must be real. I will it so."

She rolled her eyes. "Welcome to the new world, prince. Here we're all equal and no one cares about your will."

He leaned close and whispered in her ear. "Perhaps you ignore my will, but what will you do with my wants?"

A shiver of desire rippled through her. An excellent question, she thought, and one for which she had no answer.

That evening Rafael escaped the loud chaos that signaled the end of the Marcelli evening meal by stepping outside for a few moments. He crossed to the fence by the garden and stared up at the stars.

Usually he enjoyed the conversation and animation of the family, but not this evening. Tonight they had been an annoyance. He had wanted to command them all to leave so that he could be alone with Mia.

He had not bothered to express his will—no one would have listened. How he longed for Calandria, where his word was law and he could drag Mia into his bed without anyone interfering.

Their game this afternoon had started as a way for him to convince her to accept his proposal. He'd been sure if she felt the fire again, she would be unable to resist him. Unfortunately, the fire had burned both ways, and no matter how he tried, he could not forget the feel of her body against his.

He had been hard for hours. Every time he managed to get his desire under control, he remembered the taste of her kiss and the feel of her breasts, and blood rushed to his groin.

Nothing helped, he thought grimly. Not thoughts of sports or finance or discussing the particulars of growing tomatoes with Grandma Tessa. He simply had to hear Mia's voice or catch sight of her, and he ached to take her.

Ironic that in this one area he did not have to pretend. He meant what he said—she was spectacularly sexual and he was desperate to revisit their passion.

A sharp scent caught his attention. He turned and saw a cigarette tip glowing in the darkness. He moved toward it and recognized the smoker.

"Good evening," he said.

Kelly Reese glanced at him. "Are you going to rat me out?"

"Of course not. What you do with your life is your business."

She sighed and continued to lean against the side of the garage. "Whatever. Aren't you going to lecture me about the perils of smoking?"

He shrugged. "Do you want me to?"

"Not especially. I know it's not great for my endurance, but it helps me keep my weight down. Let me tell you, being this skinny isn't pleasant. I've been hungry since I was fifteen."

He looked her over. She had the typical dancer's build. Powerful, lean muscles without an ounce of body fat to soften the lines. She was tall with perfect posture and wild, curly red hair tumbling down her back.

"So you suffer for your art," he said.

"That's me. Cliché girl."

Her phrasing reminded him of Mia, which made him hard again. He swore silently.

"How long have you been dating Etienne?" he asked, knowing the shadows would keep his secret. He did not want this child to think he was interested in her.

"A couple of months. Everybody hates him. It's the Euro-trash thing. You'd think I'd know better. My mom married some guy who was supposed to be a count or something and he wasn't. But, hey, it's not my problem."

"Did Etienne tell you he came from a titled family?"

"No. His dad is a policeman and his mother works in a bakery."

Working class, which fit his accent. Etienne might not be much for personal grooming, but at least he wasn't a liar. Not that Rafael cared one way or the other.

"So you knew Mia from a long time ago," Kelly said.

"Obviously, what with you being Danny's father. It's weird. Why didn't you come after her before?"

"I was told she was dead."

Kelly stared at him. "Huh. So she thought you were dead and you thought she was dead. Interesting coincidence."

"More sad than interesting. I mourned Mia for a long time."

Kelly's green eyes seemed to see more than most. "At least it's a good story," she said at last.

"You do not believe me." How could she not?

"What I think doesn't matter. Mia has always known what she wanted and no one gets in the way of that. If she wants you, no one will be able to change her mind."

"You don't like me," he said.

Kelly inhaled on her cigarette, then dropped it to the ground and stepped on it. "I'm not real keen on the Euro-trash set."

He stiffened. "I am Crown Prince Rafael of Calandria."

"I know. I'm sure the housing is much nicer, but you're still the type. Playing on what you have to get what you want. Right now you want Mia."

The child saw too much. Old before her years, he thought, recognizing the symptoms. For him the reason had been his upbringing, for her it was her commitment to ballet. He could both admire and sympathize with her position.

She picked up the butt and slipped it into her pocket. "I'm going to give you some advice, I don't know why. Maybe in exchange for you not mentioning the smoking thing. Don't screw with her. Joe will kill you."

"That is not possible."

Kelly grinned. "You think those two bodyguards could

protect you? Not in this lifetime. Nobody gets to Joe's family, and Mia is one of his favorites."

Her total confidence surprised him. "He would be killed as well."

"Maybe, but you'd be dead first. This is a friendly warning, worth what you paid for it."

Kelly walked away. Rafael watched her go. The child's words did not frighten him—nor did the thought of facing an angry Joe Marcelli. But he was surprised to feel something like regret.

It was increasingly obvious that Mia could be hurt by his plan. He didn't want to wound but he did require his son. Was there perhaps another way?

He immediately shook off the question. Sacrifices would be made by all. If Mia's were greatest, so be it.

Mia sat curled up in an old leather chair in the library. She loved the room with its high arched ceilings and the tall bookshelves filled with everything from rare first editions to her old copies of *Seventeen* magazine. She loved the quiet and the fact that no one ever thought to look for her here, but mostly she loved that the room reminded her of her grandfather.

Lorenzo had been gone five years. He'd never known about Danny, hadn't lived to see Joe and Darcy marry. Right now she missed the old man and his gruff ways. She had a feeling he would cut right to the heart of the matter with Rafael.

But what would he say? Would he tell her to marry the father of her son and be a good wife or would he shake his head and say that in a world that runs by computers, who needs princes?

The door opened. Mia tensed slightly, not sure she

would welcome any interruption. Then Rafael stepped into the room and she felt her heart flutter in anticipation.

Great. She was falling for him again. Just what she needed, because her life wasn't complicated enough these days.

"I am interrupting?" he asked.

She shrugged. "Not really. I'm going over my classes for the fall term at law school. I'm getting down to the serious stuff for my specialty and it's . . ." She blinked at his look of surprise. "What?"

"You plan to continue to attend law school?"

She put the catalog on the desk and scrambled to her feet. "Did you think you would stop me?"

"Of course not, it is just if we are married, you will not be able to practice law. Not in the traditional sense," he added quickly, then smiled. "You are right. You should complete your education, so when you speak before our parliament, you know exactly what you want to say."

She wasn't totally buying the sudden transformation. "Why would I be speaking before parliament?"

"Because you will never be silent, Mia. It is, how do you say . . . Not your style? You are life and you must be a part of things. I think that if you were to come to my country, you would want to tax the casinos more to pay for education. Perhaps you would start a teaching hospital so our future doctors did not go away to France or England."

"So you're saying I could affect policy."

"Of course. As queen you can do anything."

Except live a normal life.

He motioned to the chair she'd been in and waited until she sat before claiming the one next to it.

"What troubles you?" he asked. "I know you are finding it difficult to resist my charms."

She laughed. "That pesky ego. Doesn't it ever get heavy, carrying it around all the time?"

"No. I am used to the weight." His smile faded. "Tell me, Mia. I wish to know."

She drew in a breath, not sure she could even articulate her concerns. "Calandria is very far away."

"That is true. However, you will have access to several private jets to take you wherever you want. Your family is no more than eight or nine hours away. They would also be welcome to visit us whenever they wanted."

"I'm not really princess"—she couldn't bring herself to say *queen*—"material. I'm not royal or rich or anything special."

His gaze narrowed. "What more would you require to be special? You are uniquely yourself."

She sensed that he was going to reach for her hand and snatched it back just in time. He grasped air, then raised his eyebrows.

"I know you enjoy my touch," he began.

"Too much," she muttered. "There will be no more touching until I get things figured out."

He smiled with the contented confidence of a man who knows how to please women. "You are afraid I can seduce you."

"I'm not afraid, I'm prudent."

"A good quality in a wife."

"You could say the same thing about a dog." She shook her head. "You would have to let go of the hot-and-cold-running women at your house on the rocks."

"There have been women in my life. Of course, I'm a

man. But none at the house. I take no one there, Mia. You will be the first."

Whoa. "You're serious?"

"Why would I lie? You could easily check the truth. I have not brought a woman to my house."

Good to know. "It's just I . . ." She clutched the arms of the chair. "You're different. I knew Diego. I understood him. But Rafael is a mystery to me."

"We are not so different. Not the Diego you knew."

"What about the real one?"

He shrugged. "He was angry. By a fluke of birth, he lost the crown. His brother never cared, but Diego was angry from the time he understood what it meant to be king."

"Did it change you to pretend to be him?"

"I am already a man ready to take what I want," he said. "But Diego was a fool." He dismissed the other man with a flick of his fingers. "Now he is dead."

The ruthlessness didn't surprise her. She'd seen it in him before. Men only crossed Rafael once. Which made his sense of humor and flashes of tenderness more fascinating. Rafael could laugh at the world. More important, he could laugh at himself.

"Why me?" she asked.

He stared directly into her eyes. "Because in all the years we have been apart, I have never forgotten you. I am very good at forgetting women."

He rose. "I wish to return home, Mia, but my business there will wait. You are the most important part of my world. I will stay here until you are comfortable with me."

"And if it takes years?" she asked, not sure she believed him.

"I am a young man. Despite what you have heard, I am also a patient one. You are worth waiting for. Take your time. I will be here."

He left and she was alone. A normal person would have felt relief, but suddenly she was lonely and wanted to call him back.

He'd always been a smooth talker. She had to remember that. No one came into a situation like this without an agenda. But he had an answer for everything and she didn't know how to deal with that.

Worse, she didn't know how to stop herself from wanting to believe it was all true.

8

"You're trying to make me feel bad on purpose," Mia muttered as she flopped on her bed.

"Not at all. I dance in the corps and I live in San Francisco, which, as you know, is about the most expensive city next to New York, so it's not like I have a lot of extra cash."

Mia eyed Kelly as the tall, slender redhead pulled on a skinny-strapped sundress Mia hadn't been able to fit into since before Danny was born.

"So go to the mall."

"Your closet is closer." Kelly turned and studied herself in the mirror. "It's too short."

"And too loose. God, I hate you."

Kelly grinned. "I happen to know you adore me, despite my height and lack of body fat." She spun in the pale green dress, then pulled it over her head. "What's next?"

"Have at it," Mia said, pointing at the closet. "My old clothes are your old clothes."

Kelly flipped hangers. Mia studied her narrow back and the clearly visible bones of her shoulders and ribs.

"Not to get too maternal on you," Mia said lightly, "but are you sure you're eating enough?"

"Uh-huh."

"But you're so—"

"I'm a dancer, Mia. In my line of work, they don't like chunky. I'll eat when I retire."

"Most people just want to garden."

Kelly shrugged, then dove back in the closet. She emerged with a long dress in a muslin bag. "I know what's in here."

"Me too." Mia sat up. "I haven't looked at that in years."

Kelly unzipped the front and pulled out the handmade wedding gown all the women in the family had lovingly beaded when Mia had been planning on marrying David.

"That was what, more than eight years ago?" she asked more to herself than Kelly. "I can't believe it. Was I ever really that young and foolish?"

"You were in love," Kelly reminded her. "I think it's very romantic."

"We were babies. Just eighteen and still in college. What were we thinking?"

"That you wanted to be together."

Mia remembered the heated longing of her first real love. "We were worlds apart," she said as she fingered the stunning beadwork. "I'd started college at sixteen, so I was already a junior. He was a freshman and had no idea what he wanted to do with his life. I was going to get my master's in international relations and be a diplomat."

Kelly settled next to her on the bed. "What happened with David? Was it horrible?"

"No. We both realized we weren't as in love as we thought. Better to find out before the marriage than after."

"But it was very close to the actual date of the wedding," Kelly said.

Mia fingered the dress. "Obviously." She looked at Kelly.

"Don't try to make the situation romantic. We were kids pretending to be grown-up. We could have made a disaster of our lives. We got lucky."

"I suppose," Kelly said. "Do you have any regrets?"

"Ian," Mia told her. "I don't even have to think about the question. When I think about how he tricked me. Used me."

She didn't want to get angry, but she could feel her temper growing.

"He didn't plan to use you," Kelly said.

Mia looked at her. "You're defending him?"

"Of course not. I think it's awful that he tried to kidnap Darcy and hold her for ransom. I'm just saying when you met Ian, he was a regular guy."

"He was a domestic terrorist in disguise. That doesn't exactly fit my definition of normal."

"You know what I mean. It was only after he realized Darcy was here that he hatched his plot." Kelly flopped back on the bed. "Hatched his plot. That sounds so exciting."

"Darcy nearly died," Mia said flatly.

"Oh, I know. I didn't mean in her circumstances. Just in general. Besides, you can't regret Ian."

"Why not?"

"If he hadn't been a total dick, you wouldn't have become a spy and gone to Calandria. You wouldn't have met Diego, a.k.a. Danny's father, and you wouldn't have gotten pregnant. I know you, Mia. You would never regret Danny."

Kelly had her there, Mia thought as she smiled. "I can't regret him. He's my world. But the rest of it kind of blows."

Kelly rolled onto her stomach. "I have a secret that you're not going to like."

Considering how much Mia didn't like Etienne, she wasn't sure she wanted to hear. "What is it?"

"I don't like Rafael."

"You don't know him."

"I've spoken with him a few times. He's too . . . I don't know. I can't put my finger on it, but he's not a nice man."

Mia didn't think her niece by marriage was in a position to cast judgment in the man department. "And here I thought only Grandma Tessa and Joe didn't like him. Joe wouldn't like him on principle, because he's a sweetie who loves his sister. I'm not sure what's up with Grandma Tessa."

"Does it matter?" Kelly asked. "Isn't the important question whether you like him?"

"I like him," Mia said cautiously.

Kelly rolled her eyes. "I'm not talking about the mild affection one would have for an acquaintance. I mean like as in 'This guy is incredibly cool and I must have him.' "

"Is that how you feel about Etienne?"

"We're not discussing Etienne. I know Rafael proposed."

Mia groaned. "Did he take out an ad?"

"The Grands told me, which means they've told everyone. You know they believe the phrase 'Can you keep a secret?' actually means 'Tell everyone you know.'"

"He said the words," Mia told her. "I'm not sure he means them. He's a prince. I'm not sure he's able to simply marry whomever he wants."

"A prince. Sometimes I forget that." Kelly slid to the floor and began stretching. "I want to be you when I grow up. I want your life."

"No you don't," Mia said. "I'm not a good example, Kelly. I'm the cautionary tale. Trust me, you need a different role model."

Kelly stretched her legs in front of her and then bent

over until her forehead rested on her knees. When she sat up in a graceful, fluid movement Mia couldn't dream of replicating, she said, "But you're happy, right?"

"For the most part." When she didn't think too much about everything going on. "And you?"

"Delirious. I'm living my dream, dancing with the most amazing company on the planet. What's not to like?"

Mia wasn't sure, but she sensed something was off in Kelly's world.

"You have Etienne," she reminded her niece. "Does he play into this?"

"Most of the time. I don't want to settle down," Kelly said. "I take lovers. Usually the one who buys me the best presents gets to keep me until I'm bored."

It was something Mia would have said at Kelly's age, so why did it sound so wrong now?

"Kelly, I'm all for having fun, but you should also think about finding relationships that actually mean something."

"Like Ian?" Kelly asked innocently. "I distinctly recall you saying you were just using him for sex. And aren't you the one who constantly threatened to sleep with all Joe's Navy SEAL friends and let the others watch?"

Mia winced. "I didn't mean it."

"Maybe I don't mean it either. Maybe I'm just being outrageous. Jeez." She stood and walked to the door. "You used to be fun. What happened with that?"

Kelly stalked into the hall and disappeared. Mia stared after her, not sure exactly what had gone wrong. Apparently being confused about one's life was contagious and Kelly had just caught the bug.

• • •

"Look!" Danny demanded. "I'm tall."

He stood with his back to the wall, his hand at a sharp angle, pointing up so that the place he marked on the height chart was at least three inches higher than his head.

"You are growing," Mia said, feeling both proud and wistful. Her little baby wasn't a baby anymore.

Rafael lined up several small race cars on the floor. "The men in my family are tall," he said. "You will be tall, too."

"Did you hear that?" she asked Danny. "You are going to be tall."

Danny beamed. Mia didn't bother pointing out that she was barely five foot three, the runt of the Marcelli litter by several inches.

Danny stepped away from the wall and grabbed his scepter. No matter how many times Mia managed to put it on a top shelf, it found its way to the floor. She was beginning to think Rafael had a hand in that.

"Tell me about your birthday party," Rafael said.

Danny grinned. "I have cake and presents and everyone comes."

"I'm looking forward to your party and you turning four. It is a very great age."

Danny looked at Mia. His eyes widened as if he'd just that moment understood his father would be at his birthday party. His mouth stretched into a grin as big as the morning and he launched himself at his father.

Rafael caught him and stood. "What's all this?" he asked as he swung the boy in the air.

"I think Danny just figured out you're sticking around."

"Of course I am," he told the boy. "I'm your father."

"I want presents," Danny said.

"That will put you in your place," Mia told Rafael before reminding Danny, "It's not polite to ask people to give you presents."

"But I want 'em."

"Sometimes social niceties get lost on the post-toddler set."

"I want my daddy at my party."

"I will be there," Rafael said.

"Promise?"

"Of course."

Rafael set the boy on the ground. While he appreciated Mia's attempt to educate the child on ways to behave, he couldn't help being pleased with Danny's demanding personality. He would need that strength as he navigated his way through all the potential pitfalls of growing up royal.

"There will be presents," Rafael told his son. "Many presents."

Danny grinned. He grabbed the scepter and banged it on the bed. "I'm the heir. I'm the heir."

Mia took it from him. "Not a toy," she said. "How about that race we were going to have?"

Danny collapsed to the floor and began pushing the cars around.

"You do well with him," Rafael told her as he sat on the edge of the bed.

"Practice. My mom and the Grands have really helped."

"I look forward to meeting your parents."

"They were really excited to hear all about you. They wanted to come home, but I convinced them you would still be available for meet and greet when they returned from China."

"Of course," he said, knowing he would be back in Calandria. Most likely Mia would have returned home by then and they could hear her complaints in person.

He studied the boy, then Mia, noting Daniel had the same color eyes as his mother. The boy was also very close to her, perhaps a result of her being a single parent. There would be a period of adjustment, he thought. But in time Daniel would understand why things had to be that way.

As for Mia . . . Rafael took in her easy smile, then dropped his gaze to her full breasts. She would not be so forgiving. Her fury would stir the heavens, but there was nothing she could do to him.

He briefly wished for another option, one that did not alter her world so completely and hurt her, but the choice was clear. He would do what was best for Calandria and for his son. She laughed at something Daniel had said. The sound filled him with the need to hear it again. Unfortunately, that was not his only desire where she was concerned.

"What are you thinking?" she asked. "You have the strangest look on your face."

"Just that I have missed you," he said, the lie easy and smooth.

"Are you bored here, living in the real world?"

"I am enjoying myself. Normal is more interesting than I had realized."

"Sorry, but this isn't normal. Normal means holding down a job and struggling to pay the bills and trying to save for retirement and the kids' college while hoping your company doesn't get bought out and you don't get downsized. This is a really cool vacation."

"Then I am enjoying my vacation."

She grinned. "Because you would never make it in Normal Land."

"I could get a job."

"Doing what? You'd never last, Rafael. You're too imperious."

"You like that I'm imperious."

"Sometimes."

She lowered her lashes as she spoke and his gaze dropped to her mouth. He wanted her in his bed. Not only because he sensed that once they made love he will have won, but also because he ached for her.

Their time together when he had played at being Diego had shown him that they complemented each other extremely well. She argued with him and sometimes won. She spoke different languages, understood different cultures, liked to laugh, and treated him as if he were just a man. Just as intriguing, there was a passionate fire that never seemed to go out, and no matter how many times he had her, he always wanted more.

Their recent encounter had left him hungry and restless. She might not be the most beautiful woman he'd ever known, but she was the most sexually exciting. After she'd gone home, he'd tried to figure out what it was about her that got to him. Was it the sharpness of her mind? The sound of her laughter? The way she gave herself to him so completely?

He had never discovered the answer, and now that he was with her again, he ached to claim her.

Danny crashed two of his cars and giggled. Mia glanced at her watch. "Okay, my man, ten more minutes, then we need to run through your lines again."

Danny wrinkled his nose. "I know my lines."

"All of them?"

He smiled. "Miss Valdrake will whisper them to me. She does when we practice."

"Uh-huh. Wouldn't it be totally, incredibly fabulous if you knew all your lines by yourself?"

Danny nodded as he laughed.

"This is his play for school?" Rafael asked. "He is the lead?"

"He's a tree," Mia said. "Get over it."

A tree? "But he is the heir to—"

"Actually, everyone in this room is very clear on that."

"But the teacher is not. My son will not be a tree in a play." It was not acceptable.

"I want to be a tree," Danny said, his smile fading. "I'm a good tree."

"Yes, you are," Mia said, and patted him on the back. "Don't sweat it, honey. You're going to be a tree. The Grands have worked too hard on your costume for that to change now." She looked at Rafael. "Did I mention the imperious bit, because this would be an example. Besides, it's a production for preschoolers in a summer program. There is no lead. The play is about the forest, and the trees are the really cool parts."

He was not convinced but told himself it did not matter. No one would be seeing the play except other parents. "When is the play?"

"In a couple of weeks."

Rafael wasn't sure if they would still be here or not. "I will attend."

Danny scrambled to his feet and started jumping up and down. "My daddy's coming to my play! My daddy's coming to my play!" Then he threw himself at Rafael and wrapped his arms around his neck.

Danny straightened. "You're the best daddy ever," he announced, then kissed Rafael and then Mia. "I'm hungry," he announced.

"I heard that," Grammy M said as she stuck her head in the room. "Come along, little man. I'll be gettin' you a snack." She smiled at Rafael, then took the boy by the hand and led him away.

Rafael stared after them. He was still absorbing Daniel's reaction to his attending the play.

"He wanted me to be there," he murmured. "And at his birthday party."

"Of course he did. You're important to him. That was one of the things that stunned me about being a parent. I knew there would be responsibility, but I didn't expect to be his whole world. At least until he grows up a little."

His world. Rafael hadn't expected that either. Until arriving, he'd thought of Daniel in abstract terms. A child. His child. But now the boy was more than that. He was a separate person with thoughts and ideas and dreams.

"Kind of scary, huh?" she asked.

He shrugged. "It is different. He is different."

She leaned against the bed. "Let me guess. Less well mannered."

"He has not been raised in a palace."

"You're going to have to teach him to salute."

He narrowed his gaze. "Even the mother of the heir should take care not to mock the crown prince."

She grinned. "Oooh, will the big, bad prince punish me now?"

"No, because that is what you want." He picked up one of the race cars. "When I was his age, I could already recite the lineage of my family back to the twelfth century."

"There's a party trick."

"It is not a trick. It is who we are."

"It's who *you* are. And Danny's not you. He's not even four yet. Give him a break."

Rafael appreciated her concern, but he also resented it. How strange. Perhaps if his mother had lived she would have . . .

He shook off the thought. "Before I left for school in England, I was already attending meetings of state. I would visit with my father three times a week and listen while he explained what was going on in our country and in the world."

"Arranged meetings?" she asked. "What about just hanging out. Playing, having him read you a story?"

"He is the king. He does not read stories."

"Right. Because he has a staff to do that." She leaned over and put her hand on his arm. "I'm sorry."

He stiffened. "Your apology is not required."

"I wasn't apologizing. I was expressing sympathy and compassion. That's a tough life for any kid. It shouldn't have been like that."

He stood and glared down at her. "It was exactly as it should have been. I am crown prince—"

She rose, put her hands on his shoulders, and cut him off with a brief kiss. "Get defensive much?" she asked as she drew back. "I know who you are. You've lived a life of great privilege and that's wonderful, but you've also paid a price for that. Everyone has trade-offs. Yours were different from most, but they still existed. That's okay."

He hated what she was saying as much as his body wanted to respond to her nearness.

"I do not need you making excuses for me," he told her.

"I'm not. I'm saying that childhood is a tough gig, even for a prince. No kid should have to get dressed up and have an appointment to see a parent. Parents should be the safest place in the world, and so many times they're not."

He didn't want to think about that—about how his father had been a stranger. There had been other people he could depend on. His uncle Vidal had talked to him about life and been a trusted confidant.

Mia took his hand and tugged until he sat next to her on the bed. "I have a question."

"That is hardly unusual."

"True. What would you be or do if you weren't a prince?"

He stared at her. "I *am* a prince."

"Yes, we're all totally clear on that. The flashing neon sign over your head doesn't let anyone forget. But if you weren't, what would you be? How would you make a living?"

"I have never considered such a thing."

Except he had . . . once. Rafael had spent a month his summer before university on the private island of a friend of his father's. There had been no press, no parties, no public appearances. Just the large house and its staff, along with those people indigenous to the island.

None of them had cared who he was or where he came from. They lived their lives bound by the seasons, growing crops, marrying, having children, getting old, and then dying.

"A doctor," he said without thinking, then wished he hadn't spoken.

"Really? An actual medical doctor?"

He nodded stiffly. "I would take care of people. I would also do research to fight diseases."

"You mean help them?" She sounded both intrigued and disbelieving.

"This conversation has no purpose."

"It does for me," she told him. "I'm still trying to figure you out. I wouldn't have thought a doctor."

It was a moment to push his advantage. He should discuss this more and allow Mia to believe he was everything she wanted. Instead he asked, "And you? When you were a young girl, what did you want to be or do?"

She laughed. "I wanted to rule the world. Sort of the ultimate imperial queen. It's been a joke in my family for years. Instead I decided to become a diplomat and along the way ended up, very briefly, being a spy. You know the rest."

He touched her cheek. "You would make a very good imperial queen. But why did you become a spy?"

Her brown eyes darkened. "Someone fooled me. I didn't want that to ever happen again."

Rafael stayed where he was, right next to Mia, but a part of him wanted to pull away. He was there to fool her. Perhaps in the biggest way possible. If there was another way . . .

There wasn't, he reminded himself. This was for a greater good. There was no choice. Funny how early he'd learned that in his life. For him, there never was a choice.

9

"I'm loving this," Katie said as she and Mia walked toward the gazebo behind the wine-tasting room. "I'm semi–mother of the groom. I get all the fun bits and none of the stress."

Mia laughed. "Sort of like being the grandparent? Loading the grandkids up on sugar, then sending them home to crash?"

"Exactly. Amber's mother is handling the majority of the details and only calls every now and then."

Mia raised her eyebrows. "You are so lying. You are desperate to run every minute of the wedding and it's killing you not to."

Katie sighed. "Maybe. Okay, yes. I mean I *am* a professional party planner. You'd think she'd be impressed by that. But noooo. Every conversation Amber and I have, she's very determined to make it clear she and her mother are in charge. It's David's wedding, too."

Mia wasn't used to hearing her oldest sister whine and was really enjoying the moment. "What does David say?"

"He's a typical man. Whatever Amber wants is fine with him."

"You say that like it's a bad thing."

"It's not, it's just . . ." Katie lowered her voice. "Do you know they actually considered *paper* napkins. This is a formal sit-down dinner for three hundred and they discussed paper napkins."

"Did you run screaming into the night?"

Katie sighed again. "No. I reminded them that the linens, along with the tables and chairs, were being provided by Marcelli Winery. We have weddings here all the time and like to use our own vendors. Paper napkins. Can you imagine?"

"You didn't tell them that we pay our vendor, did you?"

Katie tucked her hair behind her ears. "I didn't really see the point. *They're* not paying for it." She stopped and looked at Mia. "Am I being horrible? I know weddings are expensive, and saving money where you can makes sense. But this is for David. I adore him and I want his wedding to be perfect."

"It's okay," Mia told her, still enjoying the sight of her normally unflappable sister just a little . . . flapped. "David doesn't actually care one way or the other about the napkins, but you do. If you can make it happen without upsetting Amber and her mother, then go for it."

"I've probably put together a hundred and fifty weddings," Katie muttered. "Why can't they talk to me?"

"Because we are the Marcellis and just a little intimidating for regular folks. Plus there's the whole 'Amber worrying about David still being in love with me' thing. That's got to put a damper on events."

Katie laughed. "My God, when did you grow up?"

"A couple of years ago. It was a Thursday."

"Okay, you're right about all of it. I'm going to have to wait until Valerie and Liana are engaged to plan a wedding for my kids."

"You could betroth them now. That should be worthy of a big party."

"Gee, thanks."

They walked out from behind the tasting building and stared at the beautiful white gazebo standing in the middle of a couple of acres of grass and carefully manicured plants before stepping inside.

"Every time I come here I'm surprised by how beautiful it is," Katie said wistfully. "I'm glad David's getting married here where Marcellis have been tying the knot for eighty years."

"He's not a Marcelli," Mia pointed out. "If he had been, I wouldn't have wanted to marry him."

"He's a Marcelli by love," Katie said firmly. "Just like Kelly." There was a momentary pause; then she continued, "Was it just me or is Kelly—"

"Completely out of control?" Mia asked, finishing her sentence. "It's not just you. Kelly and I talked a couple of days ago, I guess just before she and Etienne headed out. She said she admires my life. I couldn't believe it. I'm so not doing anything right."

"You are with Danny."

"That's more luck and really great role models. I'm not an intuitive parent. I didn't think I'd survive that first year when he felt so breakable. Rafael is different. He seems to know exactly how to get right down on Danny's level and connect. Which is surprising, considering the whole royalty thing. And impressive. He's imperious about nearly everything but he'll play in the dirt with his kid. Danny is thrilled and Rafael seems taken with his son."

"Rafael is doing it right where it matters. Did you think it would be different?"

Mia sank onto the floor of the gazebo and rested her forearms on her lap. "I never thought about it. Until he showed up here, I figured he was dead. Now he's here and so friendly and romantic."

Katie sat next to her and bumped her shoulder. "Romantic, huh? Come on . . . tell your favorite big sister all the details."

"He says all the right things," she admitted. "I know there's no reason to doubt him. He's straightforward and affectionate. He's answered all my questions and he doesn't seem to be in a hurry to get back to Calandria."

"But?" Katie asked.

"I don't know. I'm jaded and cynical, I guess. He's a prince. How on earth can he marry me? Doesn't his bride need a pedigree and access to really old jewelry?"

"Maybe not. The world is different. It's a new century."

"I'd noticed the century part, but Calandria has a monarchy. How different can it be?"

"What are you afraid of? Why don't you trust him? Is this because you don't really know him? Are you getting some signal or warning from your gut? Or is this about your unproven belief that you have lousy taste in men?"

Mia turned to Katie. "Excuse me? An unproven belief?"

"You've made a couple of bad choices."

Mia shook her head. "A bad choice is a guy who cheats on you, not someone who kidnaps the president's daughter. Ian fooled me completely, and Darcy could have died because of that." She drew in a deep breath. "It's not just the bad choice thing. I don't know Rafael."

"But you're in love with him."

"What?"

Katie patted her arm. "Mia, you've been in love with him since you got back five years ago. Having Danny only cemented your feelings. Why else would you have avoided any kind of dating situation for so long?"

"I'm busy."

"Many busy women manage to date. It's more than that and you know it."

"I don't love him," Mia said flatly.

"Fine. You don't. But you're also not willing to let anyone else get close to you and there has to be a reason for that. You might want to figure out what it is."

Mia nodded. Her sister had a point. About the reason, not the love. No way had she loved Rafael all these years. How crazy was that?

Katie stood. "All right, we're here to measure the gazebo. Let's get to work."

Mia eyed her tailored linen slacks and elegant, sleeveless silk blouse, then glanced down at her own T-shirt and cutoffs. "Somehow I missed the 'dress well' gene in this family."

"It's summer, you're off from school. Why would you want to worry about what to wear?"

"I wouldn't. I'm just saying, I don't have a closet full of beautiful clothes like you and Mom and Francesca. Brenna and I are misfits."

"You're individuals."

"That's very polite. My point is, I'm not really princess material."

Katie frowned. "What? You'd marry him except you don't know what to wear? I'm going to guess that all princesses have a live-in stylist to worry about that sort of thing for them. Mia, this is a really big decision. Make it for the right reasons."

"I know. I will. Part of me wants it to be like it was before. When he was Diego." She bit her lower lip. "Well, not the illegal stuff, but how it was just us and we were nearly regular people."

"You'd like Rafael better if he wasn't a prince?"

"Something like that."

"Sorry. Princely comes with the guy. You're stuck." Katie pulled a tape measure out of her purse. "It's not exactly ruling the world, but it's being in charge of a small country. That should count."

Mia grinned. "That's true. I'll bet I could even ask Rafael to get my picture on money. Wouldn't that be thrilling?"

"My sister—the five-dollar bill. We'd all be so proud."

Mia reached for the tape measure. "So what kind of flowers are they talking about?"

Katie sighed heavily. "Daisies. Lots and lots of daisies."

Mia listened to the mantel clock chime midnight. The house was quiet and she guessed that everyone was asleep. As *she* should be. But no matter how tired she felt physically, she couldn't seem to shut down her mind.

It whirled and swirled and dipped, jumping from past to present, while completely ignoring the future because that was just too big to deal with right now. Which led her to one glaringly obvious conclusion.

The most logical solution to all her problems was to

refuse Rafael's proposal and work out an agreement whereby they had some kind of shared custody. Maybe Danny could summer in Calandria and learn all his princely duties while spending his school year here, living like a normal child.

Except she had a feeling that normal wasn't possible. Not after the world found out that little Danny Marcelli was really the heir to the Calandrian throne.

Security wasn't a problem. Sam, Francesca's husband, was an expert, and Joe had plenty of experience dealing with Darcy's welfare. But what about school? Could Danny really go to the elementary school down the road and be a regular child? Was Mia kidding herself? And if Danny really was going to rule Calandria someday, shouldn't he grow up there? Which meant what? That she would move there with him?

And if she did move there with him, what would she do with her life? She had a feeling she wouldn't be able to practice law. So then what? Being a stay-at-home mom wasn't really her style. Would she just live in the shadows while Danny became a prince and Rafael married an appropriate future queen?

Thinking about him marrying someone else gave her a tight feeling in her stomach, which she hated, because it was a definite tally in the yes column of Katie's theory.

"I don't love him," Mia said out loud. What kind of idiot stayed in love with a dead man for five years?

So if she didn't love him, wasn't not marrying him the right thing to do?

She heard footsteps in the hallway. The door pushed open and Rafael stepped into the quiet of the library.

"You hide here," he said as he approached.

"I think of it more as a retreat."

She curled up in a corner of the sofa. He settled in the middle and angled toward her.

"I have news," he said, handing her an envelope. "It arrived today, but I wished to deliver it to you privately. A most difficult thing in this household."

She took the paper. "We are a crowd," she said as she glanced at the return address and saw it was a medical lab. "The DNA results?"

He nodded.

She gave back the envelope. "I already know the results."

"As do I. Daniel is my son."

Hardly news to her, but still, hearing him say the words made her tense a little. As if the situation had just gotten more serious.

"You'll have to tell your father," she said. "I'm not sure he'll be pleased."

"He wants a grandchild and an heir for me. He will come around much quicker than Grandma Tessa. She still resists me."

Mia laughed. "You're winning her over. Tonight at dinner she offered you seconds without you having to ask. That's progress. I'm not sure your father will be as easy as you think. This can't be what he had planned for your future."

Rafael shrugged. "He will adjust. At least he'll stop parading potential brides in front of me."

"He really does that?"

"It is not a marriage mart, but yes, women are brought to different events and I meet them." He smiled at her. "So far I have found it very easy to resist their charms."

"I can relate. If my grandpa Lorenzo had thought he could have gotten away with arranging marriages for his granddaughters, he would have done it in a heartbeat."

"Would you have said yes?" he asked.

She drew her knees closer to her chest and wrapped her arms around her legs. "Not my style."

"Because you are too independent."

"It's more than that. I loved my grandfather, but he would have made the best match for the vineyard, not the best match for me. Isn't that what the king is doing to you? Parading around the grand duchess of Whosits because her father owns shipping rights to Finland or whatever? Does he actually care if you fall in love?"

"Is love so very important?"

"Hello? We're talking about living with someone the rest of your life. I suppose if the castle is big enough, you could have separate wings. Is that what you want? The right marriage for Calandria rather than the right marriage for you?"

"I think I can make them the same thing," he told her, his blue eyes claiming hers.

There was a not-so-subtle message there, she thought, not sure if she should lean in and say yes or bolt for freedom.

"I don't even know any good princess jokes," she said at last.

"You don't have to. The rules can be learned, Mia. But not the heart of a person. That is more complicated."

"What do you know about my heart?" she asked.

"That you do not give it easily. That you are loyal. That when you love, you do so without reservation."

"What happens when you love?" She lowered her feet to the floor. "Have you been in love before?"

"You mean aside from you?" he asked.

She felt herself flush. "I didn't want to pressure you."

"I loved you," he said easily. "I thought we loved each other."

His words stirred her, body and soul. Relief tasted sweet. It was as if she'd been starving for weeks and he'd finally offered her food.

He *had* loved her. All that had been real.

"Then have you been in love aside from me?" she asked.

"When I was very young," he admitted. "A long time ago. I was just eighteen. She was a few years older and very beautiful."

"Right, because in real life, the prince never falls for the ugly girl."

He smiled. "You consider me shallow."

"I consider you a typical male. Go on. You met a beautiful, older woman who seduced you with her worldly ways and seductive charms."

His humor faded. "You are right. It is a cliché, but I did not know that at the time. She could claim some minor nobility, which made her acceptable, but my father did not like her and said we were too young. Or at least I was."

Mia knew the story didn't end well. If it had, Rafael would currently be Mr. Minor Nobility and they wouldn't be having this conversation. "And?"

"And I bought a ring so I could propose, despite my father's disapproval. Then I discovered she was selling the intimate details of our private relationship to the press."

She winced. "How intimate?"

"Very. I had only been with a few other women. She

taught me how to please a woman and then she told the world about it."

"That would be horrible for anyone to have happen anywhere, but to have it play out in the tabloids . . . I'm sorry."

"As am I. But I learned an important lesson. Now I do not trust so easily."

Did he trust her? How would she know if he did? What did it take to gain his trust? Did she want to?

"It was a long time ago," he told her. "I assure you, I have recovered."

"It's still sucky that she did that. I'm sure you gave her jewelry. If she needed money, she should have sold that instead."

He chuckled. "My innocent Mia. Don't you know that to a woman like that secrets are far easier to part with than anything that sparkles?"

"No. I guess this is why I don't belong in your world."

"Don't you?"

He reached for her and she went willingly into his arms. He might think the humiliation of that young man was gone forever, but she knew some wounds never completely heal. Knowing he'd felt pain made him seem a little bit more like a regular person.

His mouth claimed hers in a kiss that demanded more than comfort. She met him as an equal, willing to do a little demanding of her own. He shifted her so that she stretched out beneath him on the sofa.

As she parted her lips and circled his tongue with her own, she rubbed her hands across his shoulders and back. He braced himself above her, his eyes closed, his beautiful, talented, sexy mouth teasing her, making her tremble.

Need rushed through her like a storm-driven tide. She melted and found herself wanting more than just a simple kiss. Her body remembered what it had been like the last time they had been so physically close. Heat filled her. Between her legs she felt herself swelling in anticipation. She knew if he touched her, she would be wet and ready and hungry.

He drew back slightly and kissed her cheeks, her forehead, her nose; then he nibbled along her jawline. She turned her head to give him more room and he licked the sensitive skin below her ear.

"Mia," he breathed before he bit down on her earlobe. "I want you."

Simple words, she thought hazily. Magic words.

"I want you," he repeated as he stared into her eyes and covered her breast with his hand.

His touch was exquisite. The weight of him, the way he moved so that his palm caressed her hard nipple. She had to bite her lip to hold in a whimper of desire. He cupped her curves in a gentle caress that loosened the last slender threads of her control.

"I want you, too," she breathed as she pushed him back. She raised herself up a few inches and tore off her T-shirt. Next she reached behind herself and unfastened her bra. That got tossed to the floor, too.

She leaned back on the cushions, feeling the cool leather on her bare skin. Above her, Rafael smiled with anticipation. It was an expression she recognized.

"So beautiful," he told her. He used a single finger to explore her breast. First the underside, then the top. Finally he slowly, oh so slowly, moved to her nipple. Once there, he lightly brushed the very tip.

Her breath caught. Need tightened every muscle in her body. She swore, then raised herself so that she was inches from his mouth.

"Stop playing."

"As you wish."

He lowered his head, then took her nipple in his mouth. The hot, wet pressure pushed her to the edge. She couldn't get enough, couldn't be close enough, couldn't feel enough. Wanting grew until it consumed her. Wanting and desire and the heavy thickness of her body slick with passion.

He sucked her nipple, then replaced tongue with fingers and moved to her other breast. She writhed beneath him, wanting it all, yet desperate to have him between her legs.

He read her mind, or understood what the frantic tugging of her hands on her shorts meant. He drew back.

"Sit up," he commanded as he pulled his shirt over his head.

She did as he requested, but first she unfastened her shorts and pushed them down, along with her panties. He stared at her nakedness for a moment, groaned, then removed the rest of his clothing. She parted her legs, desperate to have him inside.

But instead of accepting her invitation, he slid to his knees on the floor and moved between her thighs.

"Oh, God," she breathed as she remembered what he'd done to her before when he'd touched her with his mouth. It had been beyond exquisite, beyond sensation.

He cupped her hips and shifted her so she was at the very edge of the sofa, then he lowered his head toward her hot, swollen center.

At first there was only the puff of his breath. She tensed in anticipation. He parted her tenderly, then slowly, gently, lightly stroked her with the very tip of his tongue.

She felt the scream building up inside of her. She spread her legs as wide as they would go and wished she'd studied yoga more. If only she'd . . . He licked her again, this time with his tongue flat. From bottom to top, he covered every inch of her. Then he returned to that one special place and reintroduced himself.

He circled and teased and rubbed and sucked. He slipped two fingers inside of her and caressed her from the inside, the movements matching. She groaned, she begged, and did everything in her power not to come. Not yet.

She could feel herself getting wetter and wetter. She was swollen to the point of discomfort and still she held back because no one had ever gone down on her like that. But in the end, which was maybe three minutes, she had no choice. She covered her mouth with her hand and screamed her surrender.

The waves of pleasure swept her into another dimension. Muscles convulsed in rippling release, an orgasm that went on and on. Just when she thought she was surely finished, he reached up his free hand and lightly touched her left nipple. That sent her back into another release. Then he replaced tongue with fingers, keeping her going as he raised up, shifted, and thrust into her.

More, she thought, as she continued to come with each thrust. She wrapped her legs around his hips, holding him in place. More and deeper and forever.

He pumped and thrust, filling her over and over again. She felt herself begin to shatter as every cell of her body sighed in pleasure. Then he stiffened and came and they clung to each other as the aftershocks rippled through them.

She resurfaced on the sofa, his body pressing against her. They lay together, spent and satisfied. She looked at him, at the face that was familiar yet different, and in that moment she knew him.

"Just like before," she whispered.

He smiled. "Better. How I love to touch you, Mia. You are made for pleasure, and when I am with you, I am the most powerful man in the world."

Tears burned in her eyes. He had often said such things to her before, but now, knowing about his past and what his first love had done, she felt touched. She could easily use those words against him, humiliate him publicly. He trusted her to keep him safe.

"Katie was right," she said without thinking.

"Katie? Your sister? Right about what?"

Mia swallowed. It had been five years and she'd never stopped loving him. She'd never moved on. All this time she'd been waiting for the love of her life to return, and he finally had.

"I will marry you, Rafael. I'm proud to marry you."

His eyes widened slightly. "Are you serious? You are not just saying this in the heat of the moment?"

She grinned. "You're good, but you're not that good. This isn't about us making love, despite the fact that it was spectacular. It's about the fact that we belong together. I don't know how it's all going to work out, but we'll deal with that later."

"Mia." He wrapped his arms around her and kissed her hard. "Thank you. You are right. There are many things to discuss and much for you to learn, but you will see. All will be well." He grinned. "You're going to marry me."

"Apparently." She thought about the last royal wedding that had been broadcast on television. "It's going to be huge, isn't it?"

"A thousand or so guests, long ceremonies. Yes, it will be painful. Or we could elope."

She blinked at him. "Excuse me, but did you just say elope?"

He nodded. "Some formalities cannot be avoided. You must be made a princess of my country, which can happen through a different ceremony, but there is no need for us to have a big wedding if the thought of it makes you uncomfortable. Or if you don't want to wait."

"I don't want to wait," she admitted. "But more than that, I'm not ready to be the center of attention."

"Marrying me will make you such, Mia. You must be willing to accept that. You would one day rule as queen. You must not forget that."

His desire to make sure she knew what she was getting into just made her love him more.

"Are you sure a quickie wedding is legal?" she asked.

"Of course. You would officially be my wife."

"Even if we ran off to Las Vegas?"

He smiled. "Is that what you have in mind?"

"Well, any big formal thing is going to include my family. There's no way we'll be able to escape that. Which means it will take time and then the king will find out about it. So either we go for it or we stay traditional."

"Would you like to go for it?"

As he asked, he moved against her. He was already hard again. Her body tightened in response.

"All that for me?" she asked as she reached between them and took him in her hand.

"All that and much more," he murmured. "I give you my heart, my country, my history, my future. Marry me, Mia Marcelli."

He shifted so she was on top of him. She slid herself onto his erection and eased into another orgasm.

"Okay," she gasped as she tightened around him.

He reached up and teased her nipples. "Okay, what?"

"Danny's birthday is in a couple of days. We'll fly to Las Vegas after that."

He raised up and claimed her with a kiss. "As you wish, my love. As you wish."

10

Rafael woke up alone in his bed. As much as he wanted Mia there with him, they had agreed it would be better for them to keep their relationship a secret until after they eloped.

As he walked into the bathroom attached to his room, he smiled. Last night had been most pleasurable, and not simply because Mia had finally agreed to marry him. Their lovemaking had been as exciting and sensual as he remembered. She had always been able to match him, desire for desire, and time had not eroded that connection.

Although her getting pregnant had been an unexpected complication, he could not regret Daniel's parentage. Mia brought great strength and heart to the boy.

He shaved, then stepped into the shower. As he reached for the soap, he remembered how she had asked if he had loved before. As if not sure he had loved her.

He had never allowed himself to examine his feelings for her. He had known they would only be together for a short time. But he had never forgotten her. Was that love?

Did it matter? Despite the brief marriage they would share, she was not an appropriate queen. He would let her go because it was the right thing to do. His responsibility demanded . . .

Everything, he thought, both angry and resigned. It always had. This time, Mia would pay the price for who he was. He stepped out of the shower. He did not want to hurt her. Before he had arrived, she had been an obstacle. Now she was uniquely herself.

When he had dried off, he dressed. Later he would call his father and tell him of his victory. They would need to begin to draw up the required paperwork. Rafael decided that he would be generous. He would allow Mia the right to visit her son as often as she would like. There was no need to keep them apart. Having his mother around would make the transition easier for the boy.

He heard a knock on the door, followed by a low, "Your highness?"

"Enter."

Oliver stepped into the room. "Your gift has arrived and is ready."

"Good," Rafael said, knowing how pleased Daniel would be. "I will get the boy and be right down."

Oliver nodded and left. Rafael finished dressing, then walked to Daniel's room.

Mia was already there. He paused in the doorway and watched her brush his son's hair while outlining their activities for the day. She worked quickly, with the easy grace of someone who has performed this particular task a thousand times before.

Rafael stepped into the room. "Good morning," he said.

Daniel looked up and grinned, then darted forward. "Daddy, Daddy!"

Rafael dropped to one knee and pulled the boy close. "It has only been one night. Did you miss me so much?"

He asked the question of his son, but his gaze was on Mia as he spoke. She stood by the dresser, wearing her usual shorts and a T-shirt. Her hair was damp from her recent shower, which made him think of her naked, which made him want her again.

"Did you sleep well?" he asked with a smile that only she could see.

"Better than I expected."

"Perhaps it was the exercise you had yesterday."

She blushed faintly. "Yes, well, maybe. And you?"

"I slept very well."

"Good. We're all rested. Danny, come on. I can smell breakfast."

Rafael ruffled the boy's hair. "Perhaps that could wait for a few minutes. I have a surprise for him."

Mia crossed to the door. "Let me guess. A crown?"

"You mock the scepter."

"It's fairly mockable."

"Your circumstances suggest you will want to understand all of my country's traditions."

Her smile faded as something very close to panic filled her eyes. "Good point. Danny, your dad got you an early birthday present. Do you want to go see it?"

The boy nodded eagerly and took his father's hand. Rafael frowned slightly. Was it appropriate for a male child this age to hold his father's hand? He could not remember ever having such contact with his own father.

He glanced at Mia, but she didn't act as if anything

was amiss. Perhaps his childhood should not be the measure of normal, he admitted. There would be time for Daniel to learn how to behave royally.

"Where is it?" Danny asked. "Is it big? Is it soldiers? Is it lots of soldiers?"

"It is not soldiers and it is not large." Rafael looked at the boy. "It may seem large to you. Come. You will see for yourself."

They walked down the stairs. The Grands were already in the kitchen, fixing breakfast.

"Mornin'" Grammy M said, beaming at him. "You're up early."

"I have a surprise for Daniel," Rafael told her.

Grandma Tessa narrowed her eyes. "He's barely four. Still a little boy."

Rafael paused to kiss her cheek. "And here I thought you had accepted me, Tessa."

She gave him a smile. "All right. I'll wait to see what it is before I complain."

"Thank you." He reached for Mia with his free hand. "You will be very impressed."

"I'm already having doubts."

"How can you not trust me?"

"Fascinating question. We'll have to explore that later."

Later he would have her in his bed again. Later he would make her forget everything but the pleasure she felt in his arms. Later she would make plans for their wedding and he would let her.

They walked outside just as Umberto led a small pony out of a horse carrier. The animal was pure white, with a long mane and tail. Ribbons and bells had been woven into both, so the pony fluttered and tinkled as it walked.

Danny gripped his hand tightly. "For me?" he asked with a gasp. "For my birthday?"

"Yes, Daniel. This is a Calandrian pony. They are specially bred and revered all over the world."

Mia came to a stop. "You bought him a pony?"

"As you can see."

"You bought him a pony and you didn't tell me?"

He frowned. "Why would I?"

"Gee, I don't know. Because I'm his mother? Because we don't exactly have a spare stable here on our vineyard?"

"You do not have to worry about details, Mia."

"Why not? Someone does."

"All will be taken care of." He turned to Daniel. "His name is Gaspare, which means bringer of gifts."

Danny stared wide-eyed. "He's really mine?"

"Of course."

"Can I ride him?"

"Right now."

Oliver appeared with a saddle and bridle.

"There is much work in owning a horse, or even a pony," Rafael told the boy. "You will have to be very responsible. Do you know what that means?"

Danny shook his head.

"It means you will have to take care of him. You will have to brush him and feed him."

"What? He doesn't get a groom with the horse?" Mia asked.

"Yes, of course there is a groom, but Daniel needs to learn to take care of things. To be responsible."

"All part of his once-and-future-king training?"

There was something in her voice, something that

made him watch her closely. "You are angry?" he asked, not sure how that was possible.

"*Anger* isn't the right word. *Shocked.* Rafael, a pony is a big deal. How could you not have discussed this with me?"

"You worry too much," he said, then kissed her on the mouth. "Help me saddle him so Daniel can ride him."

Five minutes later a very excited boy sat on top of his pony. Mia hovered, which Rafael allowed. It was a first ride, after all. But in time she would have to learn to let her son go. He needed to be a man.

"I'm riding, I'm riding!" Daniel crowed as they made a slow circle around the backyard. "Daddy, this is the bestest present ever."

"Socks are going to be a real letdown after this," Mia mumbled.

"You did not buy him socks."

"Not exactly." She tentatively patted the pony's neck. "He seems friendly enough."

"He is very gentle, but with enough of a spirit to be a challenge as Daniel learns to ride more. In a few months, he'll graduate to a horse, but Gaspare works for now."

"I love my pony," Daniel said as he leaned forward and hugged the animal's neck.

"Keep control of the reins," Rafael told him. "It is how you control your mount."

Daniel grinned. "He's a pretty pony. Can I take him to school to show my friends and Miss Valdrake?"

"His teacher," Mia said. "Honey, I'm thinking we're going to wait on pony show-and-tell. Just until we get this figured out." She looked at Rafael. "You haven't said what we're going to do about a stable."

"The weather is mild enough that the animal can stay out."

"And in winter?"

Daniel and his pony wouldn't be here, Rafael thought. But what he said was, "I have a staff to deal with details, Mia. Please, try not to worry. All will be well."

"I don't have a staff," she said. "I'm used to solving my own problems and you're not helping with that."

"Do we really need to discuss this now?"

She smiled at Daniel, who urged Gaspare to go faster.

"I guess not," she admitted. "It's just . . . Wow. A pony. The whole prince thing is still something I have to get used to."

"You will."

"I guess I have to. What with . . ." Her voice trailed off.

He knew she referred to her acceptance of his proposal. That she would have to get used to being royal herself. He wanted to reassure her that the job would be much less taxing than she imagined for she would be only have it a few weeks.

"He bought Danny a pony," Mia said as she paced around Brenna's office at the winery. "He never said a word. He just announced he had a surprise and then there it was. An honest-to-God pony."

"It wouldn't be my first choice," Brenna admitted, "but hey, he's royal. Maybe it's a big fourth birthday thing with his family."

"I guess. It's just . . . shouldn't he have talked to me about it? I'm Danny's mother."

"Rafael is his father." Brenna rolled her eyes. "I really hate taking the guy's side against a woman, especially my sister, but this time I think you're freaking over nothing. It's a pony. It's not like he bought him an island."

"Calandria is an island. As heir, I guess Danny already has that."

"Okay, then strippers. That would have been a gift to get crabby about. Families do odd things. Grandpa Lorenzo made all of us learn about wine even though I was the only one interested. It happens. Don't worry about it. Danny is a prince, which is just too weird. Don't all princes need to learn how to ride? Isn't it in the prince handbook?"

"Probably. I should Google him again."

"Rafael?" Brenna asked.

Mia walked to the desk and sat in the large chair across from Brenna's. "Yeah. I did it once and I was overwhelmed by pictures of him with beautiful young women. It got depressing."

"Mia, you're gorgeous and smart and a lot more interesting than any high-society rich bitch he might meet at some charity event."

"You don't actually know that."

"Of course I do. He fell for you years ago and now he wants to marry you. Doesn't that mean you win?"

Mia rubbed her temples. "I can't believe we're having this conversation. I can't believe Danny is a prince."

"It's a little too late to take back Rafael as his father. You should have thought of that before you did the wild thing."

"Who knew it would come to this?" She sighed. "Who knew Diego was really Crown Prince Rafael in disguise? My life is a soap opera."

Mia looked at her sister and drew in a breath. "I said yes."

Brenna stared at her. "To his proposal?"

Mia nodded. "Last night. I can't face anything huge or ceremonial right now. We're going to Las Vegas after Danny's birthday."

Brenna stood and clapped her hands together. "I don't know what to say. My baby sister, the queen."

Mia stood and they hugged. When Brenna released her, Mia asked, "Am I crazy to do this?"

"I don't know. Does it feel right? Are you happy?"

"I was until the pony."

Brenna laughed. "What is it about that damned horse that has you so freaked?"

"I don't know. I guess it's that he didn't discuss it with me. He made his own decision."

"I can understand that, but how many of your decisions have you discussed with him? Mia, it's been five years since you were last together. It's going to take a little time to figure out how this all fits."

"You're right. Which means running off to marry him isn't what I should be doing."

"I don't want to respond to that," Brenna admitted. "You have to do what feels right. Rafael is Danny's father. Whether or not you marry him, you're going to have to deal with him for the rest of your life."

"I've been thinking about that. How exactly does one work out a custody agreement with a prince?"

"Tell me that's not why you're marrying him. To make a custody agreement easier."

"It's not." Mia sank back into her chair. "I haven't been with anyone since him. I . . . Katie said I had never fallen out of love with him, which I violently disagreed with at the time, but I've been thinking maybe she was right. I have feelings for him. Strong feelings. And he's a really great guy. I like how he is with Danny and me. He's open and honest and I still get tingles."

"So what's not to like?" Brenna asked.

"That's what I keep thinking. So I said I'd marry him."

"You can change your mind. Or put it off. There's a lot to be said for getting to know the guy you're going to rule with."

Mia groaned. "When I think about being with Rafael I get butterflies, but when I think about actually ruling a country, I want to vomit. I look at what Darcy has to go through and I know I'd hate it. She's just the president's daughter."

Brenna sat on the edge of her desk. "If you're this unsure, then put things off for a while. No one is saying you have to marry him."

Mia smiled. "But I want to. Isn't that dumb? I want to marry him. I want to know that for the rest of our lives, we'll be together."

"So if Rafael were just a regular guy, you wouldn't have a problem with this."

Mia considered the statement. "Apparently not."

"In this case, the crown comes with the guy. Can you handle that?"

"I sort of have to. Otherwise, I let Rafael go, and I can't imagine doing that. When I thought he died, I didn't want to live myself. I ached for months. Being pregnant was the only thing that got me through. I can't imagine ever surviving that pain again. But the man I loved before was different."

"In good ways or bad ways?"

"Both. I liked that Diego wasn't a world-renowned sex object. Plus I have such lousy taste in men. Seriously, Brenna, do you know how badly I could be screwing this up?"

"He's a prince, Mia. How bad could it be?"

"That's what I keep telling myself." She winced. "I don't want to move away."

"I'm thinking you're going to have to live in Calandria. But there's good news. You could be on a stamp."

"I was hoping for money, but a stamp works. My God, I can't believe we're having this conversation. I guess if I do marry him we'll move to Calandria fairly quickly. We haven't talked about it, but it makes sense. I'm sure Rafael has responsibilities, and Danny and I need to start learning to be royal."

Mia stood and plucked at her T-shirt. "Who am I kidding? I bought this for five dollars at Wal-Mart. The only designer clothes I own are my mother's hand-me-downs. I don't do jewelry or know how to waltz."

Brenna stood and moved close. "You speak about four hundred languages, you're smart, you're capable, and you're in love. Are you ever going to meet another guy like Rafael? Because if you aren't sure there's another handsome prince waiting for you, I would say learning to waltz might be the way to go."

Mia smiled. "Kelly could probably teach me."

"I'm sure she'd be delighted to. Follow your heart, Mia. That's the best advice I can give you. If I'd followed mine, I would have married Nic when I was eighteen instead of wasting nearly a decade of our lives."

"Do you regret that?"

"I try not to, but sometimes, when I'm up late with the twins, I wonder what our lives would have been like if I hadn't been afraid to take the plunge."

"Don't you hate regrets?" Mia asked.

"More than anything. Follow your heart," Brenna said again. "Don't look back and think 'if only.' If you can't imagine life without him, then go for it. If you can, then don't. He's Danny's father and that's never going to change. The bottom line is you don't have to decide today."

"I know. I have two days until Danny's birthday."

"You don't have to elope. You can tell him you need more time."

Mia considered that. "I want to be with him," she said at last. "I love him."

"Then there's your answer."

The two women hugged again; then Mia headed back to the house. She was going to do it. She was going to elope with Rafael and then figure out what she'd gotten herself into.

As she walked across the lawn, she noticed the pony tethered under a tree. "I wonder what pony poop does to grass," she murmured as she climbed the steps and entered the house.

"It's me," she yelled as she walked into the empty kitchen.

A quick glance at the clock told her the Grands were probably resting before they started dinner. She stuck her head in the family room and saw Danny curled up on the sofa, watching a cartoon video.

"Doing okay?" she asked.

Danny smiled at her and nodded.

So if her son was occupied and the Grands were sleeping, that sort of left her at loose ends. Maybe she and Rafael had time for a quickie.

Anticipation propelled her upstairs. She walked down

the hallway toward his room. The door stood open and she could hear him talking on the phone.

At first the words didn't register. She wasn't trying to listen in. She caught a word or two in Italian and paused. Was he talking business? Should she wait?

As she considered her options, she took another step and the floorboards creaked. Instantly Rafael went silent. When he continued the conversation, he spoke Portuguese.

Mia froze. Why on earth would he change languages like that? The most obvious explanation was that he didn't want to be understood. Which made no sense.

Even so, she crept forward to listen.

"Not to worry," he said, his voice low. "Yes, all is well. As I told you, Mia has agreed to marry me. We are to fly to Las Vegas in a few days. No, she knows nothing. We will go after Danny's birthday. I have the paperwork all ready."

He was silent for a moment. "We will return to Calandria as soon as possible. I know. Once we are there, Calandrian laws apply. No, Mia would never think to study such a thing. She has no idea that once the heir arrives in Calandria, he can never be taken away without permission from the throne. Of course. I will have my son and heir."

He was silent again. "Yes. A divorce. I have those papers as well. It is unfortunate she is not more suitable, but I understand my responsibilities. I will keep Daniel with me and send Mia way."

11

Mia found herself unable to breathe. White-hot fury poured through her until she felt sure she could melt steel simply by touching it. She stood as if nailed to the floor, unable to move as Rafael finished his conversation with his father. A conversation that revealed everything.

When he'd hung up, she forced herself to walk into her bedroom, where she picked up the phone and called Joe's cell.

"Get to the house now," she said, her voice low and thick. "Bring a gun."

She hung up before he could ask anything; then she stalked into Rafael's bedroom and wondered if she was truly capable of murder.

At that moment it seemed more than possible—it seemed likely. She wanted him dead. No, she wanted him in pain. She wanted to see blood and bone jutting through flesh. She wanted him writhing and begging, and she wanted to watch him disappear into a puddle of green slime.

He turned and smiled at her. "Mia. I was just speaking

with my father and we were—" He stared at her. "What is wrong?"

She could feel the scream building, but as it hadn't reached the surface yet, she spoke in a quiet voice, one laced with so much anger, it practically snapped.

"Did you think I was so fucking stupid that I didn't speak Portuguese?"

He paled slightly. "What do you mean?"

"Just what I said, you bastard. I heard and understood every damned word. Ironically, I wasn't paying attention when you were speaking Italian. I wasn't even listening. But you switched. I guess you thought I could be Grandma Tessa, who also speaks Italian. You sure as hell wouldn't want her hearing your little plan for my future."

She felt as angry about his assumption that she wouldn't understand him as she did about what he'd said. That bothered her for a second until she realized it was safe to be furious about the language he'd chosen. She wouldn't kill him over that.

"I heard you," she told him. "I heard every word. You lied. You deliberately lied. How dare you? You're not here to marry me, you're here to take my son."

The scream built and built until it finally burst free. She reached for the lamp on the dresser by the door and threw it at him.

"You fucking bastard. You tricked us all. You came here with your stories and your princely manners and the whole thing was a scam."

He'd sidestepped the lamp easily. Now he walked around the mess on the floor and moved toward her.

"Mia, calm down. You have misunderstood."

"Get away from me. I swear, if I had a gun I'd shoot you right now. Right in the gut. Or the balls. You didn't come here for me. You don't care about me or my family or anything. You want your son. You want to kidnap him."

"You're being ridiculous. Daniel is my heir. It is reasonable for me to—"

"Don't talk to me about reasonable," she screamed. "Don't you dare. You lied. It was all a lie."

"Daniel is my son."

"His name is Danny. He's a little boy. You want to take him away from me, but that will never happen. Never. Do you hear me?" She looked around for something else to throw at him and was frustrated by the lack of vases and lamps.

"He is my heir. My people have a right to—"

"Fuck your people and fuck you. Go to hell, Rafael. You're never getting him. Never. I don't care what I have to do. This is all bullshit. Why now? Why did you suddenly show up?"

She pressed a hand against her forehead as she remembered what he'd told her. "My God. The picture in the paper. That damn picture. You saw it and you recognized me and him. The age is right and he looks enough like you." She paused again and found herself unable to do more than gasp out. "The birthmark. Somehow you saw it."

"That first morning," he agreed. "The men in my family have carried it for generations."

"You didn't need the DNA test, did you?"

He shrugged. "I knew he was my son after I saw the birthmark."

"Of course. You saw the paper and knew, so you had to come here. Only you couldn't just show up. I would get really suspicious if after five years you suddenly appeared in my life. So you . . ."

She couldn't believe it. No. This wasn't happening. "You lied about everything. About being told I was dead, about missing me. You came up with that story as a way to make me trust you. You not coming after me had nothing to do with me being dead or not. You didn't care. You'd had your fling and then it was time to get back to your regular life. The prince one. You didn't give me another thought. Then you found out about Danny and suddenly you had an heir to worry about."

"Mia, you will make yourself sick."

"So what? I'll survive. You living through the day seems much less likely."

"Do not threaten me."

"Or what? You'll pretend you care about me so you can trick me into marriage and steal away my son?"

Her eyes began to burn, but she refused to give in to the tears. She couldn't think, couldn't believe this was happening.

"I was such a fool. How could you do it? How could you steal my child?"

"You are being melodramatic. Of course I would have allowed you to see Daniel. We would have made arrangements for—"

She heard footsteps on the stairs. "In here," she yelled.

Joe ran down the hallway and she was pleased to see he held a handgun.

"What the hell is going on?" he demanded.

Rafael stepped into the hallway. "Mia, you are taking this too far. Be reasonable."

"Reasonable?"

She lunged for Joe's gun, but he easily kept it out of reach.

"Shoot him!" she told her brother. "Shoot the goddamned prick right in the balls. He wants to steal Danny. He tricked me. He tricked us all. He pretended to care, but he doesn't. He wanted me to marry him so that when we got to Calandria he could take Danny away from me."

Joe grabbed her and shoved her behind him, then turned the gun on Rafael.

"Get out," he said quietly. "Get out of this house and take the bodyguards with you."

"I'm not finished here."

"Yes you are."

Rafael stared at the gun, then at Joe's face. He swore in Italian, then stalked out. As he passed Mia, he paused.

"This isn't over."

"It is," she told him. "More than you know."

And then he was gone. Mia stared into the empty room and saw the broken lamp. It was as if that shattered bit of ceramic represented all her hopes and dreams.

"Oh God," she breathed as her muscles began to shake and she felt herself go down.

Joe grabbed her and pulled her close. She went into his arms, feeling his strength and knowing nothing would ever be right again.

"I can't believe it," she whispered.

"I know."

"He lied. He tried to take Danny."

"But he didn't get him. We'll fix this, Mia. I swear."

She wanted to believe him, but she couldn't. It was too horrible.

"Danny," she said with a gasp. "Where is he? He was in the family room. What if Rafael took him?"

"Mommy?"

She turned and saw the Grands holding Danny's hands. Her son looked terrified and confused. She dropped to her knees and held out her arms. He rushed toward her and clung so tightly she couldn't catch her breath.

But that didn't matter. He was here and he was safe. She was going to make sure that never, ever changed.

They held a family meeting after Danny was in bed. Mia didn't want to attend. She didn't want to cry or breathe or eat ever again. Most of all, she didn't want to think. She didn't want to keep reliving those horrible moments when she'd found out the truth about Rafael, when she'd realized that everything he'd told her was a lie.

No, she thought as she stood at the top of the stairs and listened to the low voices coming from the family room. His lies weren't the worst of it. The true pit of her life was that she'd believed him.

Once again she'd trusted a man and he had betrayed her.

If Rafael had come after her, she could have handled it. If he'd wanted to hurt her or kidnap her or even kill her, she would have been able to cope. But he'd come after her child, and she would never forgive him for that.

She made herself walk downstairs. When she entered the family room, she saw everyone was already there. Katie and Zach, Francesca and Sam, Brenna and Nic, Joe and Darcy. The Grands were there, too, pressing food on everyone. Only her parents were missing. Since she hadn't called to tell them about marrying Rafael, she saw no reason to upset their vacation by admitting she'd almost lost her son.

Katie saw her first. "Oh, Mia." Katie held open her arms.

Mia moved into them and felt her other sisters closing ranks. They hugged her and whispered promises of revenge. The men stood a few feet back, looking angry and uncomfortable.

Mia absorbed their love and support. She'd promised herself she wouldn't cry over Rafael ever again, and she managed to get through the group hug without breaking down.

When everyone took a seat, Grammy M pressed a mug of tea into Mia's hands. She took the hot liquid but passed on food.

"I'm not very hungry," she admitted.

Grammy M started to say she had to eat something, but Tessa pulled her away.

"Mia will eat tomorrow," her paternal grandmother said quietly. "She's strong. You'll see."

Mia didn't feel very strong. She felt as if her heart had been run over by an eighteen-wheeler and left for roadkill.

"How's Danny?" Darcy asked.

"Confused. Apparently he didn't hear what I said to Rafael, but he knows we had a fight and his father has moved out. He kept asking for him tonight. He wanted Rafael to tuck him in."

Katie looked at Joe. "You should have shot him when you had the chance."

"It didn't seem the time. Besides, I can always do it later."

"We can arrest him," Grandma Tessa said to Joe. "He broke the law, didn't he?"

Joe stood by the fireplace. He shifted uncomfortably. "Technically, he didn't do anything wrong."

"All lying and cheating aside," Mia said with a lightness she didn't feel.

"Joe, there has to be something," Katie said. "He can't get away with this."

"He won't," Mia told her. "Danny is staying right here, with us. If I don't take him to Calandria, there's nothing Rafael can do. Right, Joe?"

He nodded. "I suppose he could petition the international courts, but that could take years. Appealing to the president won't help."

Darcy leaned toward Mia. "I already called my dad. Should the Calandrian ambassador try to see him, he won't be available. He also said to tell you that he would be happy to have Rafael thrown out of the country."

"I'm not sure I want this going public," Mia said. "Let's just keep it between us for now. We need a plan. We need to keep Danny safe and keep Rafael away from him."

"I don't know how this happened," Grammy M said with a sigh. "He seemed like such a *nice* man."

"He fooled us all," Grandma Tessa grumbled. "I thought I was too old and too crabby to be fooled."

"It wasn't exactly a fair fight," Katie told them. "We're basically honest people. We weren't looking for deception. Plus there's the whole prince angle. He had our attention there."

Brenna patted Mia's arm. "See? You're not the only one."

Mia appreciated the support, but it didn't help. She'd been the one who'd been willing to blindly commit her life to someone she barely knew. That impulsive decision could have cost her Danny.

"You're all forgetting something," Joe said. "Rafael is Danny's father. He might be an asshole, but he's still the father, and Mia can't keep him away forever."

"I don't want to hear that," Mia said flatly. She didn't want to be reminded of any connection to Rafael.

Francesca crossed to where Mia sat and crouched in front of her. "I understand you're beyond anger. We all are. Rafael came in here and treated us all like idiots. He tried to steal away one of our babies. I would like to spend a couple of days thinking up very special tortures for him."

Mia glanced at her sister and sighed. "You're going to be rational, aren't you?"

Francesca nodded. "You can't keep Danny from his father. Being an asshole isn't against the law."

"It should be."

"I agree, but it isn't. However much we all hate Rafael, Danny doesn't. He loves his father. He loves every minute they're together. He doesn't know what happened and none of us are going to tell him. In his world, nothing has changed. He's going to be four and he has a new daddy."

Mia understood the message. What her sister was trying to say in her calm, trained, psychologist way was that Mia didn't get to throw a tantrum. That whatever had happened between her and Prince Jerk, there was still Danny to consider, and her little boy deserved to have a father.

"I don't trust him for a minute," Mia said.

"You shouldn't," Francesca told her. "Rafael has proved he can't be trusted. Whatever you decide about custody or visitation or whatever, I'm here to remind you that you don't want to break Danny's heart."

Mia hated all of it. "You're saying I have to let him come to Danny's birthday party? That I have to let them hang out and trust him not to simply disappear with Danny?"

"I'm saying you can't refuse to let Rafael see his son. You can do things to keep Danny safe. You can make it difficult for Rafael and easy for us, but you can't stand in the way of father and son being together. As for his birthday, that's your call."

Mia heard the words and knew their truth, but she didn't want to listen. She didn't want to think about how much Danny wanted Rafael there. She turned to her brother. "Joe?"

"I hate that she's right, too," he said quietly. "I want to tell him to go to hell and maybe even help him along, but he's the kid's father and we can't undo that." He paused for a second. "Sam and I will make some calls. We'll talk to a few people and get more security here. I would like to think Rafael is smart enough not to try to take Danny, but I wouldn't bet on it."

"I can help, too," Zach said.

Mia turned to Katie's husband. "You mean legally?"

"Sure. There are laws in place to prevent a child from being taken out of the country. Danny being the heir to a throne might complicate things, but he's only four. That should be in our favor. Plus Rafael tried to trick you instead of seeking a straightforward custody agreement.

One of the lawyers in my office is an expert on child abduction. Let me get her working on this."

"Thank you," Mia told him. "That would be great."

"I can get my sister to call the attorney general," Darcy said. "Lauren's dating her son."

"Talk about friends in high places," Mia said, feeling her insides shake as a dozen emotions washed through her. "I really appreciate all of you rallying around. I would hate to go through this alone."

Katie joined Francesca, who pulled Mia to her feet. The sisters hugged.

"This is going to be fine," Katie told her. "You'll see. As you said, you're not alone. You have us, and hey, we're the Marcellis."

Brenna joined them. "You have to stay strong. Don't go beating yourself up about this. Whatever happens, it's never wrong to fall in love."

Mia appreciated the sentiment, even if she didn't believe it. "Falling in love might not be wrong," she said, "but sometimes it's pretty damned stupid."

The hotel was not to Rafael's liking. Despite the fact that Oliver and Umberto had paid off enough guests to claim an entire wing, Rafael still hated to be in such a public place. He disliked the location, on the edge of a busy highway, the flowering plants that seemed to overrun the place, and most of all he hated that he was here at all.

He paced the length of his suite, ignoring the floral wallpaper and matching drapes and bedspread. The owner had been delighted to show him all the amenities of the suite, but Rafael had not so politely closed the door in her face. What did he care about blow-dryers and heated towel racks when everything of importance had gone terribly wrong?

He had no one to blame but himself. He hated to admit that, but it was true. He'd grown complacent. He should never have called his father from the house. He knew better. Until that last call, he had been very careful.

He paused by the window and stared out at the distant view of the ocean. Mia's fury had burned with a fire so bright, he'd expected the house to ignite. He wasn't sure he'd ever seen her that angry before. In truth, he couldn't blame her for her feelings. A part of him disliked that he had hurt her. She was angry now, but later there would be tears and he would not be there to comfort her.

Comfort? What was he thinking? He had to remember his goal and how his plan had failed.

He had now shown his hand and she would be on guard against him. No doubt her entire family would be upset when she told them what she'd overheard.

He tightened his hands into fists and cursed himself for forgetting Mia's ability with languages. When he'd heard footsteps in the hallway, he'd reacted without thinking. Better to have ended the call, but no. He'd switched to a language he'd been sure Grandma Tessa would not understand. He had not suspected the footsteps were Mia's.

Oliver knocked on the open door. "Everything is taken care of, your highness. We have all the rooms on this floor. Umberto is running background checks on the other guests, but there is no reason to suspect any of them."

"Good."

"I have arranged for the menus of local restaurants to be delivered. When you are ready, one of us will order your meal and then go get it."

He nodded. "Thank you for your efficiency."

Oliver nodded. "Sir, I do not mean to presume, but perhaps it would be best to simply take the child. We could go tonight and be well on our way to Calandria before anyone knew he was gone."

"An excellent plan," Rafael said. "If we had used it that first night. Now it will not be possible. Mia's brother is more highly trained than you and Umberto. Her brother-in-law Sam is a security expert. We would not be successful."

Oliver's silence indicated he agreed with Rafael's assessment. "Perhaps a diplomatic solution," he offered. "If our ambassador spoke with the president."

"I doubt the president will be available anytime soon. You forget Joe's wife is the president's daughter. She already will have called her father. It is what I would have done. They are not fools, which is unfortunate for us."

He had been the only fool. He hated that he'd been caught. Damn Mia for being the kind of woman who would make this all difficult. He'd meant what he said—he would not have kept her from Daniel. The boy was the heir to Calandria. He belonged with his people. But would she ever see that? Would she ever be sensible?

Would she ever forgive him?

"I will come up with a plan," he said at last. "There is a way and I will find it. I always win."

12

Mia sat on the back steps of the house and waited for the limo. Joe had offered to do it for her, but she wanted to look Rafael in the eyes while she explained the new rules in play. Not that she was alone. Thanks to Joe and Sam, there were at least a dozen security personnel around the house, and Joe hovered nearby.

Anger and hurt still defined her existence, but she was learning to live with the pain and regret, along with the constant ache in her heart. Knowing she had only herself to blame was both a blessing and curse. On the one hand, she could have very heated conversations with herself about what went wrong and vow never to be that stupid again. On the other hand, no one else really understood what she was going through.

She drew in a deep breath and was pleased to feel somewhat in control. No more tears—at least not in public—and no more outbursts. She was going to stay in charge and that meant keeping her emotions in check.

The trick was not to think too much. Not to remember how she'd given her heart to a man who had betrayed her.

The long black limo pulled into the driveway. Mia stood. Joe was at her side in an instant, along with six of the guards. As the car moved closer, Mia saw Umberto behind the wheel. Which meant Oliver was in back. Unless Rafael had brought in reinforcements.

"You made sure he wouldn't have other security, right?" she asked Joe.

He patted her back. "Of course. Everything has been negotiated, from the time he could arrive to how many of my men would be on his men. He knows what will happen if he steps out of line."

"You'll kill him?" she asked brightly.

"No, I'll beat the crap out of him and then I'll make him leave."

Not nearly good enough, she thought as the rear door of the limo opened and Oliver stepped out.

Joe motioned to one of his men. Oliver was searched. The same thing happened to Umberto when he exited the vehicle. Mia tensed as Rafael stepped into the afternoon sunlight.

Damn the man, he looked perfect. Well dressed, but casual, still handsome. She half expected to see horns or cloven feet, but there was only his brown hair and expensive leather loafers. His blue eyes seemed as compelling as always and very specific parts of her body were all too happy to have him in close proximity.

"Mia," he said with a slight bow of his head.

"Judas." She took a step toward him and squared her shoulders. "Just so we're all clear, you are being allowed onto this property because it is your son's fourth birthday and he wants you here. The reason he wants you here is because I didn't tell him what a lying weasel you are. As you can see, you are severely outnumbered. The guards have been ordered to shoot to kill if you try anything."

That last bit was a lie, but she didn't care. Let him be afraid.

"You wouldn't kill me," he said calmly. "My being dead doesn't solve your problem. Daniel is still the heir."

"True, but your death gets rid of you, and for now that's enough."

"You wouldn't risk the life of your son with flying bullets."

"You want to make this about logistics, I'm making a point. You are not welcome here. No one likes you or trusts you. One false move and you are gone."

Joe moved in. "A little FYI—there are more than a dozen security guards on duty."

Rafael shrugged. "As you wish. I didn't think I was as dangerous as all that. You are taking this very seriously, Mia."

His casual attitude made her wish for long nails and a decent shot at his eyes. "You tried to steal my son. It doesn't get more serious than that."

Rafael drew in a breath. "I am sorry you are so angry and I am sorry I hurt you. That was never my intent. I should have told you the truth from the beginning."

"Do you think any of that matters?" she asked, furious he would think an apology would make a difference.

"I was never going to keep you from him. You would have been able to see him whenever you liked."

"How very generous you are. Give me a moment to catch my breath from the wonderfulness of you."

His eyes narrowed. "You do not accept my apology?"

"Not even if it came with a couple of diamonds on a gold plate. The only thing you're sorry about is getting caught before you could put your plan into action. You used me and my family. We trusted you, we believed you, and you repaid us with deception."

Anger was good, she thought. Anger kept the pain at bay.

She moved right in front of him and poked him in the center of his chest. "I will never trust you again. There is nothing you can say or do that will make me believe a word you say. You played me for a fool. I'll give you points for originality and effort. You did a hell of a job and told a great story. But you had your chance and you blew it. I don't know what would have happened if you'd been honest. It's something we'll never know. I despise you and I hate that you're Danny's father. I will do what is right because I love my son. But you are never getting a piece of me again."

She turned on her heel and walked away. Rafael watched her go. Even as he resented the situation, he found himself admiring the power of her convictions and the grace in her movements.

She was, he admitted to himself, quite a woman. Also, she was much more angry than he had thought she would be. Daniel was his heir—what did she expect him to do? Allow his son to be raised here? Away from his people?

"Impossible," he muttered.

Joe smiled insincerely. "That's what we were saying about you. The party is this way."

Rafael followed him around to the side of the house, where several large tables had been set up in the shade.

There were a dozen or so children, most likely from Danny's school, a few parents, and much of the Marcelli clan. He recognized Brenna and her husband, Joe's wife, Francesca, and, of course, the Grands.

They were all watching him as if waiting for him to pull out a weapon and hold them all hostage. He saw the anger in their eyes and knew that he didn't have to deal with just Mia's rage.

"Daddy, Daddy!" Danny raced toward him.

Rafael crouched down and reached for the boy. Daniel crashed into him and wrapped his arms around Rafael's neck.

For a moment, Rafael hugged him just as tightly.

"I missed you," Danny said. "Why'd you go away?"

He didn't have an answer for that, and oddly, he found he couldn't speak. His throat felt tight and thick.

"Daddy?" Daniel stepped back and looked at him. "Why'd you have to go away?"

"Business," Rafael managed as he stared at the boy. Until that moment, he hadn't realized he was afraid he would never see him again. "Sometimes it is work to be a prince."

"I like being the heir."

"I'm sure you do. Are you having a good party?"

Daniel nodded. "I have so many presents, and there's cake." He reached for his father's hand. "Come see."

Rafael stood and allowed himself to be tugged toward the gathering. He saw Umberto and Oliver surrounded by several of Joe's guards. While the other parents smiled warmly at him, the Marcellis all looked as if they were picturing him dead.

Mia wasn't kidding about protecting her son. She said

she would use any means and he believed her. She was strong, but he was stronger. Somehow he would defeat them all.

"I love it, Daddy," Daniel said as he fingered the new leather saddle Rafael had given him. "There's a D and a A and a N . . ." He frowned, then grabbed his mother's arm. "It's not Danny. I thought it was Danny."

Mia glanced at the saddle, then narrowed her eyes. "You're right. It's not Danny. It's Daniel. I'm sorry your daddy got your name wrong."

"That's okay," Daniel told Rafael. "Sometimes I'm Daniel, but mostly when I've been bad."

"In Calandria, you'll be Daniel all the time," Rafael said easily. "As the heir, you will go by the more formal version of your name."

Daniel stared at him for a second, then shrugged and reached for the next present. It was a remote car from Joe. Daniel gasped with delight and raced over to his uncle.

"Can we play tonight? Will you play with me? Please."

Joe ruffled the boy's hair. "Sure thing, kid. We'll have a race."

Daniel hugged the other man. Rafael watched, uncomfortable with the boy's obvious affection for the larger man. He turned back to the table of presents and scowled when he realized *his* presents—the saddle, brushes for the pony, and an expensive set of leather-bound children's stories—had been whisked away. All the other presents were still scattered about, but his were gone.

He turned to Mia. "Will you keep my gifts from him? That seems very small of you. Whatever your complaints with me, they have nothing to do with my son."

"Our son," she said evenly. "The pony supplies are near to the pony, and Brenna and Nic took the books inside so they wouldn't be ruined in the sun. Danny's not used to leather-bound books. It will take him some time to learn how to read them responsibly. Or read at all."

He felt the censure in her words, as if he'd chosen inappropriately. "Those are stories for children."

"Perhaps on your planet. Here on earth, we don't read our kids literal translations of the Grimms' fairy tales. They're just a little too brutal."

"What are you talking about?" he demanded.

"Have you ever read them? Really read them? Children do not fare well. Although I do remember a particular favorite about an evil prince being eaten by a bear. Hmm, perhaps I'll read that to Danny tonight."

"Who wants cake?" Grandma Tessa asked before he could respond to Mia.

The two grandmothers carried out a large cake decorated with race cars. The children gathered around as the cake was placed in the center of the middle table. Four candles were lit.

Mia sat on the bench in front of the cake and put Daniel on her lap. "Okay, big guy. This is it. Your chance to make a wish. Now close your eyes and wish really hard. Then open your eyes and blow out the candles. Make sure you don't tell anyone your wish, okay?"

Daniel squirmed with delight. He'd long since abandoned his party hat, and there were several food stains on his striped T-shirt. While he screwed up his whole face as he considered his wish, Rafael thought of his childhood birthday parties.

There had been other children, of course, and their

parents. Everyone had dressed formally. There had been an orchestra and some kind of entertainment. The gifts had been left on a table for him to open later, with his nanny. He'd been required to write a thank-you note after opening each present, which had stretched out the process to several days.

After he'd gone off to boarding school, birthdays had been joint affairs, celebrated with the other boys having birthdays that month. The school had prided itself on treating even royal sons like everyone else, so there had been no special celebration for him.

Daniel opened his eyes and blew out the candles. Everyone cheered.

"All right, birthday boy," Grammy M said as she hovered over the cake. "You get the first piece. Which one do you want? A corner, with lots of frosting?"

Daniel nodded, then pointed to the corner he wanted. Rafael recalled having to wait for his cake until everyone else had been served.

Grammy M cut him an impossibly large piece. Daniel took it and began to eat. The other children were served next, then the parents. Grandma Tessa passed Rafael a plate with a mint on it.

He stared at the small piece of candy, then looked at the old woman, who glared right back.

"Daddy, don't you want cake?" Daniel asked.

"Your father doesn't like cake," Mia said easily. "Isn't that true, Rafael?"

The fire in her eyes told him she would be delighted to have him defy her. That way she'd have an excuse to take him on again. But he didn't want to fight with Mia anymore. Not when the more important task was to win her back.

"Your mother is right," he said gently. "Birthday cake does not agree with me."

"I guess we'll have to put the rat poison in something else," Grandma Tessa muttered as she moved away.

Conversation quieted as the cake was consumed. Rafael was aware of how the Marcelli family kept tabs on him. If he moved close to Daniel, one of them was right there. Umberto and Oliver were never left alone. The other parents noticed nothing, but Rafael saw it all. The family had closed ranks against him.

Like Mia, he fought anger, but for a different reason. They were all acting out of ignorance. They did not understand that Daniel had responsibilities and a place in the world. He could not learn how to be king in this backwater.

At last the party ended. Parents collected their children and left. Rafael spoke pleasantly with them and waited until he could be alone with Mia. Somehow he would make her understand. But when the last guest had left, Mia picked up Daniel and walked into the house. The rest of the family followed. When he moved to go with them, several of Joe's security guards formed a line in front of the door.

"I don't think you'll be joining us for the post-party wrap-up," Joe said with a smile. "Sorry about that, but we didn't negotiate for more than the party."

Which Joe had done deliberately. "You can't keep me from my son forever."

"Were you kept from Danny? Did you miss any part of his party?"

"I must see him. I must speak to Mia."

Joe shrugged. "She doesn't want to speak to you. When

you first arrived, I warned you not to hurt her, and you didn't listen."

"I'm not afraid of you," Rafael said contemptuously. "You are all talk and very little action."

"I can't tell you how much I want to prove you wrong right now, but I promised Mia I wouldn't turn you inside out, and I keep my word. You blew it, prince. Mia's reasonable and intelligent. She could have been on your side in this. She could have respected you. But you decided to trick her and she will never forgive you. None of us will. You may be Crown Prince Bla-de-bla from some fancy island, but right now you're on my land. Marcelli land. We make the rules and the current rules are, you're screwed."

"Where's my daddy?" Danny demanded, tears spilling down his cheeks. "I want my daddy. I'm the heir and you have to do what I say. Bring my daddy back right now!"

Mia did her best not to react to Danny's tantrum. He was exhausted from the long day of celebrating his birthday and strung out on way too much sugar. But what she knew in her head didn't prevent the helpless feeling in her heart.

"I want my daddy *now*!" Danny screamed. "Why did he go away? Why did he go aw-way."

Danny collapsed on the family room floor, sobs making his whole body shake. Mia crouched next to him. "You'll see your daddy soon," she said quietly. "He came to your birthday and gave you a lot of nice presents. That was fun."

"But he went away." Danny raised his head and stared at her. "Mommy, make him come back. Please? Make him come b-back."

The Grands swept into the room. "How's the big birthday boy?" Grammy M asked as she pulled Danny to his feet and cuddled him. "What a fun day you had. So many friends and presents and just a little too much cake."

Tessa crouched in front of him and smiled. "Imagine. You're four now. Practically all grown up. You'll be driving soon."

That made Danny smile. "I can't drive. I'm a little boy."

"You don't seem too little today," Grammy M said. "You seem very big. I'm not sure I can carry you upstairs myself anymore. 'Tis a shame, because I liked that part of my day. Tessa, I'll be needing your help."

Tessa straightened and shook her head. "No, he's too big for the both of us. We'll need a crane. One of those large construction types. We'll put it right there in the hallway and it can lift Danny up to the second floor."

"I like that," Grammy M said.

Danny giggled. "You don't need a crane."

"I'm thinking we do," Grammy M said as she led him toward the stairs. "They're yellow, which means it won't go at all with the decorations. We'll have to paint it. Maybe pink with flowers."

Tessa moved closer to Mia and lowered her voice. "We'll put him to bed tonight. He's tired. Don't take it personally."

Mia appreciated the support but wasn't sure she could take the advice. Danny had bonded with his father so quickly—how was she supposed to keep them apart now? She couldn't trust Rafael, yet didn't Danny deserve time with his father?

She waited until the trio was in Danny's bedroom, then made her way to her own. She closed the door and crossed to the window.

The night was clear and cool. She could see stars, and when she opened the windows the scent of the ripening grapes filled her room like a strong perfume.

She wanted to turn back time. She wanted to have things like they were before Rafael had shown up, because his arrival had changed everything. In a matter of a few short weeks, he'd altered her world and nothing could make it as it was.

She knelt on the floor and rested her arms on the windowsill. Anger filled her. So much anger, and with it the uncomfortable realization that she was still in love with him.

Oh, she hated him and didn't trust him, but none of that meant she didn't love him. Even knowing he was a snake, her heart continued to beat out a rhythm designed to be heard only by him.

She supposed that's what happened after being in love with the same man for over five years. She was going to need some time to get over him. Having to deal with him would make the process harder.

Danny would want to see his father. She'd made the mistake of talking about him to the boy long before Rafael had ever shown up. She'd said he was brave and strong and a wonderful man. There was no way she could now tell him the truth.

She felt trapped by circumstances. Trapped and alone and clueless about her next step. At least her family would help, she thought. The Marcellis would always be there for her.

She stood and crossed to her dresser. She pulled out the small box and looked at the silver ring Diego had bought her so long ago.

Purposefully, she went downstairs and into the kitchen. There she rummaged through the junk drawer until she found a hammer; then she walked out to the porch, put the ring on the railing, and crushed it with a single blow.

After returning the hammer to the drawer, she dropped the crushed piece of metal in the trash, but as she walked back to her room, she found she didn't feel the least bit better.

The next night Brenna showed up with a box of chocolates and a bottle of Four Sisters cabernet sauvignon.

"You don't get a vote," she told Mia as she pulled her from the family room and herded her upstairs. "We're going to curl up on your bed, get drunk, eat too much chocolate, and call everyone who's ever pissed us off really bad names. You get extra points for creativity."

Mia smiled as she plopped on her bed. "I'm in."

"Good." Brenna set the wine on the nightstand. "It was a great year. Just perfect weather and the sugar in the grapes couldn't have been more right. I remember—"

"Uh, Brenna?" Mia interrupted. "Don't really care about the process. Just the results."

Brenna pulled a corkscrew from her jeans back pocket. "All my sisters are completely worthless about the magic of winemaking. How is that possible? How can I be the only one who cares?"

"A mystery you'll have to take up with the Almighty."

"I guess." She expertly pulled out the cork, then poured them each a glass of wine.

Mia took a sip. "Not bad," she said, reaching for the chocolates.

Brenna winced. "Not bad? Do you know how many medals this wine has won? Do you know how those brilliant people at *Wine Spectator* scored my wine?"

"No, and hey, don't really care. But kudos to you." She held out the now-open box of chocolates. "Want one?"

"Please."

Brenna grabbed a truffle, her wine, and sank onto the bed. "I'm the only one with a soul. That's all there is to it."

"Then speaking for the soul-free contingent, thanks for stopping by."

Brenna leaned toward her. "How do you feel?"

"Like crap. It still hurts to breathe. Most of the time I can't believe how much I hurt and how hard it is to do anything. Danny is furious. He wants his father around. It was such a mistake to have Rafael live here. Now Danny has expectations and I can't meet them."

"Rafael was only here a few weeks. Danny will get over it."

"He hasn't yet."

"He knows something is up."

Mia shuddered as she thought of her son's pain. "I never wanted him to be hurt."

"Of course you didn't. But you didn't make Rafael an ass. He did that all on his own."

Mia nodded. "I can't believe what's happened. How could I have been such an idiot?"

"We were all fooled. Like Katie said before, he had the prince thing going for him. Why would we think he was a liar?"

Mia nodded, knowing it was true and wishing it could make her feel better. "I'm going to have to deal with him, I just don't know how to get past the anger." She sipped her wine. "Nic betrayed you, Brenna. How did you recover?"

A few years ago Nic and Brenna had secretly started a relationship. She'd thought it was true love while he'd been planning to buy Marcelli Wines out from under her.

Her sister grabbed another chocolate. "It wasn't easy. I was so in love with him and I thought he cared about me and the whole time he planned to screw my family. Wow—I guess it isn't that different. I felt like you do, honey. I felt broken and stupid and empty. The difference was, we didn't have a child together. I could tell myself I never wanted to see him again."

"At least Nic came crawling back," Mia muttered, remembering how her now brother-in-law had begged for forgiveness. "Rafael doesn't even think he's done anything wrong. I can't believe the weasel apology he gave me at Danny's birthday. 'I'm sorry you were distressed. I'm sorry I got caught,'" she mocked, her voice low. "He should have started with 'I'm sorry I'm a lying worm bastard and here's a knife so you can run me through.' Now *that* would have been an apology."

Brenna reached over and patted her arm. "I wish I had magic words."

"Me too. I wish I didn't love him." She sipped her wine. "I was going to marry him. Can you believe it? We were going to run off to Las Vegas the day after Danny's birthday. What if I had? What if I'd gone to Calandria with him? I would have lost Danny."

"But you didn't. You discovered the truth in time."

Mia hung on to that slim thought. "I just don't know how I'm supposed to protect him from his father. Obviously I can't keep Danny from Rafael and I can't let him go to Calandria."

"Deep breaths," Brenna told her. "There's no need to panic right now."

"Because I can always panic later?"

"Exactly." Her sister smiled. "Come on. We have this under control. Or we're getting there. Isn't the lawyer in Zach's office looking into this for you?"

Mia nodded. "Her name is Sandy and she's amazing. We've already talked a couple of times. She has some excellent ideas and ways we can use the law. Darcy's been talking to the attorney general, and how many people can say that in casual conversation? Joe is looking into some interesting security measures. When I next have to face Rafael, I'll be ready."

Brenna shook her head. "No you won't."

Mia swallowed. "No, I won't. I'll have plenty of armor, but I won't be ready for the war. How can I still love him? How can I have feelings for him? I hate him, Brenna. I loathe and despise him and I still miss him."

"You can't just turn your feelings off because he's a jerk. You're doing everything you can to protect your son. That's the most important thing. But you've loved him for years. Why would that go away overnight?"

"But he's a bastard," Mia said. "Shouldn't that change my feelings?"

"Wasn't Diego a bit of a ruthless guy? He was a villain and you fell for him. Has Rafael really acted so out of character?"

Mia shuddered. "Yuck. What does that say about me and my taste in men? I was right to give them up. I should think about becoming a lesbian."

Brenna laughed. "Oh, right. *That's* going to happen. You could never do it."

"I guess not. Once Danny's grown up, I'll become a nun or something. Use my life for good works. If I'm never having sex again, I'll have plenty of energy to spare."

"You'll have sex again."

"I don't think so," Mia said. "I don't really see a romantic happy ending for me, do you?"

"Not with Rafael."

Mia wasn't sure there was another man for her. Which really sucked the big one.

"I wish I—"

The bedroom door opened and Joe stuck his head in. "Sorry to break up the girlfest, but we have a problem downstairs."

Mia sprang to her feet. "Danny?"

"No. He's fine. The Grands put him to bed. I just checked and he's sound asleep. It's Kelly."

Mia and Brenna followed him down the stairs. Mia heard voices coming from the kitchen. She walked in and saw Kelly leaning against the counter.

"Mia," she said, her voice thick. "Hey, how's it going?" Her gaze locked on the glass still in Mia's hand. "Is that wine? Can I have some?"

As she spoke, her entire body swayed.

"She's drunk," Brenna muttered. "This is perfect. Just perfect."

"Just a little taste," Kelly said. "Want me to dance for it? 'Coz that's what I do. Dance for my supper." She giggled, then tried a pirouette.

She managed half a turn, then she grabbed for the counter, missed, and sank slowly to the floor. By the time Mia reached her, she'd already passed out.

13

Francesca closed the bedroom door. As she turned, Sam caught her in his arms and held her close.

"I don't know what's wrong," Francesca murmured. "Why is she doing this?"

"I have no idea," he admitted.

Mia shifted uncomfortably, feeling that she was intruding. But before she could leave, Francesca looked at her.

"Tell me this is the first time she's shown up like this."

Mia made an X over her heart. "Trust me. If Kelly had been showing up here drunk and passing out, I would have been on the phone to you in a heartbeat. I don't get it. She's always been a pretty decent kid. Happy, interested. It's awful."

"I know." Francesca took Sam's hand and led the way down the stairs. They went into the kitchen, where the Grands had prepared a late-night snack that could easily feed thirty.

"Brenna went home," Grammy M said. "She's going to call you in the morning."

Francesca nodded. "I know she will. I know everyone is worried. I just wish we had some answers. I want to say this is typical acting out, except Kelly is twenty and she's always been so mature for her age. Shouldn't this have happened a few years ago?"

Grandma Tessa ushered them to the large table where sandwiches, cold pasta dishes, and salads waited. There were pots of decaf and tea, along with a pitcher of ice water and two open bottles of Marcelli wine.

Francesca reached for one of the bottles. "She was drunk," she said, as if she couldn't believe it. "Kelly's been tasting wine for years. She's never been interested in drinking to excess. Last I heard, she didn't even like hard liquor and she had trouble getting through a glass of wine in an evening."

Sam put his arm around her. "She's always been complicated."

"I know and I even understand why," Francesca said. "She went through some tough times. But I thought we'd worked through all that. I thought she felt happy and loved and wanted. We still ask her to come home when she's on break from the company and I was sure she knew we meant it. We've kept her room as it was. The twins adore her."

Tessa nodded. "She's doing well with the ballet company, isn't she?"

"Absolutely," Sam said. "Everyone was very impressed with how she did last year, and this year, she was given several important parts." He frowned. "Or is it dances?"

Mia grabbed half a sandwich. "There's something going on," she said. "Kelly was hanging out with me about a week ago. She stayed here for the night. We did a whole clothes–girl talk thing."

Francesca and Sam both waited expectantly, which made Mia feel bad. "She just said she, ah, admired my life. That it was romantic." When she finished speaking, she braced herself for the groans and recriminations.

Sam looked at Francesca. "I could live with Kelly being like Mia."

Francesca smiled. "Me too. Thanks, Mia. You're making us feel better."

Mia blinked at her. "Excuse me? Kelly is talking about patterning her life after mine? I'm the queen of poor choices in the male department, I'm twenty-seven and still living at home, I have no job, and I'm a single mother. On what planet is that a success?"

"On this one," Sam told her. "You're very intelligent, you go after what you want. You're not afraid to work for your goals. You have a master's and now you're getting a law degree. You're raising a great kid."

"He's right," Francesca told her. "Besides, a lot of women make poor choices with men. Not all of us can get lucky." She smiled at Sam.

"I wouldn't describe what I've done as a poor choice. Disaster maybe." But she didn't speak with a whole lot of energy. Hearing Sam and Francesca talk about her in such glowing terms was the first positive thing to happen to her in nearly a week. She'd never thought her very successful, very happy older sister would consider her much more than a screwup.

Francesca sank down onto a chair. "I hope Kelly isn't acting this way because of Etienne. I don't know what she sees in the man, and it would break my heart to have her behaving this way because of him."

"She didn't seem especially interested in talking about

him," Mia said. "Not in a romantic way. Usually Kelly can't stop talking about a guy who interests her. So that's something."

Francesca looked at her. "So Kelly is sleeping with someone she doesn't actually care about?" She touched her stomach. "Oh, God, I feel sick."

"No, I didn't mean it that way," Mia said quickly.

Sam shook his head. "Mia, please. Don't worry about it. We both know what you're saying. It doesn't seem that Etienne is the love of her life. That's good news. The rest of it we'll figure out how to deal with."

Francesca stood. "You're right. Oh, Mia, we've been bothering you with this when you have so much going on already."

"I don't mind," Mia said, and meant it. "As soon as you're gone, I'll only have my own life to think about, and right now, that's not a thrilling prospect."

The small hotel seemed to have more in common with a B and B than a large chain, Mia thought as Joe parked in the nearly empty lot in front of the long building. She took in the ceramic animals in the garden, the seasonal flag over the front door, and a large plaque proclaiming "Our Guests Are Our Family" by the porch.

The whole place screamed *cute*, and she had a feeling Rafael would hate every second he was there. The thought cheered her as she climbed out of Joe's SUV and walked to the reception area.

"He bought out a whole wing," her brother said as he fell into step with her. "They have the second floor. It's ten rooms. They're using three of them and leaving the others empty."

"At least it will be quiet for him," she murmured. "He can catch up on his sleep."

There was a young woman sitting behind the counter. She had an open biology book next to the registration log. A student, Mia thought. Probably from UC Santa Barbara.

"Hi," Mia said with a smile. "We're here to see Prince Rafael."

The girl glanced around, as if looking for spies, then spoke in a low voice. "We're not supposed to tell anyone he's here. He's been very clear about that. Not that anyone has been asking." She flipped through several papers. "Are you Mia Marcelli?"

Mia nodded.

"You're allowed to go see him." She glanced doubtfully at Joe.

"I'm her brother," he said easily. "Rafael and I go way back."

The receptionist nodded. "Okay. They have the second floor of the beach wing. The stairs are right out there. He's in room twenty-three." She smiled again. "It's our biggest suite. A really pretty room. He said it reminded him of when he stayed in Paris. Can you believe it? I've never been anywhere. He's so gorgeous and a real prince. I Googled him." She giggled.

"All right, then," Mia said. "Thanks for your help."

She and Joe found the stairs and climbed them. Before they reached the top, Oliver had stepped out onto the landing.

"Morning," Joe said cheerfully. "Great place. Can you see the ocean from your rooms? I'll bet they serve a nice breakfast. I heard the chefs are all culinary arts students."

Oliver glared without speaking. Umberto joined him. Joe moved forward until he reached the landing. Mia followed.

"You're not allowed in," Umberto growled. "Only her."

"That would be almost-princess Mia to you," Mia said brightly. "And I'm not going anywhere without Joe. He's not armed, though. We figured you'd get fussy about that. But feel free to check him out yourself. I always thought you got a bit of a thrill patting the guys down."

Umberto growled, then motioned for Oliver to search Joe. The pat-down was quick and efficient. Oliver shook his head.

Mia wore a cropped tank top over a long cotton skirt. She'd left her purse in the car and held nothing in her hands.

She spun in a slow circle. "As you can see, I'm not armed, either. Don't worry, as much as I want him dead, I don't want to be obvious about killing him."

The men exchanged a glance, then waved Mia and Joe through. Mia checked the numbers on the doors and knocked on 23.

Rafael answered immediately. She ignored him as she stepped into the suite. Just being close to him was enough to send her into a fiery temper, and right now she wanted to avoid any strong emotion. Far better to just get through the conversation without feeling anything at all. Emotional neutrality would be a win for her.

She took a moment to absorb the floral wallpaper and how it carefully matched the drapes and the cushions on the sofa. There were silks and satins and laces. Plants, tiny tables crammed with pictures in frames, and tiny crystal vases and knickknacks. There wasn't an inch of clear tabletop or a foot empty of furniture. The rooms were crowded and fussy. She knew instantly he would despise them. How lovely.

She turned back to Rafael. "Interesting room."

He shrugged. "I wanted to be close."

"I'm sure you did. All the better to kidnap Danny."

"Mia, please. That was not what I had planned."

She held up a hand to stop him. "This is my meeting and I'm in charge. You're going to listen." She reached into her skirt pocket and drew out a piece of paper. After unfolding it, she handed it to him.

"We've been to a judge," she said. "This is a restraining order. I'll give you the highlights, although I'm sure you'll want to read it all yourself later. You're not allowed on Marcelli land without first making an appointment to see either Danny or me. You must notify me first, and telling someone else in the family doesn't count. You must speak directly to me."

"So you can avoid me for as long as you would like," he said bitterly.

"Actually, I can't, and I wouldn't, but I don't care if you believe me or not. You're not allowed to see Danny on your own. I will be with you at all times. If you try to see Danny on your own or without setting it up with me first, you will be deported."

He stiffened. "That is not possible."

She tapped the paper. "Read it and weep, big guy. It is possible. I will supervise your visits and if you try to take him or influence him or anything else I don't like, you will be deported."

She nodded at Joe. "Why don't you do the next part."

Joe smiled. "Happy to. Danny has been fitted with a

small wristband that constantly monitors his position. If he is removed from the property, an alarm will sound and an APB will go out. Local and federal law enforcement will be notified and all airports within a fifty-mile radius will instantly be closed. When you and Danny are found—"

Rafael raised a hand. "Let me guess. I will be deported."

"I think you'll be charged with some serious crimes," Mia said. "Then your government will get involved because they won't like that you've been arrested. That will be messy. And I'm pretty sure you'll be fined for the whole airport closure thing. *Then* you'll be deported."

"Should you try to remove the wristband," Joe continued. "An alarm will sound."

Mia glared at Rafael. "Unlike you, I won't try to keep you from Danny. I think it's important he have a relationship with his father, regardless of how ratty that man may be. I was willing to trust you and you blew that, so now we do this my way. You may see him, you may be a part of his life, but you may not take him to Calandria. Not until he's eighteen, and then only if he's willing."

Rafael's anger was a tangible creature in the room. "You cannot do this. Daniel is the heir to the Calandrian throne. He has much to learn about his country and his people."

"I guess he's going to have to take his classes over the Internet."

"This is unreasonable."

"Unreasonable?" She felt her own temper flaring. "Let's talk about unreasonable. Let's talk about a man who slinks into my life, telling lies at every turn. Let's talk about someone willing to deceive my entire family. I would have worked with you," she yelled. "That's what really bugs me. I would have *been* reasonable. I would have done the right thing. Because that's the kind of person I am. But you weren't willing to find that out. The very first thing you did was to lie to me. You used me in every way possible to get what you wanted."

She curled her fingers into fists and wished she were strong enough to hurt him if she hauled off and socked him. "Do you think I like having to do this? Oh, sure, there's the initial thrill of getting a little revenge, but then what? How do I explain this to Danny? How do I tell him that his father is a liar?"

"You do not understand," Rafael said between clenched teeth.

"Actually, I understand perfectly." She moved toward him. "Why didn't you even ask? Why didn't you try telling the truth?"

"If you said no, I would be left with nothing."

"Which is pretty much what you have now."

He grabbed her by the upper arms. "Mia, Daniel has a great future. He will one day be king. You have no right to keep him from his destiny. Do you think he will thank you when he learns the truth?"

Joe hovered close enough to rip Rafael away if he tried anything. Mia hated that Rafael's touch made her blood heat and parts of her ache. So much for fury burning away baser desires. She'd been so hopeful, too.

"How do you think Danny will feel when he finds out that you were planning to steal him away?"

His blue eyes darkened with emotion. "He will understand why I thought it necessary."

"As a rule, four-year-old little boys don't appreciate losing their moms."

He released her. She hated how she instantly felt about twenty degrees colder.

"You keep saying that," he growled. "I would not have kept you from him. I planned for you to see him whenever you wanted."

The last of her emotional restraints snapped. "*You* planned? Where the hell do you get off making statements like that? You planned. That's bullshit. You don't get to make those kinds of decisions without me. A person planning visitation talks about it. He doesn't try to trick his child's mother into a fake marriage for the sole purpose of divorcing her and stealing her son."

"I know," he said. "I am sorry."

The apology surprised her, but it wasn't nearly enough. "It's done," she said. "We deal with where we are now. Danny stays here until he's eighteen."

"He needs to be in Calandria."

"Sorry, he's not going to be. If you want to compromise, then get your law changed." She smiled tightly at his look of surprise. "Oh, yeah, we looked it up. The second Danny is on Calandrian soil, he cannot be taken away without his father's permission. It's an heir thing. Change the law and we'll talk. Until then, we play by my rules."

He glared at her. "I am Crown Prince Rafael of Calandria. You can't do this to me."

"Watch me."

Rafael arrived at the Marcelli house fifteen minutes before his first scheduled visit with Daniel. While he was furious with the fact that Mia was able to dictate all the terms of his seeing his son, he also admired her strength and tenacity.

She dared to stand up to him. More impressive, she managed to broker a legal deal that put him at her mercy. He would not have thought her capable of such machinations.

Unfortunately for him, her legal maneuverings were proving most difficult to escape. The top lawyers in Calandria were investigating ways around what she'd put in place, but they were not hopeful. An appeal could be made to an international court. The most likely outcome was that Daniel would live part of the year in both places. But that would satisfy neither of them. In addition, Rafael was not yet ready to go public with this complication. He did not relish being made a laughingstock in the tabloids for a second time.

Something Mia could have done, he thought as he climbed out of the limo and saw the four security guards standing by the house and in the yard. She could easily have taken her story and her plight to any one of several television news shows. But she had not, and he appreciated her restraint.

Not that his appreciation blinded him. He knew her decision had nothing to do with him and everything to do with keeping Daniel out of the limelight. Something else he appreciated.

He had handled everything badly from the first. In truth, he had never considered compromise because that was not his way. But he had also forgotten Mia's determination.

He missed her. A foolish waste of time, but there it was. He missed her and Daniel. He missed how they had laughed together. With the two of them, he could be himself.

If things had been different . . . , he thought, not for the first time. If she had been from another family with different lineage. Except then she would not be the Mia he knew, and he would not have her change. Despite everything, he wanted her exactly as she was.

His father would not agree, he thought as he walked up to the back door and knocked. His father wanted Mia punished and Daniel returned at any price.

Joe opened the door and motioned for him to come inside. Oliver came with him while Umberto stayed outside. Rafael wasn't sure what the other man expected to do—he was outnumbered and outgunned. Still, he appreciated the show of support.

"You have ninety minutes," Joe said, then walked out of the kitchen, leaving Rafael alone to face the Grands.

Both old women stared at him. He could read the anger and hurt in their eyes. Grandma Tessa held a butcher's knife in one hand and he sensed she very much wanted to use it on him. Grammy M chose a different tack.

"I'm very disappointed in you, Rafael," she said, her voice sounding low and frail. "You were to be a part of this family."

Her words cut him in a way he had not thought possible. "I did not . . ."

Did not what? Plan to hurt them? Expect to steal Daniel away?

Tears filled her eyes and she trembled slightly. "So much for being a prince," she said, then left the kitchen.

He stood there, feeling uncomfortable in a way he had not experienced before. People were supposed to do *his* bidding. *He* was the one who decided what was right and what was wrong.

Daniel ran into the kitchen. "Daddy, Daddy! You've been gone so long!"

The boy raced right up to him. Rafael bent down and instinctively caught him as he jumped. Then he pulled him close and smiled at him.

"I am here now," he said.

"I missed you."

He stared into familiar brown eyes. "I have missed you as well."

"Look what I got." Daniel held out his wrist and rubbed a small metal band. "Uncle Joe says real soldiers wear one just like this. Now I'm a real soldier."

The tracking device. Of course. "Very nice," he told his son.

"Come play with me," Daniel said. "We can play soldiers and then I want to ride my pony and then read a story. Five stories."

"That is much to accomplish. Do you know how many stories five is?"

"A lot."

Rafael chuckled. "It is indeed."

The boy felt good to hold, he thought. He'd been telling the truth when he'd said he'd missed Daniel. In a matter of weeks, the boy had become important to him. In time he, Rafael, would have to return to Calandria and then what would happen? Would he truly be forced to leave Daniel behind?

Mia walked into the kitchen. Rafael stared as need flooded him. Not just to have her in his bed, but to talk to her, be with her. Ridiculous. He would stop needing her this instant.

"It's a little hot for pony riding," she said from the doorway to the kitchen. "Let's leave that for next time. But you can play soldier in the family room. I cleared off a big space. You can have a whole war."

"Mommy, no!" Daniel protested. "I want to ride my pony. I'm the heir and I said."

"I think your mother is right," Rafael said. "It's not good to be out when it is so hot. Not good for you or Gaspare."

Daniel pouted for a moment, then squirmed to be let down. "I'll get more soldiers. I'll get them all."

"Sounds like fun," Mia said. She turned her back and returned to the family room.

Rafael followed her. All right, perhaps he *had* expected some acknowledgment of him for taking her side, but if she chose not to give it, he would survive.

He found pieces of white satin scattered on the coffee table. There were several bags of open beads nearby.

"I did not know you sewed," he said.

"I don't," Mia told him as she sat down and picked up a small piece of satin.

The Grands came in and took their seats across from Mia. Each of them went to work on a larger piece of satin without speaking to him.

"We're beading a vest for David," Grammy M said grudgingly into the silence. "It's a tradition in the Marcelli family. Generally we bead the bride's wedding dress. Actually, we make the whole thing by hand. Katie's in charge. She made all the girls' dresses, which was a lot of work, let me tell you."

"Mary!" Tessa snapped. "He doesn't need to know."

Mia set down her beadwork and looked at him. "Maybe he does. Maybe he needs to understand that a family doesn't have to be royal to have traditions. Maybe then he could start to understand how much we all matter to each other and know cutting off an arm or a leg would hurt a lot less than losing a member of that family."

There was another pause, but this one felt much more awkward. Three pairs of eyes glared at him. He felt their combined anger as it grew and moved closer to him.

For the first time, he understood that he hadn't just upset Mia—he'd alienated the entire Marcelli family and anyone remotely associated with them. If they had their way, he would disappear, never to be heard from again.

He'd faced adversity before. Many people resented who he was, pointedly reminding him that he was a prince only by an accident of birth. In school, other boys had wanted to be smarter or stronger or faster. They had taken great pleasure in defeating him in the classroom or on the playing field. There were women who wanted to be with him simply to say they had, and others who wanted to make him fall in love so that they could break his heart. Simply because he was Prince Rafael of Calandria.

But this was different. This was personal. The Marcellis hadn't especially cared he was a prince before, and that title certainly didn't influence them now. They hated him for what he had done. For his acts, not his title.

Which meant they could have liked him for the same reason.

Over the past few days, he had wrestled with his own temper and frustration. He resented having to come up with a new plan and take more time to achieve what he wanted. He'd never once considered what he might have lost.

Not just Daniel, but all of them. Mia and the rest of the Marcellis.

Did he care?

He couldn't answer the question. Shouldn't he be able to instantly say no? He was here for a single purpose. Nothing else could get in the way.

Yet sometime in the past few weeks Daniel and his family had become entwined. He wasn't sure he could have one without the other. He wasn't sure he wanted to.

If he lost, he would lose more than the heir, his son. He would lose his family and the woman he had never been able to forget.

14

"Back to the hotel?" Oliver asked as he and Rafael walked toward the limo.

It was the logical choice, Rafael thought. He had finished his visit with his son. It wasn't as if he had business in town or knew other people.

Perhaps that was the problem. He had too much time on his hands. At home there were matters of state and different organizations to occupy his day. But here, now that he was in exile at that ridiculous hotel, he had nothing.

"A computer store," he said. "I will purchase a laptop and work from the hotel."

Oliver nodded and opened the rear door of the limo. Rafael glanced back at the house. No one stood at a window watching him go. No doubt the women inside had carefully distracted his son so Daniel would not miss him. He had been in the boy's life for such a short time. Would he now be forced out of it?

He knew that technically Mia couldn't exclude him forever, but there were subtle ways to make him matter less. If he had always been in the boy's life, she would have a more difficult time, but he had not. He was new and exciting, but not permanent. Not yet.

The thought of not seeing Daniel, of not watching him grow from a small boy to an active teenager, made his chest ache. The sensation was unfamiliar and uncomfortable.

"Your highness?" Oliver prompted, still holding open the door.

Rafael took a step forward then stopped. He would not lose his son, nor would he lose Mia.

But how? How would he make things better with her? How could he . . .

A bit of information came into his brain. Before flying out to meet the Marcellis, he had asked his staff to research them thoroughly. If he recalled correctly, Brenna Marcelli had had a rocky start with her husband. Nicholas Giovanni had planned to secretly buy the Marcelli vineyard and strip the family of everything. His plan had been discovered in time to stop it.

Yet Brenna had still married him. So she had forgiven him.

"The winery," Rafael said as he stepped into the limo. "The main offices."

"Yes, your highness."

Brenna's office was large and cluttered, with a huge map of the winery filling one wall. The massive desk had a heavy masculine style, and when Rafael entered the room and saw it, he wondered if it had belonged to her grandfather.

She was on the phone. When she glanced up and recognized him, her entire body stiffened. Her expression closed, her mouth tightened, and she quickly ended the call.

"Get your slimy royal ass out of my office," she said as she came to her feet and pointed at the door. "I don't want to see you or talk to you. I hope you get some horrible wasting disease brought on by a congenital defect inherent in lying, selfish, bastard princes."

He closed the door behind him and crossed to her desk. "I see that Mia gets her verbal skills honestly. It is a fascinating trait in the Marcelli women. I wish to speak with you."

"I have no interest in listening." She reached for the phone. "I can call security. Actually, I can call my brother. The ex-SEAL. He doesn't like you much, and seeing as he's a man who could take you out with a Q-tip, I'd be a little worried if I were you."

Rafael held out both hands, palms up. "Am I so frightening as all that? You have to call in reinforcements because you are afraid that by listening to me you might change your mind?"

"You're manipulating me."

He smiled slightly. "I doubt it will work on you, but it is necessary to try." He stepped closer. "Hear me out, Brenna. What harm is there in that? We both know I'm unlikely to influence you in any way. Later, when I am gone, you can call Mia and mock me behind my back. Think how that will bring you both pleasure."

She sat back in her chair. "Fine. But only because of the mocking. I'm really going to do that."

"I'm sure you are." He claimed the seat opposite hers and wondered how to begin. "I wish to make amends with Mia."

"Why?"

"I did not plan for things to go this way."

"Right. You just wanted to steal Danny, then leave town. I'm sorry we got in the way of that. What a serious bummer."

"Brenna, you deliberately misunderstand me."

"Oh, no. I understand you perfectly. Mia's right. You're sorry about getting caught, but you're not the least bit sorry about what you tried to do. You don't care about anyone, not even Danny."

He narrowed his gaze. "Of course I care about my son."

"I don't think so. Oh, sure, Danny as heir is really important to you, but that's about your country and tradition. It's not as if Danny is a real person to you. It's not as if you care about his happiness."

He stood and glared at her. "How dare you speak to me this way?"

"I believe you came to me, not the other way around. So I can pretty much talk to you any way I'd like. You're free to leave." She pointed at the door.

He sank back into the chair. "I'm not leaving."

"Then you have a problem, because I'm going to continue to talk to you any way I want." She leaned toward him. "Rafael, no one who genuinely cares about a child could imagine ripping a four-year-old little boy away from his mother and the only family he's ever known. Do you have any idea how that would devastate him? Of what he would go through?"

"He is my heir," he said, but the words came automatically. Without meaning to, he remembered a time long ago. He had been about Daniel's age when his own mother had died. He recalled the activity around her room and then nothing but quiet. No one would speak with him. For days he only saw his nanny. Then one evening his father had appeared and announced his mother was dead. The funeral was the next day and Rafael was expected to behave appropriately.

He'd understood nothing, except the fact that his father was obviously very angry with him. It wasn't until nearly a week later that he'd begun to figure out his mother was gone forever.

He remembered feeling lost and afraid. Sometimes he would creep into her room and curl up on her bed, closing his eyes as tightly as he could, hoping that when he opened them, she would be there.

"I had no intension of keeping Mia from her son," he told Brenna. "I had very specifically planned for her to . . ." He paused, not sure how to explain what he hadn't decided yet for himself.

"To what?" she asked impatiently. "See him for fifteen minutes every quarter? Don't give me that crap. You didn't have a plan. You didn't think of anything but what *you* wanted. You're like a kid who only discovers he's interested in a toy after someone else has taken it from him. It's not as if you cared about Danny until now."

"I did not know about him until recently."

Brenna leaned forward and gave him a cold smile that warned him she was about to trap him. "Did you bother to find out if Mia might be pregnant? Did it occur to you to send one of your minions to do a little reconnaissance work? Six or seven months after the last time you two got personal, it would have been really easy to tell. My God, Rafael. You let her think you'd died. What kind of weasel behavior is that?"

"It did not occur to me she *could* be pregnant."

"Why? Hadn't the little soldiers been potent until then?"

"I used a condom."

"Which obviously failed. Still, you had a responsibility and you're avoiding the question about just letting her go. Not even a good-bye? Wouldn't that at least have showed good manners?"

He shifted in his seat and glanced out the window toward the vineyard. "There were reasons."

"Uh-huh. Let me guess. You didn't want her to know who you really were. You didn't want to risk an American groupie. How embarrassing. Plus she could have told the world how you'd been playing dress-up."

He swung back to her. "I was protecting the heritage of my country. That is hardly playing dress-up." Brenna was a most annoying woman. Nearly as difficult as her sister.

"Call it what you like," she said with a shrug. "What do I care?"

"We are getting off the subject at hand," he said between clenched teeth. "I would appreciate your assistance in finding a way to communicate with Mia."

"I don't think so. I mean, come on. To what end? You had an affair with her once and let her go. Now you tried to steal her kid. You're not a really good catch, despite the title."

His frustration flared into anger. "What did you expect?" he asked heatedly. "That I would marry her?"

"You're the one who proposed."

He stood again and paced the length of the office. "I had no choice. I had to secure Daniel for my people. You think because I have money and a title it is all so easy for me, but you are wrong. With great wealth and power comes responsibility. I must not only think of today, I must think of five hundred years from now. Each law, each pardon, each act has consequences. Like ripples in a pond, they continue endlessly."

He paused by the map on the wall and traced the outline of the Marcelli land. "There are times when I wish it could be different. That I were a man like any other. That my life was my own. But it is not."

Brenna leaned back in her chair. "I wish I had some tissue here so I could weep for your sad little life. Poor rich boy all alone." She straightened. "I don't actually give a rat's ass about you or your sob story. The bottom line is you lied. You lied and you're not even sorry. If you had come to Mia and explained the truth from the beginning, she would have worked with you. She's intelligent and reasonable. But that never occurred to you. I guess *compromise* isn't a word in the royal vocabulary. You didn't bother to find out anything about her when the two of you were together before or you would have known that number one, she's more than willing to do what's right, and number two, she will die before she lets you take her child away from her."

"You speak of compromise," he said slowly. "I have been thinking about the concept."

"A little too much after the fact. Welcome to the real world, where people actually negotiate things like child custody agreements and stealing is against the law."

He looked at her. "You do not like me."

"No one does, except maybe Danny, and that's because he doesn't know any better. But he will."

"You will turn him against me?"

"I won't have to. I'm guessing you'll do that all on your own."

Her statement insulted him. "You do not know me."

"I have a good idea about you. You've never had to work for anything in your life. You get what you want and people just get out of the way. That's not happening this time. We're a strong family, and when you screwed Mia, you screwed us all." She paused. "Figuratively, of course, because otherwise, to quote my baby sister, ick."

"I will win."

"I can't see that happening. From where I'm sitting, there is only one win. You really fall in love with Mia and then somehow convince her it's for real. But what are the odds of that? Oooh, you'd have to go against Daddy and marry a commoner. I don't think you have the balls for it."

His blood ran cold. "If you were a man, I would call you out."

"Swords at dawn? I'm all a-tremble."

"You will not speak to me this way."

"How, exactly, are you going to stop me? This isn't Calandria and you can't throw me in the tower. Or is it a dungeon? I can never keep that straight."

"I will win, Brenna. I will defeat you all."

"Not even in seven lifetimes." She stood and walked to the door. "The funny thing is, I'm kind of glad you stopped by."

As if he believed that. "Why?"

"Because I'm not angry with you anymore. I actually feel sorry for you. You're so busy chasing after the moon, which you'll never get, that you can't see the beauty in the moonlight. You hide behind duty and privilege. There's a real world out there, Rafael. You should try leaving the titanium credit card at home and experience how the rest of us live. You might find what you've been missing."

• • •

David was being force-fed by the Grands. Mia grinned when she saw him and rushed to his side.

"Do you need rescuing?" she asked as he stood and hugged her.

"Apparently. I'm in danger of exploding."

"A man on his own," Grandma Tessa said. "I know you don't eat right."

"You can't make up for it in one meal," he protested.

"We try," Grammy M told him.

He released Mia and patted his stomach. "I'm going to take Mia for a walk. When I get back, you can ply me with desserts."

"I made a tiramisu just yesterday," Tessa said.

"I have fresh blueberry cobbler," Grammy M offered.

David had spent enough time at the house to know the right answer.

"I look forward to both," he said, then grabbed Mia's hand. "Get me out of here," he whispered.

She laughed and led the way outside.

The afternoon was warm and sunny, as often happened in August. They strolled to a shady tree, then plopped down on the grass.

"Where's Danny?" David asked. "With his dad?"

"Not without me around to supervise. He's at school this afternoon. His preschool class is doing a play and this is their final practice. I almost stayed, but I get so nervous watching him." She smiled. "I don't know how I'll get through the performance."

"You and Rafael are still at odds?"

"What do you think?"

"That you're stubborn and you won't forgive him easily."

That surprised her. "You think I should?"

"You're going to have to eventually. He's Danny's father."

"He's an asshole."

"That doesn't change the whole father part."

She stared at him. "You don't think what he did was so horrible."

"I didn't say that."

"You don't have to. I can see it on your face. What is all this? Guys sticking together?" She couldn't believe it. This was David. She trusted him.

"Mia, I'm not on his side. What he did was inexcusable. I'm simply pointing out that he's Danny's father and nothing is going to change that. You can try to keep Danny from Calandria all you want, but eventually you're going to have to let him go for a visit."

"No way. There's a law that says once he's on Calandrian soil, only a royal parent can say if he's allowed to leave. I would have no rights at all."

"Laws can be changed. You can make that a condition of his visiting." David put his arm around her. "Don't shoot the messenger. You know I'm telling the truth. The reason you're going to have to give in sooner than you'd like has nothing to do with Rafael and everything to do with Danny."

She pouted. "You're saying he'll want to visit Calandria."

"If you were him, wouldn't you want to?"

She couldn't even imagine her reaction if her mother had come to her when she was ten or twelve and told her she was a princess of some country. There was nothing that would have kept her away from visiting. Not even her mother's tears.

"So I should talk to Rafael about changing the law," she muttered. "I did before, but sarcastically. You're saying I should do it for real."

"I would use it as leverage now, before Danny starts making decisions on his own." David touched her chin. "I agree. Rafael is an ass. He acted badly and you shouldn't trust him. But you also have to be realistic about the situation."

She stared into his eyes. "You're the only sensible male in my whole romantic life and we broke up. Why is that?"

"We realized we weren't in love."

"If I'd known how much I was going to screw up every other relationship, I would have tried harder."

"You don't mean that."

She sighed and leaned against him. "I want to, but I know we weren't destined to be each other's great love. Still, I can dream about what if . . ."

"We wouldn't have made it a year," he told her.

"Stop being so damn practical. Did I say the word *dream*? Can't you go with that?"

"Sure."

She closed her eyes, but instead of a pretend future with David, she saw Rafael's face and remembered what it had been like to make love with him.

Instantly her body began melting from the inside out, which really pissed her off. How could she still want the man? Did he have to become a serial killer before her hormonal self let go?

"I want to talk about you," she said. "I need the distraction."

"Not exactly the level of interest required to get me to spill my guts," he told her.

She smiled. "You know I'm interested. How are things with Amber?"

When he didn't answer, she glanced at him and was surprised to find him staring off into the distance.

"David?"

He leaned his head back against the tree. "I don't know. The same, I guess. Maybe worse."

"Worse? Worse as in Amber still isn't convinced we're not an item?"

"Something like that. Imagine if she could see us now."

Mia considered their position, sitting close together, David's arm around her. "Okay, it might look bad, but there's nothing between us. You won't even let me fantasize about what could have been."

She'd been hoping for a smile. Instead he shook his head. "What if she doesn't love me?"

There was stark pain in his voice. Mia shifted until she faced him.

"She loves you. She adores you. Women who don't care about guys generally don't marry them."

"What if it isn't enough? She has to get over this, Mia. We can't spend our entire married life fighting about you." He smiled. "You're not all that."

"You've been talking to Grandma Tessa, haven't you?" she muttered as she considered the problem. "How much of this is about me and how much of it is a manifestation of Amber's insecurities?"

"I'm a guy. I haven't a clue."

"Maybe we should ask Francesca."

"Maybe we should keep it between the two of us," he said. "I don't want this being talked about at dinner. That would humiliate Amber."

"Good point." Mia knew her sister would keep a secret, but she didn't want to stress David out any more than he was.

"I have to know if it's just nerves," he said, "or something more serious."

"I agree. So bring her out and we'll prove there's nothing romantic between us."

"How?"

"I'll come up with something. Then, if she still doesn't believe you, there's a bigger problem."

His eyes darkened. "I'm not sure I want to know that. I don't want to lose her."

"She loves you," Mia told him. "I'm sure of it. And she is, too. I don't think her fears about me are all that big. I think I'm just the object of all her prewedding jitters. But we'll find out for sure and then you two can live happily ever after."

"Promise?" he asked.

And because she wanted him to be happy and live a wonderful life, she said, "Yes."

Rafael drove onto the Marcelli property a little before two. Mia had insisted that they go to Daniel's play together, which was fine with him. He wanted time alone with her so that he could explain . . . Explain . . .

He swore, still not sure exactly what he was supposed to say. All she had accused him of was true. He could claim he was the prince and that he had a right to his son, both of which were accurate. Yet neither excused his behavior.

Of all the statements Brenna had thrown at him the other day, one continued to haunt him. "No one who genuinely cares about a child would consider ripping him away from his mother and the only family he has ever known."

Rafael had never viewed the situation from Daniel's point of view. He had not thought how a small child could be scarred by such an upheaval. He had only thought about what he wanted and what was best for Calandria.

He turned onto the Marcelli driveway and found humor in how closely the black sedan followed him. Umberto and Oliver had strongly resisted his decision to drive himself. Although he had assured them he was unlikely to be assassinated between the hotel and Mia's house, they had protested his autonomy. He had agreed to allow them to drive behind him in another vehicle, but had refused to let one of them sit with him.

He wanted to be alone with Mia. He sensed that the fewer reminders of his royalty, the better. She was not the type of woman to be easily won and his position was only a source of contention between them.

He parked next to the house and climbed out. Kelly stood by the fence, a cigarette in her fingers. She glanced at his new ride.

"I didn't know they made them that big."

Rafael nodded proudly at his new SUV. "It is a Hummer. Such things are not practical in Europe, but here, where the roads are wide and gas is plentiful, it is appealing."

"I guess." She inhaled on her cigarette. "The good news is I don't have to worry about you giving me away anymore. No one in the family would bother listening to you. They all hate you. It's kind of cool."

He frowned. "What is cool about it?"

"You were a real dick. I like that Mia is going to make you crawl and then refuse to give in to you."

He did not like her choice of words, nor did he appreciate her assessment of the situation. "Mia and I will reach a point of compromise."

Kelly laughed. "Oh yeah. I want to be there for *that* meeting. Are you clueless about all women or just Mia?"

"I am very successful with women."

"Right. We're all in awe of how you handled *this* situation. I mean, come on, Rafael. It was sneaky and really low. You're a prince. Aren't you supposed to be held to a higher standard than the average guy?"

"Why do all the women in your family feel so comfortable pointing out what I did wrong?"

"Because it's fun and we're all highly verbal. Besides, it's not like Mia screwed up. She was honest with you from the beginning. The way I heard it, she didn't even try to keep Danny from you. She told you about him within seconds of finding out you weren't dead. Face it. You're the skanky one here."

Were there any names they weren't going to call him? "I will not stand here and be insulted."

She inhaled again. "Then take a seat."

He glared at her. "As if your life is so perfect."

"I'm twenty. I'm allowed to make mistakes. What's your excuse?"

"What was the mistake? Etienne?"

She shrugged. "I don't know. Maybe."

"Have you told him?"

"No, I just broke up with him. No big."

He studied her. "You are not wounded by your parting?"

"Wounded by our parting? You might want to think about communicating in a way slightly more relevant to this century, your highness. As for Etienne, no, I'm not wounded. I wanted him gone and now he is."

Which sounded correct, but in Rafael's experience, young women did not heal so easily from relationships.

"You were sleeping together?"

She frowned. "Get personal much?"

"If you were sleeping with him, then you should miss him."

"Thanks for the news flash."

"Why don't you?"

"I never really liked him."

Kelly immediately looked as if she wanted to call back the words.

"Why would you sleep with someone you don't like?" he asked.

"Don't you have a grovel appointment with Mia?"

"I am early."

"Lucky me."

"You are avoiding the question." He folded his arms across his chest. "Why would you sleep with . . ." He nodded slowly. "Because your parents wouldn't approve of him."

She took a step back. "Whatever. I have to go."

He didn't take the hint. "So you *wanted* them to be upset. I have seen you with your parents. You have a good relationship with them, so you are not trying to upset them out of spite."

"I would never do that," she snapped. "Now just shut up."

"I will not and you can't make me."

"That's mature," she muttered as she crushed out her cigarette, then picked up the butt.

"How is your dancing?" he asked.

"What?"

"You are doing well with the company?"

"Of course. They like me. I'm a hard worker. I'm moving forward with my career."

There was something in the way she said the words. Something brittle and filled with pain. He felt he was close to the truth.

"Most girls your age are in college," he said.

"I'm not a girl, you sexist pig, and so what? Why would I want to spend my day studying in some stuffy classroom when I can be on the stage? Do you know what a rush that is? Do you know how many really cute guys send me flowers after every show?"

He could relate to nothing in her conversation and yet he knew exactly what she felt. Perhaps because he had lived his whole life in a state of duty—doing what was expected rather than what he wanted.

"You must have spent a lot of time working at your ballet," he said casually.

"Well, duh. Of course. Hours and hours. Francesca used to joke that we should get some kind of frequent flyer miles for all the times we went back and forth to the studio. She was great, staying with me through class and really encouraging me. My dad was just as proud. He . . ." She glared at him. "Why are we talking about this?"

"Because you feel guilty." He felt triumphant, knowing he had found the key. "You thought this was what you wanted and your entire family sacrificed to make it happen. Perhaps not with money, but in time and effort. Perhaps the younger children had to give up time with their mother. Now you have what you vowed you always wanted and you hate it. You're acting out in the hopes that you'll so anger your parents that they will insist you quit and come home. You might even want them to punish you by sending you to college."

Her eyes widened in shock. "You're wrong!" she yelled. "You're wrong and you're stupid and you're a liar."

With that she turned and ran away. Rafael watched her go and knew he was right.

"What on earth have you done now?" Mia asked from the entrance to the rear of the house. "Was Kelly crying? Were you mean to her? I swear, Rafael, you're really an amazingly useless human being."

He turned to her. "Kelly is upset because I discovered her secret."

Mia didn't look convinced. "You're not exactly someone any of us want to confide in."

He walked toward her. "You're right. She didn't think she had told me anything significant, but she did. I recognized the symptoms. She is bound by duty."

Mia rolled her eyes. "Oh, please."

"She isn't happy dancing. She regrets her career choice, but because of all the sacrifices her family made for her, she feels too guilty to tell them. She's acting out, hoping to shock her parents enough so that they will punish her by bringing her home. She may even want to go to college."

Mia moved back into the house and he followed her. "You know I'm right," he said.

"I do not."

"Think about it. How unusual is her behavior? Hasn't it come on fairly quickly? The drinking, Etienne. She admitted she doesn't even like him. What twenty-year-old sleeps with a man she doesn't like?"

Mia leaned against the kitchen counter. "Maybe," she admitted. "I don't know. I'll have to think about it."

"I have solved the problem of your niece, Mia. Admit it. That should be worth something."

She glared at him. "This isn't a barter economy."

He eased toward her, enjoying the fire in her eyes. "Of course it is. You have something I want and I have something you want."

"You have *nothing* I want."

He touched her arm. She wore a sleeveless summer dress and he brushed his fingers down her bare skin to her elbow. He was close enough to feel her shiver and see the goose bumps that erupted.

Interesting. All her fury had not burned away her desire for him. He was pleased, because he still wanted her as well, but that wasn't what he spoke of.

"I wish to have a relationship with my son," he said. "You wish that as well."

She opened her mouth, then closed it. He had suspected she wouldn't be comfortable saying she *didn't* want him to be close to Daniel. What mother stood in the way of a boy and his father bonding?

"You're still a pig," she said.

"So Kelly informed me. The women of your family are not afraid to speak their minds."

"We're good at it."

"I have noticed. Come. We will go see Daniel in his play and you will think about what I have said about Kelly. In time, you will admit I was right. I am not as insensitive as you think."

"Don't push it," she grumbled as she collected her purse.

"I will not." He held open the door. "I have a surprise. I bought a new car so that I would fit in with the other parents."

She stepped out and stared at the massive SUV. "That's the biggest thing I've ever seen. You think it's inconspicuous?"

"It does not have diplomatic flags. And see? Oliver and Umberto are driving in a different car. No one will notice them. We are just like everyone else."

"Oh, right," she muttered as she walked over to the SUV and eyed the high step. "We're the walking, breathing definition of *normal*."

15

Although Mia had mocked Rafael about his new SUV, she was actually pretty grateful to arrive at Danny's preschool in it rather than in a limo with diplomatic flags. As promised, Oliver and Umberto stayed in the background and did their security guard best to blend in. Which left her the yet unsolved problem of how to explain Rafael.

While she wasn't close with the other mothers in the school, she did chat with them from time to time. She'd never mentioned a father for Danny. Not that anyone had asked. In today's world of single mothers, no one thought it was unusual to be manless. But showing up with a well-dressed, gorgeous man who looked like a fallen angel and spoke like Antonio Banderas was bound to create just a little too much interest.

She stopped at the edge of the parking lot and looked at him. "I don't know how to explain you," she admitted. "To the people here."

"Will they ask?"

"Danny's been enrolled just over a year and this is

your first time showing up. Not to mention the fact that you haven't exactly been a subject of conversation."

"All right. Tell them I am his father. We will smile pleasantly and keep moving. If you do not give them time to gather their thoughts, they will not be able to ask questions. Most people are too polite to pry in a setting such as this." He smiled. "You may get a few phone calls later."

She'd already figured that out. As for his plan, it was the only one they had.

"Let's go," she said, and led the way into the low, one-story building.

There were several small classrooms, three playrooms, and a big meeting room that currently had a stage at one end. Mia smiled at several of the mothers she knew and did her best to ignore their wide-eyed stares at Rafael. Oh yeah, there would be *plenty* of phone calls later.

The two of them took seats on the far side of the room, by a fire exit. There weren't any other parents sitting there yet. She had a feeling that spot had been prearranged and that Umberto and Oliver were hovering just outside. She subtly shifted her chair a bit farther away from Rafael's so there would be no accidental touching. Right now she didn't need the distraction.

"I hope no one recognizes you," she muttered. "I'm not a big tabloid reader, but lots of other people are. I wouldn't enjoy someone standing up and screaming out your identity."

"Nor would I." He glanced around. "We do not have a camera. I did not think to bring one. This is Daniel's first play. We must have pictures." He started to rise. "Instruct them not to begin the play until I have returned."

Mia put her hand on his arm. "Settle down. I have a camera." Then she realized they were touching and that the heat from his skin burned her in a way designed to make her rip off her clothes and beg to be taken right that second.

She casually removed her hand and reached into her bag for her digital camera.

Why did he still have to get to her? If only they hadn't made love. If she didn't have such incredible and recent memories, she would be able to ignore her physical attraction to him. She loathed the man with every fiber of her being and she absolutely hated suspecting that if they were alone and he started to seduce her, she wouldn't be able to say no.

In her head, she knew the opposite of love was apathy. That as long as she had energy in her feelings for Rafael, she was far from being over him. But in her heart, she wanted to slice her feelings away, like an unwanted disease. She wanted to forget how good he was with Danny, how he could be sensitive at the oddest times, how, until the Portuguese incident, he respected her intelligence.

Two months ago, her life had been relatively uncomplicated. Now it was fodder for a cable movie of the week.

"You told me Daniel is the star of the play," Rafael said.

"No I didn't. He's a tree. I told you he has three lines, just like every other child. This is preschool, not Broadway. There are no stars."

"But he is . . ." He lowered his voice. "He is the heir to the Calandrian throne."

"Gee, you know what? I didn't have that information when they were casting the play. What a shame, because if I'd told them I'm sure they would have made him the star."

Rafael stared at her. "Do you not believe your son is special?"

"Of course. But because of who he is on the inside. Not because of his relationship to you. I thought he was the most amazing child back when he was the son of an antiquities smuggler."

He frowned slightly. "I had not considered that. Were you angry when you discovered you were pregnant?"

"No. Not angry. Shocked. But I was going through a bad time, and finding out I was pregnant got me through it."

She really didn't want to talk about this. Why couldn't they be arguing about the light bill like the other parents?

"You mean because you thought I was dead," he told her.

"Whatever." She stared straight ahead.

"Mia." He leaned close until his mouth was almost touching her ear. "I did not mean to hurt you by letting you think I was dead. I did not consider that you would mourn me."

She turned to glare at him only to discover their faces were very, very close. "I told you I loved you. I don't say that to just anyone. I thought you were a real bad guy. I was violating every belief I had by being with you."

"I see that now. I am sorry for not understanding it then. Returning to my real life was traumatic. My father was very angry. I had neglected many duties. There were complications, but I should have considered your feelings."

It wasn't much of an apology, but considering the source, it wasn't bad. Unlike the last one, when he'd been whiny and had complained about being caught rather than being wrong.

"Fine," she muttered, and faced front again.

"This is nice," he said. "The preschool. The play."

"If you're going to launch into some sob story about how you never had a normal childhood with the hopes that I'll feel sorry for you, forget it."

"My childhood was fine," he told her. "One of great privilege. I had a series of very nice nannies and tutors until I was sent away to school."

He spoke so matter-of-factly that she couldn't tell if he was being casual or playing her.

"I'm glad Daniel will have more than that," he continued. "Different experiences."

"Which you wanted to take him away from."

"He would have carried the memories. They would have shaped him."

As if that was an excuse. "He's four. How much would he remember?"

"Enough." He glanced at her. "I did not mean to take him from you."

That got her attention. "Excuse me? That was your entire plan."

"Yes, I know. I am saying now, after considering what would have happened, I was wrong. I wanted my son in my life. I still want that. I want him to understand who he is. His history, his place in the world. But I see . . ."

When he paused she turned toward him. The urge to be sarcastic and cutting pressed in on her, but she resisted. Maybe, just maybe, she and Rafael were actually going to get to the truth for once.

"It would have been difficult for him," Rafael said

slowly. "He would have missed you and your family. I would not have known what to say to comfort him. My father would have insisted he act like a prince and a new nanny would have been hired. I'm sure neither would have helped a four-year-old boy heal from that kind of wound."

"You're right. No child should have his whole world ripped from him. Sometimes things happen and it can't be helped. But it shouldn't happen like this."

His blue eyes darkened. "You know you can't keep him from me forever. Some point of compromise will have to be reached."

"You're ruining a perfectly good moment," she muttered as she fought against anger. "You have no right to talk to me about compromise after what you did."

"I know, but that does not change the truth. I want things to be different for Daniel. Better. I do not know how to make that happen. I would need your help."

As he spoke, he reached for her hand. She snatched it away. Any touching would only muddle her brain. It was just her bad luck that the first sex she'd had in nearly five years turned out to be with a lying weaselly dog.

"You would need my help if you were taking him away, but you're not, so there isn't a problem."

He settled back in his chair. "You're a very stubborn woman."

"It's a Marcelli trait. Something I'm very proud of."

She stared at the stage and was grateful that no one had come to sit near them yet. Talk about a fascinating conversation to overhear.

"You think I walked away from you and never thought of you again," he said.

Unable to resist the bait, she spun to face him. "Don't

even go there. Don't try to convince me that you pined for me for even one second. We both know you didn't. If you had cared, you would have come after me. You would have told me you weren't dead. You would have done something. I was a way to pass the time while you were playing at being the bad guy."

"So much anger," he said as he touched her cheek.

She jerked her head back. "Stop touching me."

"As you wish."

He dropped his hand to his lap and she immediately wanted him to put it back on her.

"You've already done this dance, Rafael," she told him. "Stop lying. You can't sell me on believing in you again, so just let it go."

"I did not come after you," he said. "When I returned to the palace, my father was furious with me. He thought I had been studying abroad. When he found out I'd risked my life, he nearly locked me in the dungeon. I pointed out I was of age and free to live my life. He disagreed. I am, after all, the heir."

She rolled her eyes. "Is there an actual point?"

"I am the heir, Mia. I am expected to marry a particular kind of woman."

"I wasn't asking you to marry me, you egotistical creep. A postcard would have been nice. You let me think you were dead."

"I did not have a choice." He shook his head. "I chose not to have a choice. You were not someone I could have married. There was no point in caring about you anymore."

There were too many emotions, she thought, wishing she could simply leave. Anger and hurt and confusion and a deep, stupid desire to believe him.

"I did not know what to say to you," he told her. "I did not know how to explain we could not be together. To say why seemed . . ."

"Arrogant? Stuck up? Presumptuous?"

He shrugged. "All of those. So I took the easy way out. I said nothing. I let you walk away."

"Why are we having this conversation?" she asked, wishing the damn play would start or someone would come sit by them so he would stop talking.

"Because I want to apologize for that. I behaved badly."

He sounded sincere. She would swear that she could see the truth in his eyes. And she hated that. Hated that after everything they'd been through, she still wanted him to be one of the good guys.

"You can't honestly believe I'm going to trust you," she snapped. "You're an expert at playing my emotions. You came here with the express purpose of seducing me in order to steal Danny. Why is this any different?"

"Because it is. I do not know how else to explain myself to you."

"Then stop trying, because I'm done listening."

"Mia—"

But whatever he'd been about to say was cut off when a family moved into the row in front of them. Mia breathed a sigh of relief. It was a testament to his charm that even knowing what she knew, she still had trouble resisting him. The man was the devil.

Maybe that was problem. Women had been losing their souls to the devil's brand of temptation since the very beginning of time. Who was she to buck tradition?

• • •

Francesca hesitated outside the bedroom door. "I'm scared," she whispered.

Mia squeezed her hand. "You love her. That's what matters."

Francesca nodded, then knocked once and pushed open the door. "Hi, sweetie, how are you?"

Mia followed her sister into Kelly's room. Kelly lay on the bed reading a fashion magazine. She barely glanced at them.

"What are you doing here?"

"I wanted to see you," Francesca said. "Just to talk about how things are going."

Kelly threw down the magazine and pushed herself into a sitting position. Her gaze narrowed. "So why is Mia here? And why is your face all scrunchy? You're not just here to talk. What's going on?"

Francesca glanced at Mia. "She was always really bright."

"Beats the alternative," Mia told her. "Want the chair?"

Francesca nodded and pulled out the desk chair. Mia settled in the window seat. Kelly folded her arms over her chest in a position even a layperson like Mia recognized as defensive.

"What?" she demanded.

Francesca drew in a breath. "Kelly, your dad and I love you so much. I hope you know that. We only want you to be happy."

"I am happy. Perfectly happy. I have a great life. I'm a dancer with the San Francisco Ballet. It's a fabulous company and I'm working really hard. Everything is fine."

"I don't think so."

Kelly rolled her eyes. "Because you're going to believe Rafael's bullshit? Isn't he the liar prince?"

Mia admired her sister's patience. Francesca didn't lose her composure. She kept eye contact and spoke in a low voice. Obviously she wasn't a real Marcelli—she must have been spawned by aliens from a galaxy far, far away.

"I think what you do is amazing," Francesca said. "When you dance, you move with such grace and beauty, it's as if you're one with the music. You're right. You are working really hard. You've given up so much for your dance. Maybe it's too much. We were all so caught up in the dream of you being a ballerina, maybe we never considered the reality."

Kelly opened her mouth, then closed it. "This is stupid."

Francesca continued as if she hadn't heard. "So many women your age are in college. They're going to classes and frat parties and changing their minds about their majors. Sometimes their biggest problem is how to fit all the dirty laundry in the trunk of their car. But not you. You're living in the real world. You have an apartment, you pay your bills. You're a working woman. I can't imagine that at your age. Of course I was a student at twenty-eight."

Francesca smiled as she spoke. Kelly's lower lip quivered a little.

"We want you to be happy," Francesca told her. "Sometimes you have to try something to know if it's what you want. Sometimes you have to stumble and fall before you can fly."

Mia shifted on the window seat. "Francesca, you would try the patience of a saint. I swear, if you have any more analogies, I'm going to have to scream. Jeez. Just spit it out. Tell the kid you don't care if she doesn't want to be a dancer anymore. That it's fine. She can move home or go to college or whatever."

Francesca shot her a very clear "would you please shut up" look.

"I'm not a kid," Kelly said, then burst into tears.

Francesca moved onto the bed and pulled Kelly into her arms. Kelly clung to her.

"I'm s-sorry," she breathed between sobs. "I hate being a dancer. I know you guys g-gave up so much for me. I know it c-cost a lot. But I hate it." She raised her head and wiped her face with the back of her hand. "I hurt all the time. The physical work is grueling. I'm tired and I'm hungry. I don't have what it takes. I don't. Even if I do, I don't want to anymore."

Francesca hugged her close. "Then you can stop right now." She smiled at Mia over Kelly's curly red hair and mouthed "Thank you."

Mia didn't bother to point out that she wasn't the one to be thanking. Rafael had figured out the truth none of them had been able to see. She wouldn't have thought he had the sensitivity or awareness, but she'd been wrong.

Kelly continued to cry. "I'm sorry. I'm sorry."

"You don't have to be," Francesca said. "You're only twenty. How can you know what you want to do with your life? You're allowed to change your mind."

Kelly raised her head and wiped at her tears. "Really?"

Francesca nodded. "Of course."

"Then I want to go to college. Maybe community college at first. I want to be a physical therapist, get married, and have kids. I could teach ballet on the side or something. I don't want to let it go, but I can't make it my life anymore."

"Then you won't."

Kelly smiled. "Thanks for making me talk about this."

"Not a problem. I want you to know you can always come to me or your dad if you need to."

"I know, I just felt so stupid. I finally had what I'd always wanted and suddenly I didn't want it anymore. And . . ." She ducked her head. "I'm really sorry about Etienne. He was another mistake."

"You were trying to get our attention."

Kelly grinned at her. "Did it work?"

"Big-time."

Kelly hugged her, then slid off the bed. She crossed to Mia and caught her in a hug. "Thank Rafael for me, okay? Maybe he's not such a big butthead."

"I'll keep that in mind."

Kelly straightened. "I'm gonna go call Dad, then ask the Grands for some leftovers."

"Good. He'll want to talk to you, and you know how the Grands feel about feeding you. You'll make their day."

Kelly raced from the room. Francesca watched her go. "I'm so relieved," she said with a sigh. "I feel so much better about things. I know Kelly does, too. It's just . . . how could we not have figured it out before? She's been crying for help and no one noticed."

"We noticed," Mia told her. "We just weren't sure what was wrong. To quote your daughter, it took the butthead to see it."

"Which means he isn't as completely self-centered as we thought."

"Actually he is. He told me with the idea of getting points in return."

Francesca shrugged. "Still, it took a little emotional awareness for him to figure it out."

"You say that like it's a good thing."

"It's not bad. Mia, we're talking about Danny's father. You can't ignore him forever."

"Watch me try."

"Oh, that's mature."

Mia shook her head. "I know what you're saying, but I'm not prepared to be mature right now. I'm still angry and I don't trust him."

She thought about all they'd discussed while waiting for Danny's play to start. What bugged her wasn't what he said—it was her desire to believe it.

"Maybe he's learned his lesson," Francesca said.

"People don't change."

"Of course they do. Look at you. You're not the same person you were six years ago."

"We're talking about days, not years," Mia reminded her. "People change if motivated. Do you really think Rafael is? Right now he's pissed because he didn't win. He'll get tired and go home."

"Do you really believe he's going to walk away from Danny?"

Mia drew in a deep breath. "No," she said slowly, knowing anything else was wishful thinking on her part. "He'll come up with another plan. Maybe he already has. Whatever happens, I refuse to trust him."

Francesca winced. "Be careful about drawing a line in the sand. You don't want to get trapped by your own words."

"It's a risk I'm willing to take. There is nothing Rafael can say or do to make me ever believe him again. He knows it and I know it."

"I'm riding, I'm riding," Danny cried as he circled the lawn behind the house.

"You look great," Mia called to the boy.

"Excellent," Rafael said. "Just like that. Very good."

Mia watched her son on the pony and realized that with the trip to Calandria off, she was going to have to find a place for Gaspare. She couldn't keep him tied up by the garage under Joe's makeshift tent/stable.

"I need to find a stable," she murmured. "Are they listed in the phone book?"

Rafael stiffened, but didn't protest that Danny and his pony would soon be leaving.

"You have land here," he said instead. "You could build a small stable."

"In theory, but unless the plans came with a way to build a little someone to care for Gaspare then we'd still have a problem. Danny's too young to care for the pony and I'll be busy with school. Even if you're still here, you don't strike me as the type to muck out a stall." She glanced at him. "It is 'muck out,' isn't it?"

"That is the term."

His expression was tight, his eyes narrowed.

"You're all pinchy," she said, feeling suddenly cheerful. "Is it the thought of being forced to stay here or the knowledge that the little prince won't be returning with you?"

"I am enjoying my time here with you," he said, avoiding the question. "Daniel has an excellent seat."

Not exactly a smooth change of subject, but that was okay. She glanced at Danny and saw he really did seem to have an instinctive understanding of how to ride.

"He must get that from you," she said. "I don't think a Marcelli has been on a horse in eighty or ninety years."

"Then perhaps it is time. I could arrange for the three of us to go riding."

"No, thanks. I think the pony is dangerous enough. I don't want to see a real horse."

"You are afraid?" he asked, his voice taunting her.

She refused to be trapped by threat of being called chicken. "Sensible. Very sensible."

"I see. How is Kelly?"

She groaned. "You love that you were right, don't you?"

"I'm glad she was able to tell her parents the truth and now she's happy."

"Oh, please. You're desperate to do the happy dance," Mia said. "You think you're Mr. Sensitivity."

He smiled. "I assure you, that title never crossed my mind. I meant what I said. I like Kelly."

"You're not fooling me, Rafael. I know all this pleasant chitchat is just part of your master plan. You're trying to lull me into liking you again. It's not going to happen."

He glanced at her, then returned his attention to Danny. "Is it so impossible to believe I might regret what happened? That I now wish for a chance to make things right between us?"

"Yes. It is impossible."

"Because I am so horrible?"

"It's not about being horrible. It's about being used to getting your way. You're not used to regular rules. You don't believe in them. Why would you play by them now?"

"Because they are all that is left to me." He looked at her again. "You are right—I planned to steal your son from you. But in my mind, I didn't take the idea any further. I did not consider that Daniel would be devastated by the loss. I would have, and then I would have realized we needed to come up with another way."

"That's it?" she asked, incredulous. "That's all you got from this?"

"What is wrong with what I said? I have admitted I was wrong. I would have hurt Daniel and that was never my plan. I have also told you several times that I intended for you to be able to see Daniel, that I wasn't going to keep him from you, but you choose not to believe that. So why would I continue to repeat myself?"

"That's it?" she demanded again, even as she smiled and waved at Danny as he continued to circle the lawn. "That's the best you can do?"

"What more do you want from me? Blood?"

"It would at least be a start."

"Be reasonable, Mia. I cannot undo the past. What would make you feel better now?"

"There's nothing," she said between clenched teeth. How she loathed the man. How she wished he'd never seen that stupid picture, had never come here. If only—

"Change the law," she said suddenly. "I was kidding before, but I'm not now. Change the law that says once Danny is on Calandrian soil I have no rights. Make us equals in Calandria law."

"Will that be enough?" he asked, surprising her. She'd been so sure he would protest.

"It will be a start."

"I will call the leader of parliament in the morning," he said. "I give you my word."

He held out his hand as if they were supposed to shake on it.

She didn't want to shake hands with him. She didn't want to touch him at all. Whenever she did, she was reminded how weak and rebellious her body could be. But there was no polite way to avoid the contact, so she braced herself and slid her hand against his.

The sparks were instant. Need exploded like a firecracker trapped in a box. There was light and heat, which she hated almost as much as his knowing smile.

"It's just physical," she snapped as she pulled back and stepped away from him.

"The body and the spirit are not so easily separated," he said. "They influence each other."

"Not in this case. Don't go getting any ideas." She glanced at her watch. "Your time is up. You need to leave."

She expected him to protest. Instead he walked over to Danny and lifted him down from the pony. "You have done well," Rafael told him. "I'm very proud of you."

"I don't wanna stop," Danny said.

"It is time for me to leave."

Danny's lower lip thrust out. "No!" he yelled. "You stay. Mommy, tell Daddy to stay."

"Danny, it's time for Daddy to leave."

She tried to gather him in her arms, but he pushed away and ran to Rafael.

"Stay, Daddy," the boy cried. "I'm the heir and I say you stay."

"Danny . . . ," Mia started.

Her son turned on her. "Why did you make him go away? Why can't my daddy stay with me? I want him to stay. I want him to live with me. I'm the heir and I say so. I say so!"

The last sentence came out as a shrieking scream. Mia was stunned when her normally reasonable, rational, emotionally stable child threw himself on the ground and began kicking and yelling.

"Danny," she said quietly. "It's all right."

"It's not. It's not."

"Mia," Rafael murmured.

She looked at him. "Just go. I'll deal with this."

"I will not leave you alone while he is like this."

Which, in theory, was lovely. But in reality, the longer he stayed, the worse it would get. Still, she couldn't force him to go.

She sat next to Danny and Rafael sat next to her. Danny cried himself out of his tantrum in about three minutes, then crawled on her lap. He put one arm around her neck and one around his father's, forcing them to lean toward each other. Then he cried as if his heart were breaking.

Parts of words tumbled out. It took her a minute to figure out what he was saying, and when she did, her heart broke, too.

"I want a mommy and daddy at the same time."

16

Mia stood by David in the hallway. He smiled at her and then said, "You look like hell."

She fingered her hair and realized she was in desperate need of a trim and maybe some highlights, but she didn't think that's what he meant. The stress wore on her until she had arguments with Rafael in her dreams.

"Things have been better," she admitted. "It could be worse. At least I don't have classes. I don't think I could deal with all this and tort law at the same time."

He patted her arm. "I wish I could help. Want me to beat up Rafael?"

"Thanks, but Joe already called that one and I haven't said yes to him yet."

"I don't want to stand in the way of Joe and a mission," David told her. "Is there anything else I can do?"

"Just being here with Amber helps," she said. "Watching the two of you gives me hope. Not every relationship is destined for disaster."

He smiled and she saw the love in his eyes. For a moment she felt a twinge—not because she wanted him to still be in love with her, but because just once she wanted a man to look like that when he talked about her.

"I got lucky when I met Amber," he admitted. "Even more lucky when she agreed to go out with me. I couldn't believe she didn't have a serious boyfriend or wasn't already married." He chuckled. "I nearly proposed on our first date. I knew she was the one, but I figured if I said so, she would think I was crazy and disappear into the night. So I waited and played the dating game, but all the time I knew."

Mia sighed. "Now you're getting married."

"I know some guys think of it as a loss of freedom, but why would I want time away from Amber? To do what? Meet other women and be disappointed? She's the one. I want to wake up next to her every morning. I want to plan a future and have kids and curl up in the dark just breathing in the scent of her body."

Mia listened to his words and felt another twinge. Sure, David was doing what they'd talked about, but he also meant every word. He spoke from the heart about the woman he loved.

"She's going to be a great mom," he continued. "She loves kids and she's patient. What?" he asked with a frown.

"I didn't say anything."

He touched her cheek. "You're crying."

"I'm not." She felt the dampness. "Okay, maybe, but just because it's so wonderful. I want you to be happy."

"I want you to find what I have," he told her. "Mia, you're great. You're smart and beautiful and I want you to find the right guy."

"I'm sure I will," she lied. "But until then, I have you two to inspire me."

"I've never been an inspiration before."

"You were never marrying Amber before." Mia hesitated. "David, I need you to talk to her for me."

"About?"

She drew in a breath. "The Grands. They really want to bead something. You know we have the tradition of making the bride's wedding dress. Obviously Amber has picked out a dress already. The wedding isn't that far away. The Grands have beaded your vest and they loved it, but it's not the same. The thing is, it's about more than just helping. It's their way of showing Amber they love her and really want her to be in the family. But they're afraid they'll say it wrong, or she'll think they're weird or pressuring her. They mentioned something about working on her veil, if that would be okay."

"I'll talk to her," he said as he leaned against the hallway wall. "She really likes the family, but sometimes they're a little much."

Mia laughed. "Of course we are. I get overwhelmed and I was born into this craziness. I hope you can explain how much we already love her and how happy we are that she's going to be one of us. Even if that does mean having to marry you."

"Hey!"

She grinned. "I've seen you at your worst."

"I could say the same."

"You could, but you're a gentleman and you won't." Her smile faded. "I love you and I'm incredibly glad we're not the ones getting married."

"Me too." His expression turned serious. "We were kids. What did we know about marriage and forever?"

"Plus you probably would have met Amber eventually and left me for her."

"I would have felt bad about it."

She laughed. "And that's supposed to make it all better?"

He shrugged. "What can I say? She's the love of my life."

"David?"

They both turned and saw Amber stepping out of the dining room where Grammy M had carefully sent her to polish the silver. The preplanned move had allowed Amber to hear every word while staying out of sight.

"Amber." David shifted uncomfortably. "We were, uh, just talking. Mia and I. It doesn't mean anything."

Amber's eyes were bright with affection and understanding. "I know." She turned to Mia. "I'm sorry I've been so foolish about so many things. It's just you're amazing and I'm just . . ."

"The woman David loves," Mia told her.

Amber stepped into his embrace. "I am, aren't I? Wow. How did I get so lucky?"

David hugged her tight. Over her head, he mouthed, "Thank you."

Mia nodded, then turned away to give them privacy. Not that they cared. As far as they were concerned, they were the only two people in the world.

Mia returned to her room, where she could have her breakdown in private. This was the Marcelli family, after all, and if anyone saw her crying they would all want to know what was wrong, then work as a committee to fix it. Right now, she just couldn't handle that.

She closed the door and then threw herself on the bed. But once there, the tears refused to come. She squeezed her eyes shut and tried not to think about everything going on, but it was impossible.

She hurt. Every bone, every hair, every inch of skin. She ached with disappointment and a strong sense of having lost something that could have been—should have been—wonderful. For a few days, a couple of weeks even, she'd been in love with a caring, smart, funny guy who'd pretended to love her back. She'd allowed herself to believe. To have hope. It had been a long time since she'd had hope in the romance department.

So many pretty words, she thought. So many lies and she'd fallen for them all. Apparently she only looked smart.

Now everything felt broken. She knew Rafael was trying, but so what? How could she ever believe him again? How could she trust him? Or was that not her problem? Did she have to trust him? If he changed the law, then they would have to negotiate some kind of visitation for Danny in Calandria.

She rolled onto her back. If . . . There was no if. Rafael was nothing if not determined. He wanted his son to grow up knowing about his people and his duty. He wanted Danny to understand that being the heir meant more than waving a scepter and making pronouncements. Rafael would get the law changed and then she would lose Danny.

Her eyes burned as the tears came at last. Perhaps it was dramatic to think she would lose her son, but everything would be different. He would probably summer with his father and go to school in Los Angeles with her. He would have major life experiences without her, learn things, be independent. She'd expected that when he was a teenager, but not before he was eight.

She wanted to hate Rafael for all this. She wanted to

blame him for everything, but she couldn't. In truth, Danny was his son and he had as much right to the boy as she.

She closed her eyes and felt the trickle of moisture run down her temples and into her hair. Her chest ached. How would she survive without Danny around? The summer would be too long. She could—

Eventually he would have to go to school in Europe.

Mia sat up. He would need exposure to a larger world. An international one. She had the sudden hope that he'd inherited her ability to learn languages. It would certainly make his life easier.

But what about her? Should *she* move to Europe? Would that help Danny? There had to be law firms that would want to hire her. And then what? Make a life for herself living quietly somewhere while her son trained to be king and Rafael married someone appropriate?

She picked up a pillow and threw it across the room. "Damn you, Rafael," she cried as more tears poured down her cheeks.

"Mommy."

Mia froze and looked at the now open door. She'd been so caught up in her thoughts, she hadn't heard it open.

Danny stood there, his eyes wide as he stared at her. "Mommy?"

She quickly wiped her face. "Hi, sweetie. I'm okay. What's going on?"

"I want to do a puzzle."

He still wasn't very good at them. Even the ones with the really big pieces.

"Sure. I can help. Let me go wash my face and we'll head downstairs."

He crossed the room and climbed up on the bed. "Are you mad at Daddy?" he asked.

Her first instinct was to deny that she was, but based on what Danny had just seen and heard, that seemed kind of stupid.

"I am, right now, but that's okay. Grown-ups get mad at each other and then we talk and make up."

"Does Daddy have to 'pologize?"

"He has."

"But you're still mad?"

She sighed. "I'm mad about a lot of things."

"You could make a list."

She laughed, then put her arms around him. He hugged her back, his body small and sturdy.

"I love you, big guy," she whispered. "So much. You're my whole world and the best thing in it."

"I love you, too, Mommy."

She couldn't let him go, she thought as she continued to hold on to him. Not even for a summer. She couldn't survive. Which meant she and Rafael had a whole lot of stuff to work out.

But how was she supposed to negotiate with a man she didn't trust?

She straightened. "Okay. Let's go find that puzzle."

"Okay."

He smiled and slid off the bed. She followed him. In the hallway, he reached for her hand. She held on to his small fingers and vowed that no matter what, she was never letting go.

Rafael walked toward the back door of the Marcelli house. He'd had two angry phone calls with his father that morning. The king was not a patient man and he expected his grandson in residence before the end of the summer. Rafael didn't see how that was possible. He was no longer willing to simply spirit Daniel away, as he had been before. Mia had worked legal magic to keep Daniel with her in any other circumstances. It was a problem without solution.

The door opened before he could knock. Daniel stood there.

"Good morning," Rafael said pleasantly. "I thought we could go into town today. There is a children's museum that is—"

"You made my mommy cry," Daniel told him. "You made Mommy cry and say a bad word. Go away."

With that, the door slammed shut, leaving Rafael standing alone outside.

Mia looked up when Grammy M walked into the library. "What's up?" she asked.

The older woman was twisting an old dish towel. "It's Danny," she said, then quickly added. "He's fine."

"Okay." Mia stood. "Did he do something wrong?"

"I'm not sure you'll think so. Rafael was here."

Mia glanced at the clock and swore. It was ten after two. Their appointment was for two.

"I was trying to figure out my class schedule," she said. "I wasn't watching the clock." Her heart froze in her chest. "Oh, God, Rafael didn't take him, did he?"

"What? Of course not. None of us would be lettin' that happen. It's nothin' like that. Danny answered the door and told his father that he'd made you cry and that he should go away. Then he slammed the door in Rafael's face and ran up to his room. He's there now."

Mia winced. "He walked in while I was having a personal pity party last night," she admitted. "I didn't think he would take it so hard. What did Rafael do?"

"He left."

Mia blinked. "You're kidding. I would have thought he would demand his son."

"I think Danny hurt his feelings."

Mia couldn't imagine a building falling on the man and causing pain, but stranger things had happened. "Okay, I'll take care of this."

Danny first, then Rafael, she thought.

"Rafael really left?" she asked again.

Grammy M nodded. "He got in his car and drove away."

"So not like him to walk away." She couldn't believe he'd given up on Danny, which left what? He'd been shocked, maybe? Because the hurt thing . . . so not happening.

Thirty minutes later she pulled into the hotel parking lot. She'd had a very productive talk with her four-year-old, explaining he didn't get to say who came and went in the house, and now she was here to . . . to . . .

She parked and stared at the small hotel as she tried to figure out what she was there to do. Telling Rafael he was welcome to come over was the sort of thing she could say on the phone. So why had she left Danny in the very capable hands of the Grands and driven here herself?

Oh, well, now that she *was* here, she might as well deliver her message.

She walked up to the second floor and was immediately stopped by Oliver.

"It's me," she said easily. "I'm not armed and I'm not

going to let you feel me up to confirm that, but you can check my purse if you want."

She held out the bag. He quickly went through it, then handed it back.

She walked to Rafael's room and knocked.

"It's open."

She stepped inside and found him sitting on the sofa, reading what looked like a very thick report.

"Hi," she said as she entered. "I came by to, ah, talk about what happened with Danny."

Rafael rose and pointed to the sofa. "Please, have a seat. Would you like something to drink?"

"No, I'm good."

He waited until she was seated before claiming his own chair again. She studied him, trying to figure out what he was feeling, but his dark blue eyes gave nothing away and the half smile hid all his secrets.

"I heard what happened," she began, again wondering why she hadn't just phoned it in. "I'm sorry Danny did that. I didn't coach him."

"I did not think you did. Two days ago he was furious with you because he thought you were the reason I no longer lived at the house. Today I am the villain."

Bad guy, she thought, but didn't correct him. "Okay. Well, I thought maybe you were upset."

"So you came to gloat?"

"Ouch. That's not fair. I said I'm sorry."

"So you did. You are sorry and I am sorry. Where do we go from here?"

He was asking her? "I haven't a clue," she admitted. "We'll have to find some middle ground."

"Difficult when you don't trust me."

Difficult, yes. But impossible?

"I want to trust you," she said slowly.

"You say that as if it's a horrible thing."

"It is. How many times do you get to fool me?"

"I'm not fooling, Mia. This is very real. We're talking about our son and his future and how best to be parents. What is more real than that?"

"You're still an arrogant prince who doesn't believe he has to play by the rules."

"Perhaps, but you didn't come here because of Daniel."

He was on his feet before she had a chance to absorb his words. Once she did, she stood and glared at him. "If you're saying what I think you're saying . . ."

"You're here because of me. Because of the connection that exists. You're here because there is a need and a hunger and because when you close your eyes at night, I'm the man you see."

She started to stalk out, but he grabbed her arm and spun her toward him. They were inches apart. She could feel the heat of his body and hear the soft rhythm of his breathing. His eyes were as dark as midnight and she recognized the passion burning there.

"Admit it," he commanded.

"Never."

"But you must, Mia. You were never a liar."

"Of all the arrogant, self-centered, egotistical—"

He cut off her rant with a kiss. She knew what he was going to do the second before his mouth touched hers and she braced herself for the assault.

Only it never came. Instead he released her arm and pressed his lips to hers in a gesture so tender, so soft and tentative, she felt herself strain toward him to deepen the contact.

All the anger and uncertainty drained away, leaving nothing in their wake but desire. Her body remembered what it had been like to be touched by this man, and every cell called out to him. Her breasts ached, her thighs tightened, and between her legs, she was already wet.

All this and they were still kissing like schoolchildren.

"Mia," he breathed against her mouth. "How I've wanted you. How I've thought about what it was like when we made love. We have always had the fire. When I touch you, I feel your pleasure."

She felt the same. As she ran her hands over his body, she knew his response as if it were her own. But she didn't say that. She might be foolish enough to sleep with him again, but she wasn't going to get sucked in emotionally.

This was just sex. Fantasy and friction. Nothing more.

Still, when he pressed against her mouth, she turned into him. And when his arms came around her waist, she raised hers to his shoulders. Then she tilted her head and parted her lips and surrendered.

His tongue swept inside her mouth. His heat and taste combined with incredible sensations of delight. She surged toward him, wanting to feel the hardness of his body against hers. Even as he explored her mouth, he rubbed his hands up and down her back. She did the same to him, then went lower, to cup his rear and squeeze.

He immediately pressed his hips toward her, driving his erection into her belly.

He was already hard, she thought happily. Hard to her wet. She closed her lips around his tongue and sucked as she remembered what it had been like last time, when he'd driven into her so deeply, she'd been forced to come over and over.

He reached for the hem of her T-shirt. She released him long enough to step back and hold her arms up over her head. He pulled the shirt free, then expertly unfastened her bra.

Then his mouth was on one breast with his fingers matching the movements on the other. As he stroked and sucked and licked, she ran her fingers through his hair and tried to remember how to breathe.

It was perfect, she thought, her head falling back. With each tug on her nipples, she felt an answering contraction between her thighs. Her shorts confined her. She needed to be naked, her legs spread, him between them. Going down on her or plunging inside of her, she didn't much care. Just *something.*

He straightened and claimed her mouth again. She didn't complain because he covered her breasts with both hands and continued to caress her. Even as he kissed her over and over again, he nudged her back. She allowed him to urge her into the bedroom where the high four-poster bed beckoned.

When she bumped into it, he lifted her onto the mattress. She scooted back, only to be stopped by him unfastening her shorts. Somewhere along the way, she'd kicked off her sandals.

When he released her, she continued to scoot while he held on to her shorts. Her panties came off with them. When she was naked, he grinned and went to work on his own shirt.

Minutes later, he was next to her, touching her everywhere. She traced the muscles of his chest and skinny line of hair that led to his arousal. He teased her belly button before moving lower and slipping his fingers into her wetness.

They lay on their sides, facing each other, eyes open as they pleasured each other. He kissed her cheeks, her forehead, then her nose.

"The difference is," he said quietly, "that I very much want to make you come, but you do not have the same goal."

She continued to stroke his hard length. "Are you sure about that?"

"Of course. If you make me come now, how will I slide deep inside you later? How will I part your legs and move faster and faster?"

"We'll have to wait, what? Ten minutes?" she asked with a smile.

"Any time would be too much."

He had a point, she thought as she reluctantly released him. He, however, kept touching her, rubbing back and forth, occasionally dipping his fingers inside of her. She had a leg over his hip and they were so close she could see the various colors that made up his irises.

Not that she could really focus on them. Instead her attention kept slipping to the building tension in her body.

This was just sex, she reminded herself. Really great sex. And she wanted more. She wanted more touching and rubbing and dipping. She wanted to come like this, then do it all again.

"You have always been difficult," he said conversationally.

"What? We're naked and you want to discuss that now?"

"I can think of no better time. You never do what you're told."

"I take great pride in that," she said, finding it difficult to speak, especially when he bent down and licked her nipple. She was close and getting closer. The rhythm of his fingers drove her crazy, but in the best way possible.

More, she thought. She just needed a little more.

"But sometimes instructions are a good thing. For example . . ."

He eased her onto her back, all the while continuing to touch her. He positioned himself between her legs. He had to be millimeters from entering her, but he didn't. She strained toward him.

"Rafael," she breathed.

He stared into her eyes. "Come for me, Mia. Come now."

The unexpected order shocked her. She felt him pushing slightly, but he didn't enter. He waited.

Suddenly she knew he would thrust inside of her the second she started to climax. She tightened in anticipation of his hardness filling her over and over again.

That was all it took to push her over. The first shudder of her release claimed her. She arched her body.

"Now," she breathed. "Do it hard, Rafael. Do it."

He plunged inside of her. At that first thrust, her contractions increased. Pleasure poured through her as she wrapped her legs around his hips and held him in place. Again and again, thrusting deep and fast, claiming her.

She held on to him, climaxing until his body stilled and shuddered.

• • •

Rafael lay still on the bed. Mia lay next to him. The sound of their breathing filled the quiet of the room.

Once again the power of their lovemaking surprised him. He hadn't thought she would really give in, but now that she had, he felt the first whisper of hope.

Perhaps all was not lost. Perhaps there was still a way to make her believe in him again. Because that is what he wanted. Over the past couple of weeks, he'd begun to see all he had lost with his deceptions and arrogance.

He wanted to make things right with her. He wanted her in his life because she wanted to be there. He needed her.

"Mia," he began, not sure what he was going to say.

She smiled, then stood. "I'll give full points for that one. It was great."

Her lush body distracted him until she reached for her clothing.

"What are you doing?" he asked.

"Getting dressed. I need to get back. I don't want to miss dinner."

"You should stay here," he said. "We can talk."

Talk? Had he really said that?

"I appreciate the invite, but I'm okay." She pulled on her panties and picked up her bra.

"You can't leave," he told her.

"Actually I can and I'm going to."

She quickly finished dressing, then walked to the door. "It was sex, Rafael. Nothing more. I haven't forgiven you and I'm still pretty sure I don't like you. Unfortunately, I have a mindless reaction to your body. I'll get over it. I did before."

And then she was gone.

17

Mia held her bravado until she'd driven out of the hotel parking lot and was confident she was out of sight of anyone watching from a second-story window. Then she pulled to the side of the road and tried to catch her breath.

What had she done? The why was easy—no point in wondering about that. The why was the incredible sexual chemistry that had always existed with Rafael and the things that happened to her body when he touched her. But the what . . . now *there* was a question.

What on earth was she supposed to say the next time she saw him? How was he going to take her seriously if she fell into bed with him every time he smiled pretty? Because the man smiled pretty on a daily basis. He was born to smile pretty.

She leaned back in the seat and did her best to hold back tears. Lately she'd produced as much waterworks as a class 2 hurricane and her emotions were about as unpredictable. She had a good excuse, but still, where was her pride? Bad enough the man could make her come without breaking a sweat, worse if he also got to her heart.

Except her heart was the main problem. Her brain was firmly on the side of "Rafael, bad." Her body was weak, and despite physical evidence of the bones in question, spineless. Still, she could control her body simply by never being alone with him again. Wanting didn't necessarily have to lead to doing. But her heart. Her traitorous still-in-love-with-him heart . . . what was going to happen there?

She wanted him but knew she couldn't have him—at least not again. She hated him and still had to deal with him. She loved him and couldn't trust him.

She wasn't just fighting him, she was fighting herself, and that was one battle she didn't know how to win.

Mia found Joe looking for her when she got home.

"I wanted to give you an update on the—" he started as she climbed out of her car, then stopped. "You look like hell. What happened? Did Rafael threaten you?"

Not in the way Joe meant, she thought, trying to find the humor in the situation and failing badly.

"He didn't see Danny today," she said instead. "At least not for very long. Danny walked in on me having a meltdown and blamed his father. Basically the kid slammed the door in his face."

"I like his style," Joe said.

"It's a little volatile, but that comes with being four. I'm just a little shaky right now, but I'll get over it. What did you want to tell me?"

"That I've been doing regular equipment checks on the tracking system and it's fine. The alarm kicks in as soon as Danny leaves Marcelli land and the GPS instantly boots. It doesn't automatically work on the property, but we can always program it in manually. That wouldn't take much more than half an hour."

"In case Rafael kidnaps him and hides out in the vineyards? I can't see that happening."

"Me either, but it's an option." He stared at her. "Are you really okay?"

"No, but trust me, you don't want to know details."

He sucked in a breath as if bracing to have a fingernail or two removed. "I can listen."

For the first time that day, Mia laughed. "Darcy's done a very nice job with you. You're practically domesticated. But as much as I appreciate that very heartfelt offer, I'll pass. But I do have a question."

He nearly glowed with relief. "Sure. Ask me anything. I know a lot."

"And you're so modest." She hesitated, then asked, "Can men really change?"

The relief faded and his face took on a trapped expression.

"Dammit, Mia, don't drag me into this. As far as I'm concerned, your prince is a real bastard. I don't care if he changes, I just want to beat the crap out of him."

"Which I really appreciate. But that's not the point. He's saying he's sorry, and while I didn't believe him, I kind of do now. Or I want to, which isn't at all the same thing. Can he change?"

"Him specifically? I have no idea. Guys in general? Maybe. If they're motivated. Do I have to get into this with you?"

"Since you're the only brother I have, yes."

"Then it's possible, but not likely."

"How do I know for sure? How do I get proof?"

"Hell if I know. Look, you want to believe him because he's Danny's father and for a couple of other reasons I don't have to hear about. But proof, Mia? How do we prove anything in a relationship? It takes time. Is he going to be there when things get hard? Is he willing to make sacrifices? Are you equals?"

"I can't answer the first," she admitted. "The answer to the second two are probably no. How does a prince make sacrifices? Sleep on two-hundred-thread-count sheets instead of five? As for us being equals, in some ways we're not. He's royal. I'm the girl he knocked up. He certainly wasn't willing to come after me until he found out about his son. Apparently I'm not princess material."

Joe stared at her. "Do you want to be?"

"What? No. Of course not. Nothing about that life appeals to me."

"But you're pissed he didn't come claim you."

"Only in the sense that we'd had a relationship and he ended it by pretending to be dead."

"You have to give him points for creativity."

She punched him in the arm, then wished she hadn't when his muscles hurt her fist.

"I can almost understand that," she said as she rubbed her knuckles. "I mean, I was some American spy and he's got to marry Euro-trash, as Kelly would say. But there's a level of tackiness I just can't support. Plus there's the whole pretending to be in love with me so I'd marry him and he could take Danny. That's annoying."

When she thought of all the things he'd told her, she got mad all over again.

"Do you know he actually implied that I'm the reason he didn't get engaged to any of the appropriate women his father brought around. That he didn't realize it at the time but as soon as he and I were back together, he understood what had been going on."

"You think he's lying."

"As much as I think the sun is going to come up tomorrow."

Joe shifted. "The guy's not married."

"What? You're taking his side?"

"No way. I'm just pointing out that for whatever reason, the guy's not married. He's what, thirty?"

"Thirty-two," she said, fighting the urge to hit him again. Only, seriously, who would get hurt in *that* encounter?

"He didn't know about Danny, so he had to be under some serious pressure to produce an heir. Why isn't he married?"

"I'm sure there are a thousand reasons."

"Such as?"

"He's not willing to give up the babe banquet. Once he gets married, he'll be in a permanent relationship. Rafael doesn't like to cheat. I know it sounds strange, but it's true."

"He told you and you believed him?" Joe asked.

She rolled her eyes. "Yes, and yes. But I have confirmation from other sources. The woman he'd been with before me, plus when I Googled him, all the write-ups indicated he was pretty faithful to his girlfriends. Cheating was never listed as a reason for a breakup. I'm sure part of the reason he's resisted marriage is that the thought of having sex with the same person for the rest of his life is horrifying."

"Not so much as you might think," Joe told her with a grin. "Some of us like it."

She knew that her good-looking ex-Navy SEAL brother had never lacked for female companionship. Still . . . "I'm not sure your babe world compares with a royal one."

"You're saying he didn't come after you because he wasn't willing to give up the possibilities."

"Maybe," she said cautiously.

"So it wasn't personal. He could have been madly in love with you."

"Or not."

"Did you ask?"

She glared at him. "Ask him if he loved me? When, exactly, was I supposed to ask that and why would I believe him now?"

"I'm not saying you should, but the answer could be interesting."

Maybe to him, but to her, not so much. If she didn't care about Rafael, then the question wouldn't matter. But she did, and she didn't want to have him flat out tell her he'd never loved her. Thinking it herself was one thing—she could always secretly hope she was wrong. But once he said the words, all her illusions would be shattered forever.

"I need therapy," she muttered. "Long term. I might have to check myself in to a facility."

"We'll miss you, but I'm sure the Grands will visit regularly."

"Your support is overwhelming."

"I'm here to please." He put his arm around her. "Seriously, whatever you want, I'll do."

"Can you turn back time?"

"Except that."

"Then I guess I'm okay for now."

Rafael walked into Brenna's office without knocking. She looked up from her computer and rolled her eyes.

"You again."

He closed the door and crossed to her desk. "How do I prove myself to her?" he asked by way of greeting.

"The her in question being Mia?" Brenna asked.

He nodded. "She won't listen to me. She won't believe anything I say. How do I change her mind?"

She turned away from her computer screen and faced him. "The first thing that comes to mind is maybe you leaving her and Danny alone until the kid is eighteen."

She toyed with him, he thought impatiently. Didn't she understand he was serious? That he needed help? "Daniel is my son. I cannot ignore him."

"Your government will survive—"

"This isn't about my government. I have a child I did not know about. Now that I have found him, I will not let him go."

Brenna eyed him, then pointed at a chair. "You can sit down if you want."

He sat and leaned toward her. "Mia and I have to come to some agreement. I have already spoken to several members of parliament and they are writing a new law that gives Mia equal rights in Daniel's life. But that will take time. Weeks. Perhaps months. I am willing to wait—I will stay here as long as necessary—but something must change."

"I believe that something you're talking about is you."

He straightened. "What do you mean?"

"Here we go," she said wearily. "The whole 'I'm Crown Prince Blah de blah. You are nothing but dust beneath my feet.'" She sipped her coffee. "It gets old."

He had a feeling she was not referring to her drink.

"I *am* the crown prince."

"No one is unclear on your title. So what? I'm married, but I don't go around referring to myself as the wife of anyone. I'm my own person, separate from that. You're still Rafael, crown prince or not."

"I am not a separate person. My future has created the man I am today."

"See, that's the problem. If you had a little less prince and a little more man, you'd have a shot."

"I do not understand."

"Let's say you and Mia had just met and dated and you weren't a prince. You were just a regular guy. You broke up, she went back to America, and you didn't see each other for five years. Then, suddenly, you discover she had a son, but she had never told you. She didn't want to, didn't think you'd be a good father, whatever. What if she had willfully withheld that information from you? When you found out and confronted her, she had a lot of good reasons, but nothing you really bought. Would you ever trust her again?"

He did not want to answer Brenna's question. He didn't want to understand the analogy. He wanted to tell her that his circumstances were different. That he hadn't done it on purpose . . . only he had. He had let Mia leave Calandria thinking he was dead.

"It was easier that way," he said quietly. "I adored her. She was lovely—bright, beautiful, fearless. But an American with no important family."

"You're rambling, so I won't take issue with that last bit," Brenna said, "but don't push it too far."

"There are traditions," he continued. "Expectations."

"Is one of them for you to wear a condom so there isn't an unexpected pregnancy?"

"I told you. I had used . . ."

Protection. That was the next word. He'd always been careful. Always. Except for two times. The last two times with Mia.

She could be pregnant. Even this second, there could be another child growing inside of her.

He was torn, wanting to experience every moment he'd missed with Daniel, and uneasy at the thought of more complications in an already difficult situation.

"Earth to Rafael," Brenna said. "Where did you go?"

"I must make her understand I am sincere," he said quietly. "That I understand things now."

"Do you love her?"

Love? "It is not relevant."

"That's where you're wrong," she told him. "Love is the biggest relevance there is. It would help a lot, as would humility. Putting her on a stamp would work, too."

"You're mocking me."

"A little. Just for sport." She shrugged. "I like you, Rafael. I don't want to, but I do. Still, I would never advise my sister to trust you again. How could I? You blew it so badly, I don't know how you can recover. It would take a step of faith, and I don't know if Mia's that much of a believer. I'm sorry." She frowned. "Wow—I really *am* sorry."

He had been hoping for a miracle and she didn't have one to offer. "I appreciate how honest you have been."

"It's my strong suit. I live to tell other people what's wrong with them. Come anytime."

Rafael helped Daniel from his pony.

"You are doing well," he told the boy. "I see much improvement."

"I want to ride more," Daniel insisted, and stomped his foot. "Take me out more."

"This would be the imperious child," Mia said lightly. "He's closely related to the overtired one. I like the funny one and the loving ones much better."

"There's just me," Daniel told her. "I'm your only little boy." He frowned. "No more little boys."

"Wouldn't you like a little brother or sister?" Rafael asked, keeping a close eye on Mia as he spoke, but she didn't react.

"No! Just me."

Daniel stalked off to sit on the bottom step by the back door. Oliver led Gaspare away.

"I believe he gets his ill temper from you," Rafael said. "I was a most good-natured child."

She laughed. "Oh, please. You were imperious, too. I'd bet money on it."

She wore a pale summer dress and had bare feet. The loose fabric made him think of what was underneath. Of what had happened the last time they had been together. He wanted her, yet he sensed that making love with her again wasn't the answer. In truth, he didn't know what to do.

Uncertainty was not a familiar or comfortable state of being.

"Mia," he said, his voice low. "There is something we must discuss. About being together."

"No," she said firmly. "It happened, it's over. There will be no recaps or repeats."

"There is another issue that concerns me, although the topics are related."

"What on earth . . . Oh." Her mouth curved up in a smile. "I don't remember you being so carefree before. One could say you were almost fanatical about protection." She glanced at Daniel, but the boy was busy pouting and grinding his toe into the lawn.

"I agree. It has always been an issue with me, just to avoid certain complications."

"And yet here we are, filled with complications."

"Filled?"

"I meant Danny," she said. "It's fine." She moved close and whispered, "I'm on the pill, and it's not something I ever forget to take."

He braced himself for the wave of relief, but it never came. Instead there was a small twinge of regret. Why? Because Mia's being pregnant would have forced them into marriage?

Or would it? Mia was just stubborn enough to refuse him.

He reached for her hand. "How can I convince you I am truly sorry? What words are there? What actions?"

She jerked her fingers free. "None. I don't mean to be cruel. I'm only speaking the truth. There is nothing you can ever say or do to convince me that you're doing anything but playing a game."

He stiffened but didn't retreat. "I will not give up."

"I feel bad, Rafael. I don't want to be a complete bitch. I know about the law you're trying to change. I know that's for me. When it goes through and I've had a couple of lawyers read it over, then we can talk. I won't be unreasonable. In time, Danny has to learn that being your heir is about more than giving orders and getting his way. But not for a while. Not while he's still this young."

"I can't be gone forever."

"I won't let you take him."

"Then come with him. Live with me in Calandria. We can be a family."

"What will your future princess have to say about that?"

"There is no future princess, Mia. Unless you would like the job. We could be married."

He braced himself for the explosion, but there wasn't one. Instead she sighed.

"You're one for surprises, I'll give you that," she said. "Let me guess. It would be a marriage of convenience. We get to share Danny, we have the advantages of . . ." She glanced at her son, then murmured, "The advantages of chemistry without all those messy emotions."

As she spoke, he realized she was wrong. He didn't want to avoid messy emotions. He wanted more. He wanted her temper along with her passion. He wanted her moods, her craziness, her quirks, her beliefs.

Before he could say so, Grandma Tessa opened the back door. "Mia, you have a call from the law school." She saw Rafael and frowned. "I'll stay with him if you want to take the call."

Mia glanced at him and he raised both hands. "I give you my word that I will not attempt to kidnap our son while you're gone."

"I didn't think you would."

"Now *you* are the liar."

"Rafael . . ."

"Take your call. I will be here when you return."

She went into the house. Grandma Tessa came out onto the porch and stood with her arms folded across her chest. Rafael smiled at her.

Daniel stood and crossed to him. "I want to go riding some more."

"Tomorrow," Rafael promised. "Your mother will take you."

"Mom will just say no," Daniel said glumly. "I want to ride when *I* want." The boy leaned against him. "Daddy, can I come live with you?"

Under other circumstances, the question would have pleased him. However, he was now familiar with the mercurial nature of a four-year-old's emotions.

Feeling Grandma Tessa's sharp glare, he said, "You live with your mother and her family. I know you love them all very much."

Daniel stepped back and shook his head. "I want to live with you. I want to ride my pony all the time. I'm the heir."

Rafael knew he had no one but himself to blame for the "heir" nightmare.

"I'm the heir," Daniel repeated, then began to cry.

Grandma Tessa took a step toward them, but Rafael waved her back. Then he dropped to his knees and hugged his son.

"You have had so many changes in such a short period of time," he told the boy. "I think we all need to take a little time and get used to them before doing anything drastic like moving away from home. Besides"—he kissed the top of the boy's head—"your mother would be lost without you. She loves you so much."

Daniel sniffed. "She would cry if I was gone."

"Yes, and that would make you feel bad. Do you like making your mother cry? I never did."

Daniel stared into his eyes. "You could come live here, like before. That was nice."

"It was nice. But remember all the changes? Let's get used to what we have now."

He heard a sound and saw Mia standing next to her grandmother. There were tears in both women's eyes.

He hadn't said the words for her, nor did her tears matter. She'd already made her case very clear. She didn't trust and she didn't want to trust him. He had come so very far only to realize he had lost.

He kissed Daniel again, then stood. "I should be getting back," he said. "I'll see you tomorrow."

Mia groaned at the thought of an eight o'clock class, but it was the only time the stupid subject was offered and she couldn't risk missing out. She entered the number into the box on the computer screen and hit the Enter key. The screen cleared, then offered to let her print out her fall schedule.

She turned on the printer and tried to work up some enthusiasm about her upcoming semester. She was nearly done. Shouldn't she be thrilled at the prospect of finally getting a job in the real world? After all, her compromise with Rafael might have her working in Rome or Paris.

She tried to convince herself that easy access to Italian shoes was going to be fabulous, only she knew she was lying.

"It's all his fault," she whispered to the empty room. Ever since Rafael had left, she hadn't been able to think about anything but his backhanded proposal.

Did the man really think she was willing to play that game again with him? Hadn't she made it clear she would never, ever trust him?

Apparently in his world things like trust didn't matter. He was willing to do anything to be with his son, even marry her. Well, golly, allow her to pause right here and feel the love.

A sharp pain cut through her. All the sarcasm in the world couldn't disguise how much she hurt. Love. Rafael didn't love her. She was a necessary evil in his plan to be a father. Worst of all, she couldn't blame him. Because if their roles were reversed, she would be willing to marry him just to be near Danny.

But she didn't want a duty proposal. That was almost more insulting than a pity one. She wanted the impossible. She wanted him to love her.

"Grow up," she told herself. "Men like him don't fall in love, and if they do, it's not with women like me." Regular women. Oh, sure, there was the whole Grace Kelly thing, but seriously, who would consider her normal?

The library door opened and Grammy M poked her head in. "Is Danny here?" she asked.

"What? No. I saw him about an hour ago. He was watching a video and said he'd come in when he was finished." Her stomach clenched. "He's not in the family room?"

Minutes later it was clear he wasn't anywhere in the house. The Grands were hysterical and Mia wasn't far behind.

"Call Joe," she told them as she threw open the back door and ran outside.

"Danny!" she yelled. "Danny?"

There was no answer.

This wasn't right. He never went outside without telling someone. He never went anywhere on his own. He was a good boy who loved hanging out with his family.

She raced around the lawn, checked the garage, then came to a stop in front of Gaspare's makeshift stable. The pony was gone.

She remembered how Danny had wanted to keep riding. How he'd had a fit about stopping. Oh, God. If he'd taken the pony, he could be anywhere. He could—

Rafael! Danny had wanted them to all be a family again.

But he didn't know his way to the hotel. Sure, he'd seen it but . . .

Panic exploded. He might know enough to try. What if he had? It was hot and he was so small. The hotel was eight or nine miles away, and between here and there were acres of vineyard and a four-lane highway. There were a million places for a little boy to get lost, or hurt.

Or worse.

18

The fear lived inside of Mia, growing, sucking her strength, making her want to fall to the ground and beg for mercy. Only there was no one to bargain with. She left the prayers to the Grands and their rosaries. She preferred action.

"How long?" she demanded.

Joe typed on the computer. "Fifteen minutes, tops."

"It's hot," she reminded him. "Too hot for a little boy to be out riding. The best we can figure is he's been gone an hour."

She tried to stick to facts because thinking about what could be happening to her son could very easily drive her to madness. She paced the length of Joe's office, then looked out the window.

"Rafael will be here soon," her brother told her.

"I wasn't sure he should come," she said. "Maybe he would do better to search the roads."

"It's too early. There's no way that pony is going to make it through the vineyard in an hour. I'm guessing Danny is lost in the vines, and as soon as the GPS is up and running, we'll find him. Go back to the house, get your supplies, and wait for Rafael. I'll call you in less than fifteen minutes."

Mia nodded, then ran to her car. Three minutes later she was at the house.

The Grands had already prepared a backpack containing a first-aid kit, water, and cut-up fruit. There was also a hat for Danny, to help keep the sun off him.

"You'll find him," Tessa said through her tears. "I've been praying."

"We both have. God protects the wee ones," Grammy M told her.

Mia wasn't so sure God protected little boys who willfully ran away, but she couldn't say for sure either way.

"Keep praying," she said. Maybe it would help.

Tessa touched her arm. "We're sorry."

Mia paused in the act of dropping her cell phone into her shorts front pocket. "What? Sorry?"

She looked at their stricken faces, not liking how fear aged them. "No," she said firmly. "This isn't your fault. Danny was watching a video when I went in the library to finish my on-line registration. I should have checked on him. I didn't know he was still mad about Rafael. If anyone is to blame, it's me."

"You are not to blame."

The statement came from behind her. She turned and saw Rafael standing in the doorway.

"I am the one who encouraged him to do as he pleased," Rafael continued. "He ran off because he is the heir, and the blame is mine."

Without thinking, Mia rushed toward him. He caught her against his body and held her tight.

"I am sorry," he whispered in her ear. "So sorry."

His arms were strong and supported her. He was Prince Rafael of Calandria, she thought. He would insist on finding his son. He would move heaven and earth to make that happen. For once, Rafael's imperious determination was a good thing.

"It's not your fault either," she said. "He got mad. He acted up. Now we have to find him."

"We will," he promised, and she believed him.

Just then, the back door burst open and Brenna came in with an armful of maps. As Rafael and Mia stepped apart, she put them on the kitchen table and unrolled them.

"Once Joe gets the coordinates, I'll tell you what vineyard that is." She traced the road that led to the hotel. "This is where he wanted to go, but hey, the kid is four. Who knows where he actually went."

Rafael bent over the maps. "There are dozens of acres."

"Hundreds," Brenna said unhappily. "Especially if you consider the Wild Sea vineyards butt right up to ours. If Danny headed that way, he would never find his way out on his own."

She squeezed Mia's arm. "But he's got the tracking thingy on, right? So it's okay."

Mia glanced outside and wished it were a little less hot. The weather might be perfect for grapes, but it would be hell on a little boy trapped in the sun.

Rafael traced possible paths. When Mia's cell phone rang, she grabbed it.

"You have him?" she demanded.

"Yes. Put Brenna on. I'll give her the coordinates, then meet you."

Mia handed over the cell phone. Brenna listened, then looked at the map.

"Okay, yeah. I've got it. Uh-huh." She glanced at Rafael. "Are the moron twins joining us?"

He grimaced. "Yes, Oliver and Umberto are waiting by the car."

"We have a team," Brenna said into the phone. "Uh-huh. Sure."

She hung up and handed Mia the phone. "Joe has the location. He's going to stay where he is and monitor the GPS. He'll call every ten minutes with updates. We'll take carts as close as we can, then walk in." Brenna smiled. "We found him, Mia. He'll be fine."

"I'll believe that when I'm holding him."

Five minutes later they were in three golf carts and heading out into the heart of the Marcelli vineyards. The sun beat down mercilessly. Mia drove, closely following Brenna's cart, while Oliver and Umberto maneuvered the last one. Rafael sorted through the contents of the backpack.

"Your grandmothers have thought of everything," he said.

"They feel horrible about what happened. I hate them blaming themselves."

"As do I."

She glanced at him. "I meant what I said. I don't blame you."

"You do not have to. I still blame myself. If he is hurt . . ."

His voice trailed off. Mia didn't want to think about that either. She wanted to find Danny perfectly healthy and safe, and very sorry for what he'd done.

"Thank God for the tracking system," she said. "If he didn't have on that bracelet, I have no idea how we'd find him."

"So my deception has one bright spot," Rafael said grimly.

"Not just that one," she told him. "I can see you're trying to change and I appreciate it."

"But you still do not trust me."

"At least I didn't assume you'd kidnapped him. That's something."

She slammed on the brakes after Brenna did the same. Even as everyone scrambled out of the carts, Mia pulled out the cell phone and tossed it to Rafael.

She had to. She couldn't talk, couldn't breathe, could only panic when she saw the pony standing alone in the center of the path.

"Are you sure about the location?" Rafael asked into the phone. "We have found the pony and Danny is not here."

He listened, then looked at Mia. "Joe still shows Danny about a half mile from here." His face paled.

"What?" Mia demanded. "What?"

"Danny's not moving. He hasn't moved since Joe first found him."

"Oh, God," Mia said, pressing a hand to her stomach. "Oh, God."

Rafael hung up and handed her the phone. "We must hurry," he yelled to the others. "Umberto, the pony."

The bodyguard raced to Gaspare and led him out of the way. Rafael guided Mia into the passenger seat, then pushed the backpack into her arms and got behind the wheel. Brenna took off at full speed and he did the same. Oliver came up behind.

"He's fine," Rafael said, as much to convince himself

as Mia. "It is very hot. He stopped to rest and Gaspare ran off. That is all."

Mia rocked in the seat. "Please, God, let him be all right. Please."

He heard the pain in her voice and felt it himself. At that moment, he would have given anything to have Danny in his arms. All his money, all his privilege was useless in finding one small, lost boy.

A few minutes later, Brenna came to a stop. She jumped out of the cart and pointed to a vineyard.

"In there," she yelled. "Joe has the coordinates, but we don't exactly have street signs, so we're going to have to walk through. It's this vineyard, though. It has to be."

Rafael took the backpack and stepped out. Mia hurried to his side.

"We'll split up," she said. "Brenna, go with Oliver. You have a cell phone, right?"

Both held one out.

Rafael reached for Mia's hand. "We will go this way," he said, pointing to the right section of the vineyard.

Mia squeezed his fingers. "What if he fell off? What if he's hurt?"

"Then we will take him to the hospital."

He spoke with a calmness he didn't feel, but there was no point in upsetting her more.

"Danny," she yelled as they stepped between the rows of vines heavy with ripe grapes. "Danny, where are you?"

"Danny," he called, hearing Brenna and Umberto in the distance. "Danny."

He paused to listen. There were only the sounds of insects and the rapid beating of his heart. If something had happened to his son . . .

He pushed the thought away. He would not consider it. Danny was fine. He had to be fine. Rafael could not imagine any other possibility.

They walked deeper into the vines. Both called. Brenna's and Oliver's voices came from farther and farther away. Beside him, Mia stumbled, then began to cry.

"Why isn't he answering? What if he has sunstroke? It's hot and he's so small."

"We will find him," he promised, then yelled, "Danny? Can you hear me?"

For a moment, he thought he'd heard something. Mia stared at him.

"Was that a cry?"

They listened again. Sure enough, in the distance came a small sound.

"Danny?" Mia screamed. "Danny, is that you?"

Rafael began to run. He pulled her along with him. "Danny," he called. "Danny, answer us. Answer us so we can find you."

"Over here. I'm over here. Mommy? D-Daddy?"

Rafael heard the voice more clearly now and he knew his son was crying.

"He'll be fine," he promised Mia and himself. "He's just scared."

He saw a flash of color and broke through one of the neat rows. Danny sat in a small patch of shade. His T-shirt was torn, his face dusty and red, and his eyes filled with tears.

"Danny!" Mia dropped to the ground and hugged the boy. Rafael sank next to her and put his arms around both of them.

"Are you all right?" she asked. "Are you hurt?"

"My head hurts and I'm thirsty."

"Of course," she murmured. "We have water."

But she didn't let him go. Rafael slipped off the backpack and pulled out the water. He gave one bottle to Mia, who offered it to the boy, but only let him take small sips, and used the other to dampen one of the washcloths the Grands had packed.

"Put this on the back of his neck," he instructed. "It will help cool him down. He might have heatstroke."

Mia did as he told her. He saw her hands were shaking. His weren't that steady either. Relief joined with the fear of what could have been.

Danny stared at them both. "I'm sorry," he whispered. "I was bad."

"Yes, you were," Rafael told him. "We'll talk about that later. Right now, let's get you back to the house."

He opened Mia's cell phone and called Brenna. Next he phoned Joe. Once they had been notified, he picked up Danny and carried him back to the cart. Mia walked with him, constantly touching Danny's hand and arm, as if reassuring herself that the boy was really all right.

Rafael understood her actions. Had he not been carrying the child, he would have needed reassurance as well. Danny was no longer just his heir. Danny was a piece of Rafael, as much as his arm or his thoughts or his heart. They could never be apart. Not him from Danny or Danny from his mother.

Which made for an interesting quandary.

"Wine and cookies," Katie said as she sat in the chair by the desk. "This is the good life." She nodded at Mia's barely touched glass. "You okay?"

"No," Mia admitted. "Every time I think about what nearly happened, I start to shake."

"It'll take a couple of days to feel better," Francesca told her. "The doctor said he was fine and Danny said he was fine. You need to start believing that."

"When I think about what could have happened . . ." Not that she wanted to, but she was having trouble thinking about anything else.

"Let it go," Brenna said. "We found him. You may not be drinking, but I am. Pass the wine, please."

Francesca handed the bottle over to her twin. They were sprawled on Mia's bed. Mia sat in the window seat and did her best to forget the horrible afternoon.

"You guys didn't have to come all the way over here," she told her sisters. "Katie, that's such a long drive."

"I was already on my way," Katie admitted. "More details for David's wedding. But I'm happy to stay and offer support. You must have been terrified."

"That's as good a word as any," Mia admitted. "I felt desperate and unable to cope. I know none of you like him, but Rafael was really there for me today."

To her surprise, her sisters didn't say anything. Instead they exchanged odd glances.

"What?" she demanded.

Brenna shrugged. "We don't hate Rafael so much. You're right. He was great today. He even called the kid Danny. Who knew a royal could unbend that much?"

Mia had noticed that as well, but in the trauma of the moment, she hadn't thought to mention it.

"I appreciate what he did with Kelly," Francesca admitted. "He saw what none of us could. What if he hadn't been here? How long would Kelly have gone on hating her life because she was too embarrassed to tell us the truth?"

"Good question." Brenna cleared her throat. "You know, he's, ah, well, come to see me a couple of times."

This did cause Mia to gulp her wine. "Why?"

"To talk about you and how to make things right. The first time I told him exactly what I thought of him."

"Wish I'd been there," Katie said with a grin.

"Me too," Mia said. Brenna being totally honest was always entertaining.

"Yeah, it was fun," Brenna told them. "But the second time he was . . . I don't know. More sincere, I guess. I'm kinda willing to give him the benefit of the doubt. Not totally. Just a little."

Who would have guessed, Mia thought. She looked at Katie. "What's your excuse? He hasn't saved your world."

Her oldest sister smiled. "How can I hate the guy my baby sister is in love with?"

Ouch. "You noticed that, huh?" Mia had been hoping she'd kept her feelings to herself.

"You can't turn off love," Katie reminded her. "You've loved him for over five years and you two have been apart. Being together would either destroy your feelings or make them stronger. It didn't seem to me you were any less interested."

"Great. So he's not horrible all the time and I'm still in love with him. Now what?"

She thought of mentioning his "marriage of convenience" proposal, but decided it would only make things more complicated.

"You have to decide if you trust him," Francesca said. "He should have to earn it, of course, but are you willing to let him try?"

"I don't know," Mia admitted. "How can I make myself that vulnerable again? Okay, he's getting the law changed in Calandria, which means he won't be able to keep me from Danny, but still. What's real and what's lies? How do I know he's not playing me for a fool again? He was a total sleaze."

"Total," Brenna said.

"But he's Danny's father."

"And he's not going away," Katie said. "You're stuck with him. So how stuck do you want to be?"

Mia leaned back against the window. "I don't know," she admitted. "My head tells me one thing and my heart says the opposite. Which should I listen to? How do I figure it all out?"

"You need a sign," Francesca said.

Brenna rolled her eyes. "Gee, Dr. Marcelli, is that your professional, psychologist opinion?"

"Sure." Francesca smiled. "It's as good a way to pick as any."

"I had a lot more respect for our higher education system before she said that," Brenna muttered.

Mia laughed. "Okay, fine. What kind of sign?"

"A really big one?" Katie offered.

They were all laughing when the loud noise cut through the quiet of the night. Darkness faded into an ever-growing bright white light.

"Oh, my God," Brenna said as she scrambled to her feet. "It really *is* a sign."

The four of them put down their glasses and ran downstairs. The Grands were already there, as was Rafael, who was spending the evening with Danny.

They stepped outside and saw a large helicopter setting down on the driveway.

"That can't be good," Mia muttered, wondering if something had happened to Darcy's father. She couldn't imagine anything but presidential disaster bringing a helicopter.

She heard another engine and turned to see Joe driving toward the house.

"Do you know about this?" she asked over the rising noise of the helicopter.

"No, but I'll guess he does."

He pointed at Rafael. Mia felt herself go numb.

"No," she screamed as she ran back to the small crowd. She shook Rafael by the arm. "You can't. You can't. I won't let you."

"Mommy, see the helopter? It's so big."

She reached down and picked up her son. "You can't," she repeated.

Rafael grabbed her. "I'm not. I swear. I have nothing to do with this. Mia, look at me. I'm not taking Danny away."

She tried to think, tried to breathe. Where could she go? How fast could she run?

The helicopter touched down. As the wind kicked up, she pressed Danny's face into her shoulder and wondered if it was possible to get to her car in time. Only her keys were inside the house and if she stopped to get them, it would be too late.

"Mommy, don't be scared," Danny said as he peered over her shoulder. "I won't let the helopter hurt you. Oh, look. There's people."

She turned to watch two soldiers step off the helicopter. Next a set of steps appeared. Overhead, the blades slowed to a stop.

Mia stood there clutching her son as an older man walked off the helicopter and onto her front lawn. She'd never seen him in person before, but she recognized him from the pictures.

King Xavier of Calandria.

"Rafael, there you are," the king said. "You are well?"

"Yes, Father."

The king glanced at all of them, then settled his gaze on Danny. Mia took a step back.

The king nodded at Danny. "Is that him?"

Rafael took a step forward. "Yes, he is my son."

"Good. Take him and we will leave."

19

"Liar!" Mia screamed as she thrust Danny at Brenna, who stood closest, then charged Rafael. "Liar. You sonofabitch."

She clawed at his face, and when he easily avoided her assault, she pounded on his chest.

"You lied."

She couldn't believe it. Again. She'd been a fool again and this time the price would be her son.

"I trusted you," she sobbed. "It was all lies."

He grabbed her wrists. "I did not lie. I have no part in this. Mia, listen to me."

Mia tried to twist free. She looked at Joe. "Don't let him take Danny."

Umberto and Oliver hovered in the background, but Rafael didn't call them closer. However, that didn't stop the king's guards from looking menacing.

"Enough of this," Rafael said. He released Mia and pushed her toward Joe. Her brother caught her easily. Brenna carried over Danny. Joe took the boy.

"No one is taking Danny," Rafael told his father. "We

are not taking him away. Not without the consent of his mother, and she will never give it."

The king glared at him. "I have been patient long enough. The boy belongs in Calandria, as do you. Come with me now."

"No," Rafael said calmly. "Not without Mia, and until the law is changed, she will not set foot on Calandrian soil. I will not allow it."

"*You* will not allow it," the king repeated, obviously furious. "Until I die, I am ruler of Calandria."

"That doesn't mean you're right about this, Father."

Mia didn't know what to think. Was it possible that Rafael was really taking her side? That he was standing up to the king for her? Protecting her and Danny?

"The child belongs with his people," the king said coldly. "He needs to be trained."

"He needs his mother," Rafael said flatly. "He needs to grow up knowing he is loved. It is easy to learn a history of a people, but much harder to replace family. He's only a boy. I will not allow his life to be destroyed because you want to turn your grandson into a miniature version of yourself."

The king stiffened. "You forget yourself."

"I remember everything," Rafael said. "I remember more than you realize. I was wrong to come here and attempt to deceive these people. I was wrong not to speak to Mia in good faith. The law will be changed, and when it is, she and I will come to terms."

"You allow yourself to be dictated to by a mere woman?" the king bellowed.

"Hey," Katie snapped. "Watch it. Not just any woman. Not a mere woman. A Marcelli."

Rafael glanced at Mia and smiled. "She is right. A Marcelli. Smart, funny, irreverent, beautiful, and capable of so much love." He returned his attention to his father. "She is far too verbal, but it is a flaw I can live with."

Mia hated that her brain, which so far had been the rational one in all this, instantly focused on the "beautiful" part of his sentence.

"Rafael, everything about this situation is unacceptable," the king announced

"Then you will need to learn to compromise. Danny stays with his mother and I stay with them both."

Stay? Mia stared at him. "You're staying?"

"No, he is not," the king said, glaring at her. "He belongs in Calandria."

"I belong with my family." Rafael took her hands in his. "I belong with you, Mia. With you and Danny." He stared into her eyes. "I have changed. I know you do not trust me, and I accept that I am the reason. I will have to earn my way back into your good graces. I am more than willing to do so. I will wait patiently and then perform whatever tasks you set out for me. I want you to believe that I am the right man for you."

She'd spent a lot of the past couple of months in a state of disbelief, but this was certainly going for the record.

"I don't understand," she said.

"Nor do I," the king announced. "You are Crown Prince Rafael of Calandria. You do not humble yourself in front of a woman."

"You are wrong, Father," Rafael said, never looking away from Mia. "I humble myself in front of *this* woman. Have you ever wondered why I refused to marry those others? Did it ever occur to you that the reason was my heart was engaged elsewhere? I didn't understand until I came here and nearly lost the only thing that has ever mattered."

She hung on to his hands because the world had started to spin. There were no words, no way to do anything but stare at him and pray this was all really happening.

"I will stand against my father for you," he said sincerely. "For you and for Danny. I will be there for you, and seek your counsel, and love you for always, Mia. I love you."

At that exact moment, the helicopter blades shut down and his words echoed in the sudden silence.

"I will not have this," King Xavier said. "Rafael, take the boy and get on the helicopter immediately."

Rafael ignored him. "I see doubt in your eyes," he told her. "I know why. I have earned that doubt. There is no reason for you to believe me now. Just accept that I am staying."

"You are not staying," the king said.

"Can someone shut him up?" Brenna asked.

"It's so romantic," Grammy M breathed. "Oh, Mia, it's so romantic."

"I don't know," Mia admitted as she pulled free of his touch and stepped back. "There's too much happening."

"You see," the king said. "She doesn't even want you."

Rafael ignored him. "Mia, I understand. No one is asking you to say anything. I want you to know I love you and Danny."

Mia hated how much she wanted to believe him. He was saying all the right things—especially the part about not going back to Calandria until the law had changed. But what about Danny being the heir? And how was she ever supposed to take that step of faith?

She looked at Katie. "What do you think?"

"That your life is never boring." Katie held up both hands. "I'm not weighing in on this. Are you crazy?"

"You must have an opinion."

"I'm keeping it to myself."

Mia looked at Brenna, who had never been one to stay silent. Her sister sighed.

"He's not a slug," Brenna admitted reluctantly. "I thought he was, but he isn't. He's standing up to his father and when Daddy's the king, that can't be easy. I don't think he's lying. Xavier there looks ready to have a heart attack and no one is that good an actor. I say give him a chance."

The king glared at Brenna, "I will have you arrested."

She smiled. "You'd have to catch me first, your highness."

Mia looked at Francesca. "And you?"

"He was great about Kelly. I think being with Danny has changed him. Is it enough? Only you can answer that, Mia."

Grandma Tessa sniffed. "I still don't know about him. He hurt you, Mia, but when he thought Danny was lost, he was devastated."

Mia looked at Joe. He shook his head. "I'm only on your side, kid. Rafael doesn't matter to me."

"You will stop this immediately," the king demanded. "You will not speak of my son or myself this way. It is unspeakably rude."

Grandma Tessa moved toward him. "What would you

call swooping down in the night and trying to steal a child? Good manners?"

The guards took a step forward, then hesitated, as if unwilling to take on a woman pushing eighty.

"This is not for you to decide," the king said. "Daniel is heir to the throne. He belongs in Calandria and he is going there now."

"No he's not," Rafael said. He looked at Mia and smiled. "I know what to say," he told her. "I know how to make you believe."

She was torn between wanting his words to be true and knowing it wasn't possible.

"Rafael, don't do something you will regret," the king said.

Rafael took her hand and then faced his father. "I have regrets, but none of them have anything to do with this. You only want Danny because he's your heir. Allow me to solve that problem. I, Rafael, Crown Prince of Calandria, do hereby abdicate as heir to the throne."

Mia's mind went blank. "You can't," she and the king said at the same time.

"I can and I do," he told his father. "I am tired of living with all the rules and restrictions of office. I am not interested in an arranged marriage. I love this woman and I will spend the rest of my life proving myself worthy of her. I'm hoping that, in time, she'll be willing to marry me. I told you, Father, I'm staying here."

Mia felt her heart stop. As far as gestures went, this one ranked right up there with going through time. "You'd give up the throne for me?" she asked, her voice a squeak.

"You are more than worth it."

She wasn't sure about that.

The king's face turned the color of a tomato. "Rafael, you dishonor me and our country. No woman is worth the throne."

"You're wrong. I'm not the first man to walk away from his duty because of love."

The king glared. "Do not compare yourself to an English ruler." His eyes narrowed. "What is it about American women?"

"We're sassy," Francesca said.

Rafael turned to Mia. "If I'm not the heir, there's no danger to Danny. I can stay here permanently."

"Oh, you will get a job and live in the suburbs?" the king asked contemptuously.

"Perhaps."

Mia pressed her hand to his chest. "I can't let you do this. You can't walk away from your heritage. Being the crown prince is who you are."

"Who I am is the man who loves you," he told her gently.

"You will be king," his father insisted. "You must be. There is no one else."

"My cousin."

"Quentin? A gay clothing designer?"

Brenna snorted. "There's a coronation I'd want to see."

"Mom loves his clothes," Katie whispered to Mia.

Mia ignored everyone else and stared at Rafael.

"You can't do this. You can't give up your future."

He kissed her. "I give up only my past. You are my future. I think I would like to study medicine and be a doctor."

"Never!" his father yelled.

"Rafael, no," she told him, sure she would wake up at any second. There was no way this was happening. "Trust me, you're not going to like living in the ordinary world."

"I will enjoy it as long as I have you."

She bit her lower lip. "I don't know what to think, let alone say."

"Arrest her!" the king yelled, pointing at Mia. "Arrest this woman. All of this is her fault."

The guards didn't move toward her. If anything, they seemed to be inching toward the helicopter.

Rafael sighed. "Father, you cannot arrest Mia. You're on American soil and she has broken no laws. Even if she had, I would not allow it. You have lost. I'm staying here. Quentin will be king next."

"Never! You are my son. I command you to return to Calandria with me."

Rafael shrugged. "I'm sorry, Father. No. You made me choose and I have made my choice. I want to marry Mia and be Danny's father."

"She hasn't even said she loves you. She hasn't accepted. You've been the one baring your soul and what has she done?"

Rafael smiled at Mia. "I owe her."

"You are Crown Prince Rafael of Calandria! You owe her nothing."

Mia pressed a hand to her stomach. It was all too much. "I think I'm going to be sick."

"Then we should get you inside." Rafael put his arm around her. "Father, we will end this discussion for now. Perhaps we can talk later, when we are more calm."

"I am the king. You do not dismiss me. I dismiss you."

Katie shook her head. "I'll bet he was a real tight-ass when you were growing up."

"Arrest that woman, too!" Xavier insisted. "Arrest them all."

"He was a good king," Rafael said. "But a distant father."

"I'm sure it's how he was raised," Francesca said. "People often find it difficult to break with tradition. It's comfortable and there's a sense of guilt in forging a different path after so many years. In your case it would be what? A thousand?"

"Something like that."

They all started for the house. The king continued to rage, but no one paid attention.

Once they were inside, Brenna opened bottles of Marcelli wine. The Grands did another of their instant meals-on-demand tricks. In a matter of minutes food covered the kitchen table. Mia sat with Rafael on her left and Danny on her lap.

"Are you really staying?" Danny asked tentatively.

"Yes," Rafael said. "I will always be in your life."

"Are you going to live here?"

Mia wasn't sure how he would answer the question, but Rafael jumped right in.

"Not for a while. Your mother and I have to get to know each other again. That takes time. But we're still a family. You're my son and I love you very much."

"Do you love Mommy?"

"Yes."

Mia still had trouble getting her mind around that one.

"You abdicated," she said.

"I am aware of that."

"How could you? You're supposed to rule your country."

He shrugged. "I'm not losing you, Mia. I have waited my entire life to find you. What is a kingdom when compared with that?"

"It's a kingdom! It's being king. Your face on stamps and having buildings named after you."

"None of that is important."

"Fine. Then it's about fulfilling your destiny. You were born to rule. Your people deserve a good leader. Do you really think Quentin is up to the task?"

"He can learn."

"But—"

Rafael leaned in and kissed her. "Stop. If I am an ordinary man, you will see me as someone worthy of a second chance. As Prince Rafael, I will always be the man who deceived you. I am content."

She found herself getting lost in his eyes. On a scale of one to ten, abdicating had to at least be in the twenties.

He picked up her hand and kissed her palm. "I will court you, Mia Marcelli. I will be here no matter what. I will love you with a devotion that leaves you breathless. When you are ready to trust me again, tell me, and then I will convince you to marry me."

There were five other women in the kitchen and Mia heard every single one of them sigh. She would have, too, except she was already breathless.

"Rafael," she whispered. "You know I never stopped loving you."

"I know. I was a fool to let you go and a bigger fool to try to trick you. My time would have been much better spent realizing what was in my own heart and then convincing you we belonged together."

"I'm sort of convinced."

"Good."

Grandma Tessa reached for Danny. "What would you like to eat?" she asked. "Some pasta? It's your favorite."

"That one," he said, pointing. "Mommy? Daddy? Where are you going?"

"They're just going upstairs," Grammy M said as she pulled out a chair for the boy. "To, ah, talk."

Katie poured him some milk. "They'll be talking awhile. But that's okay. After we eat, we can watch a video. Or play a game."

"Can I go talk with them?"

Francesca smiled. "Not this time. It's grown-up talking."

"Talking, huh?" Brenna said with a grin. "Who would have thought it would come to this?"

Grammy M sighed. "I always liked that man."

Tessa rolled her eyes. "If the devil had a title, you'd like him as well."

"That I would."

Hours later, when the house was quiet and stars filled the sky, Rafael leaned over Mia and kissed her.

"You're not saying much," he told her.

"I don't know what *to* say. You abdicated, said you loved me, proposed, and then walked out on your father in a matter of twenty minutes. My head is still spinning."

He kissed her again. "Good. I always want to make your head spin."

She rubbed her hands across his bare chest. "Do you mean it? The not-being-king part?"

"Yes. I have no desire to change my mind." He smiled. "I love you, Mia. I would do anything for you."

"Even walk away from everything you are?"

"I am more than just a prince. It is time to discover the man."

She believed him. There were no doubts, no questions. She opened her mouth to tell him so but what came out instead was, "You have to be king."

He laughed. "Mia, no."

She sat up, not caring she was naked. "Rafael, I'm serious. You have to be king. It's what you were born to be. Plus I think you'd be a good king."

"No. I'm serious about wanting to study medicine. Besides, you don't want to be a queen, do you?"

She grimaced. "Not really, but I would. You owe yourself, and your people. And Danny."

He pulled her down next to him and bent over her. "I think it would be best to discuss this later."

She sank back onto the bed. "Fine, but don't think for a moment I can't change your mind."

He lowered his head. "Mia, I have long since learned never to doubt you."

Epilogue

One year later

"I swear, if anyone from the press tramples through my grapes, there will be hell to pay," Brenna muttered as she adjusted the front of her dark green sheath. "I will kill anyone who so much as bruises a grape."

Francesca rolled her eyes. "Mia, I told you to wait until after harvest. Brenna, you're like an old woman about those grapes."

"I am a protective bear mother of twins," Brenna muttered. She walked to the window and stared out toward the vineyards. "I can feel them inching closer to the grapes. I hate the press. Have I mentioned that? Mia, you should have gotten married in the spring."

"I suggested that, too, but Rafael didn't want my law school graduation eclipsed by wedding plans. He wanted both days to be special."

"I think I liked him better when he was a jerk," Brenna said. "He's so nice now. So caring and thoughtful. It's not natural."

"Ignore her," Katie said as she adjusted Mia's veil and fingered the tiara. "These are real diamonds, aren't they?"

"That's what I'm told," Mia said. "About thirty-five carats."

"Cool," Kelly said with a grin. "Can I borrow it when I get married?"

"Maybe."

Amber turned sideways in front of the large mirror that covered one wall of the bride's room. "I look huge."

Mia smiled at the pregnant woman. "You look beautiful. Radiant."

"You're barely showing," Brenna said. "At six months, I was a cow. Trust me, you're lucky."

"You were a beautiful mother-to-be," Colleen Marcelli said. "I'm a mother and I know about these things."

Darcy walked into the room, closed the door behind her, and leaned against it. "It's done. The president and the king have officially shaken hands. It was a beautiful moment. Joe looked surly, but he often does. I tried to get him to come up here, but he was afraid there were too many women in one place and the estrogen would asphyxiate him." She looked at Mia. "You're gorgeous."

"Thanks. I owe a lot to you guys."

"You're right about that," Francesca said, coming up to stand beside her. "Do you know how many hours of beading went into this thing? I bled quarts on your dress."

Mia stood in front of the mirror and tried to convince herself this was all happening. That she was really getting married to Rafael in front of eight hundred of their closest friends.

The guest list had been just one issue to be dealt with. There had also been the logistical nightmare of housing so many foreign dignitaries and their families. Something, the king informed her on a regular basis, that would not have been a problem had she been married in Calandria, like every other princess.

But then he'd smiled, because after all this time, he'd gotten used to the fact that Mia wasn't like other princesses.

Rafael had resisted revoking his abdication for nearly six months, but after the law had changed allowing Mia equal say in her children's future, he had agreed to once again be heir to the throne.

She stared at herself in the mirror, at the yards and yards of beaded silk. The design for the dress had come from a modified version of an eighteenth-century ball gown. The infamous Quentin had flown out himself to fit Mia. He'd directed the Marcelli women on the beading, which had taken months. Now it was finished and she was about to marry Rafael.

She smiled at the thought. He truly had changed. He was a good, caring father and supportive of her. He had moved into the house and taken care of Danny while she'd crammed for finals, and he had been patient as she had then tried to learn a thousand years of Calandrian history in just two months.

Her father walked into the bride's room. "It's time," he said.

The women collected their bouquets and hurried out. Mia's mother lingered.

"My baby is getting married," she whispered as she kissed Mia's cheek.

"Don't make me cry," Mia pleaded. "We don't have time to redo my makeup."

"Or mine." Her mother lowered Mia's veil over her face. "I'm glad you're happy. That's all I ever wanted."

Her father grinned. "Sure. We don't actually care about being related to royalty. Although I've been thinking. Now we have the perfect in for the European market."

His wife slapped his arm. "You will *not* discuss exporting Marcelli wines during the reception. Do you understand me?"

Marco grinned again.

Then Mia was alone with her father. He squeezed her hand. "You can still get out of this if you want."

She laughed. "Not even on a bet. I love him, Daddy."

"I've offered the same escape to each of my girls and you have all refused. I guess that means you're really in love."

"I am."

"You put him through the wringer. I'm not saying he didn't deserve it, but he came through."

"He did. He loves Danny and me."

"He's a good man," her father said. "I like that I can say that about all my sons-in-law. Come on, Mia. It's time."

They walked down the wide staircase and through the arched doors that led to the wide expanse of lawn. She could hear the royal Calandrian orchestra playing and smell the thousands of flowers arranged for the event. Then she and her father turned and she could see the dais where the ceremony would take place, the beautiful arch, and a seemingly endless sea of guests.

"Katie outdid herself," her father murmured.

Mia nodded in agreement. Her sister had worked with the Calandrian protocol officer to pull off a massive wedding in far too short a time. Everything looked perfect.

"I'm ready, Mommy," Danny said as he stepped in front of her. He held a pillow with two gold bands clipped in place.

"You look very handsome," she told him.

"I look like Daddy." He grinned and tugged at his miniature bow tie.

"All right, kids," Katie said, motioning Danny to join his cousins. "Let's go. Just like we practiced."

Mia watched her sisters' children begin the long walk down the aisle to where Amber, Darcy, and Kelly waited. The girls scattered rose petals. Brenna and Francesca stepped up next.

"Thanks for the great dresses," Brenna said with a grin.

"Thank Quentin," Mia told her.

The twins started their walk.

Katie squeezed Mia's arm. "I love you."

"I love you, too," Mia swallowed to hold back tears. "You did an amazing job with the wedding."

"I loved it. And there isn't a single daisy anywhere."

Mia laughed.

Katie turned to face the arch, then began her walk. Mia slipped her hand into the crook of her father's arm.

"Ready?" he asked.

She nodded, her gaze drawn to the handsome man waiting for her. Her eyes locked with Rafael's and she felt the warmth of his love surround her.

A handsome prince. Who would have thought it would ever come to this?

The music changed to the traditional wedding march. The guests rose and turned toward her and her father. He covered her hand with his and squeezed her fingers. Then they stepped onto the petal-covered path.

Once again, she found Rafael and let him draw her in. Everything about this moment felt right—as if she'd finally found her destiny. Today she would be his wife, and Calandria's new princess. In time, she would be queen.

Today Calandria . . . tomorrow the world.